AF668507

# THE SHARK AND THE DOLPHINS

# THE SHARK AND THE DOLPHINS

## THE MAKING OF THE DREAM STARTUP

PRABHU SUBRAMANIAN

NU VOICE PRESS

First published by NU VOICE PRESS 2023
An imprint of Hubhawks Pvt. Ltd
www.nuvoicepress.com

Copyright © Prabhu Subramanian 2023

The moral rights of the author have been asserted
Database right NU VOICE PRESS (maker)

ISBN: 978-81-963184-20

This is a work of fiction and all characters and incidents described in this book are the product of the author's imagination. Any resemblance to actual persons, living or dead, is entirely coincidental.

All rights reserved. Enquiries concerning reproduction outside the scope of the above should be sent to NU VOICE PRESS at the address above.

Typeset by Saanvi Graphics, Noida
Printed at Thomson Press
Published by Nu Voice Press

*To,*

*First and foremost, myself and my midlife crisis*
*The engineer I could never become (thankfully!)*
*Of course, my wife, my parents, my son Kabir,*
*And, last but not the least, the incredible power of friendship, science, and the enormous powerhouse of talent and genius that my country India is.*

# PROLOGUE

Adv. Nivedita Das
1005, Block G
C.R. Park
New Delhi—110019

I picked up the envelope from the table amidst the clutter of all the case files and legal documents. I wondered if I should open it or just stay focused on the big battle ahead. Not that I haven't been put to the test before, but this one was different.

There is so much that is not adding up here, and both sides seem to be correct. Again, not a first. Both sides have been right before. We just defend the story we believe in.

*You will be fine, Nivi.* I told myself, ignoring the envelope and sipping on my green tea.

Interrupting my train of thought, my six-year-old son Vihan called out to me, 'Mom, I am ready!' He frolicked about at seven-thirty in the morning. Overjoyed at wearing his school uniform all by himself today, he ran from room to room, bragging to his father, his nine-year-old sister, and even the house helps.

'Well done, my little genius!' I cheered him on and gave him a hug after rearranging some of his shirt buttons.

'Vinay Uncle!!!' he yelled and charged towards Vinay Aggarwal, a full-time prankster and a part-time engineer. Only his part-time genius could trump most full-time engineers anywhere on the planet. Vinay, when outside the workshop, could be sillier than my six-year-old, what that meant was both bonded like buddies on a playdate, and Vihaan would drop anything at the mere sight of Vinay.

Accompanying him were his two friends and Co-Founders, Aman Trivedi, a Chartered Accountant and the scheming, calm, conscious keeper of the company. Along with him was Bharat Srinivasan, the man who once dreamt and would stop at nothing to fight for his dream.

Together, these three thirty-something men created the world's best electric car, hundred percent made in India—The Zila, under their company Bharat Kinetics.

And why were they here? Well! That's the big battle.

Shantanu Vashishta, the man who was once their mentor, investor, and guide, was now out to get them, and standing in the way was me, Advocate Nivedita Das, correction, Senior Advocate, Delhi High Court, Nivedita Das.

'Let's go back to the day when this whole thing blew up,' I said after we kind off settled in took our places on the couch. This was perhaps the twentieth time in this week when I had asked him to go back to the day.

# 1

# MUNICH

## BHARAT

It was the 2017 Munich All-Electric Global Championship (MAEGC). The first and the only of its kind. This all-electric global motorsport championship was more than just a speed contest. It tested the machines on a whole host of things, such as speed, resilience, charge time, handling, acceleration, etc. Even today, the MAEGC is the holy grail for all-electric car reviews; because of this. The mightiest of auto corporations from around the planet have yielded and started building all-electric grand racing teams. The best part about this event is the level playing field it offers. They set clear limits on how much a team can spend, whether drivers, pit staff, or the car itself. Any increase in the budget and participation can either be annulled or be shifted to another higher category contest. In a world where so much of your success in sports depends purely on how much money you can blow up, a contest like this was a godsend for a company like ours operating on a low-cash diet.

I came across this opportunity and once I was smitten by the vision of the first Made-In-India electric car dominating the global stage, it was only a matter of time before it spread to the rest of us. We wasted no time enrolling ourselves for the event. By now, most of us only had memories of a contiguous stretch of sleep, and with this announcement, our preparations went up by a factor of ten.

Except for one person. For him, this was nothing more than a battle of the Might. He was convinced that we were no more than his henchmen, or, at best, skilled mechanics, who had no business outside the garage. He was the guy with the tie, the face of it all.

We should have known better. We didn't expect Shantanu to drag things this far. He didn't take the fact lightly that we were lifting the company on our own to this unimaginable world stage. We achieved more than what we could, and now he was going to stop at nothing to thwart our progress. But, each time, he kept hitting a wall, a wall named Bharat, one he was still trying to breach. Not sure how many blows I will be able to handle before I start to see some cracks.

Tiding over everything he threw at us, we continued to work resolutely for the contest. Hoping, once Zila took the ship, it would be smooth sailing. Finally, Munich it was. A sense of liberation ran all through my nerves. The moment we set foot inside the sports village, developed for the event with the team flags, country flags, and giant screens showcasing cars from all participants with our baby Zila among them—we felt so proud and maybe even intimidated with all the grandeur.

Everything was perfect, except for one man who could not let go of his ego and pride. I think my dad once told me to never overestimate logic and never underestimate pride. I didn't care much. As they say, those who don't learn by advice learn by experience.

The Americans, the Germans, the Japanese, the Chinese, the Koreans … you name it, everyone had their cars on the track. Some claimed 0–100 miles in five seconds, while others claimed 400 miles run on a single charge. Most of them boasted massive crews, the world's best technicians and pit crews, with a pit timing of fewer than five seconds. Competing against them was our modest crew, still learning on the job, trying to hold its own on the big stage

As for our machine that was going to grace the tracks of Munich, there was nothing modest about it. The first fully India-produced pocket dynamite powered by a Zinc-air battery with a top speed of 300 kmph, 0 to 100 in six seconds, that ran 350 miles on a single charge. Zila could go up to 100 percent charge in less than twenty-five minutes, a feat even the mightiest of corporations couldn't claim to have achieved. What this also meant was a naturally heightened level of interest in this dream machine from India which no one considered to be a serious contender. We were seen as a bunch of boys armed with investor money and no real product.

It was a two-hour race with fifty laps of a 4.5 km long circuit, which meant any car driving at less than 115 kmph average speed could forget about even finishing the race in time. The results, though, were not limited to just speed. It wasn't only about who gets past the post first but through a weighted average score on four parameters: Top Speed, Range, Peak Power, and Handling.

The stalls, the meetings, the venue, the track, the stadium, and the crowds were enough to overwhelm a first-time spectator, and here we were as participants! We could sink under our own weight. So, our brief to ourselves and the team was to keep it simple like we were still working from our makeshift garage; no pressure, just the basic routine, day after day after day.

To boost our chances, we even hired a coach and contract crew with experience in the circuit. 'Boys, this is the track we need to scale fifty times over. Take a hard close look and imagine the car right up there dominating this stretch of 2.2 miles like no one ever has. Even though it looks lovely from a distance, it's as crooked as it can get, and you need to know each one of these bends and traps like the neighborhood you grew up in,' announced our coach, Kevin, on day one of coaching.

'Let's take a look at the corners first, there are thirteen of them, but the trickiest ones are 2, 4, 6, and 9, also known as 2, 4, 6, and 9,' he said and burst out in a fit of laughter. For a change, there was someone with a worse sense of humor than us.

Every morning our drivers, Neel and Aditya, began practicing on the adjacent race track, a replica of the real one, only half the length at about 2.5 km. After a ninety-minute grind, our drivers practiced in the virtual gaming environment using their Virtual Reality (VR) headgear inside a mock-up car, creating a race-day-like vibe.

While Vinay was in charge of managing the racers and the engineers, Aman and I took the responsibility of handling the rest; Shantanu, media, investors, payments, team morale, etc. Because of the bias that media often shows, we relied heavily on freelance vloggers who were kind enough to create some buzz. So those who were actually interested would tune in to the championship page or YouTube, where it was going to be live-streamed. No channel was going to air this at home, which was understandable, given the cold shoulder Formula-1 gets in India. An event like this didn't have a chance in hell, especially when it clashed with an Indian-Australia cricket battle, and honestly, I, too, would have chosen Dhoni over an electric car challenge.

But this is precisely how we wanted things to be. No media, no pressure, just us, our ambition, and preparation. There were a few Indian auto and car magazines around who would pass by the Zila stall from time to time, but they seemed more interested in the big American eye candy.

'You are up against top teams from around the world. Do you think your entry was pre-mature?' one of the editors from the top car magazine asked.

'The contest itself is for pre-launch models. We are here to dominate the circuit. Zila will, at the very least, have a podium finish,' we responded with confidence.

We had practiced some standard answers like saying that we respect everyone but are here to win or that the time for Indian engineering has come, which we are here to showcase.

'So, nervousness in the camp?' a British journalist once asked. 'You should drop by, perhaps!' Aman responded with a thumbs-up and a smile.

Friday was allotted for practice on the main tracks. While Saturday was for individual runs to decide the line-up sequence. The car with the best lap time would secure the pole position. To the surprise and shock of many, we finished fifth. We beat the Chinese, the Korean, and even the French, German, and British teams.

Finally, it was the Race Day. Our entire crew was dressed in Polo T-shirts with Zila branding on our hearts over the left side and Bharat Kinetics written on the sleeves. Half the team wore black while the others wore white T-shirts. A few of us also donned Bharat Kinetics blazers.

The atmosphere was other-worldly, the likes of which we had only seen on television. The tracks were pristine, barring their mild blemishes of the tire marks from the two days of rigorous practice and qualifiers. A giant arc that could presumably be spotted from space was erected right in the middle of the circuit, sponsored by a famous wheel maker. Despite not being a top motor racing event, we were going to race in a sold-out venue, and *boy*, it was electric! A cacophony of cheers was rising and reverberating across the stadium. The country and the team flags were fluttering with pride. Amidst them stood the modest yet spirited Zila fan group. Busy pits, nervous team owners, interviews, and photo-ops, it was only then that it began to sink in how far we had come. *MAGICAL*!

I wouldn't say it was unimaginable or unthinkable since this is all I dreamt of for as long as I can remember.

Commentators were doing their best to pump up the adrenaline.

*'Hello and good evening, everybody! Vistared Energy brings to you the third All-Electric European Championship. Let's go straight to the circuit and find out who all do we have behind the wheels today.*

*'In the pole position, we have Mark Johnson and his american supercar. Kim Zu is in charge of the Telan by the Koreans, Neel Krishnan is behind the wheel for the Indian Zila, Li Wei for the Zongfeng from China, the Munich local boy Karl Schumer with his Wagen E, Benjiro Hama for the Japanese Esuzu, Nicholas Ferrero with his Cheval from France, Davis Peter with his Bolt from Great Britain, the Italians are here too with three models: the Levin, the Ghepardo, and the Fulmini.*

*'Drivers… start your engines … oops … I mean, switch on your motors. It's time to electrify Munich!'*

And so it began.

The Americans and the Germans were able to build up an early lead, but with Neel driving, Zila hit a 99 km/h record in 3.6 seconds faster than our claims. This shot us up to the fourth position, with the Chinese and the Italians close behind. We retained our fourth position until Lap 15, while Neel remained sublime at 175 km/h.

*'The Korean machines are closing in, but Zila seems resolute in its handling. Neel is packing a punch. This is getting close. The Wagen E and Zila are tied for third position. Neither is ceding an inch. Wagen E is still in the lead, and Zila is inches ahead*

*now in third position. Wagen E is closing. Neel is still keeping his lead. Will there be a collision? The drivers are almost bullying each other… Oh, did we just see the cars brush off each other? This contest has simply lit up the circuit!*

*'Zila has a disadvantage in the turning angle. It looks like Karl will regain his podium position… Neel retreats a little as Zila seems slightly out of control and seems to be straying towards the edge of the lawns.*

*'But wait a minute! Wait a minute! What is Neel trying?*

*'This is unbelievable acceleration! He has taken a wider angle, and with insane acceleration, he has zoomed right past Karl and is zipping ahead of even the american supercar! It's a rocket on the roads, and this zinc-powered machine is now in second place!*

*'Is it the man or the machine? This is the stuff of legends! the Indian Flag is soaring at the Munich International Moto Circuit.*

### Lap 20 of 50

*'Zila is sprinting away, extending its lead, but Neel doesn't seem to be content. He's going in for a win. This is unbelievable!!!'*

'Send him a message that we are happy with a podium finish. I don't want blood on the tracks! What has gone into this guy?' I was getting nervous.

'He is fine! You just watch! He is in perfect control,' Aman assured me.

'This is getting dangerous now. We have made our mark. I don't want him seriously injured or, worst– dead! I promised his parents that he would come back in one piece. Besides, we are not a race team!' I yelled.

'Oh well, we are now,' Aman said casually.

Vinay was already in touch with Neel through the walkie.

'Neel, you gotta slow down right now. We haven't tested at high speed for such a long period. Don't do this. I am warning you. Don't! We are going to be back next year to win.'

'Let's do it now, boys! You have created a beast!' Neel was on a roll.

'No, no, no, bloody hell, Neel. If you don't slow down now, you are fired! I swear to God. I am not kidding. We just need a podium finish in attempt one. Even the first five would do,' Vinay was absolutely furious with him by now.

'Yeah, okay, I am not going for a win,' responded Neel disinterestedly.

'Win or no win, even if we risk a podium finish, you will not go beyond 175. Is that clear?'

'Copied, captain,' Neel assured.

## Lap 21

*'Mark Johnson is in the lead, but Neel is keeping him nervous. The circuits are on fire, and the Indian contingent is out with their dance. Well, we are now in an eyeball-to-eyeball contest here, but wait, Neel seems to be retreating! Seems to be a signal from his crew. Mark is now extending his lead, and Karl is closing on the Zila.*

*'Neel is operating at peak power. He is trying to maintain his second place against this spirited rear-guard action by the German racers. It looks like we are in for another mouth-watering contest. The cars brush against each other once again, and again*

*and again. Karl is now retreating, and Zila survives the German scare keeping the lead.*

## Lap 36

*'The Koreans are now picking up pace. They are up to the fourth position. Karl is trying hard to secure a podium finish as Zila and the American Supercar are fighting it out for the championship. Mark doesn't seem as invincible as we would have imagined but beats Zila for the fifth time in a neck-and-neck contest, this time more comprehensively than before!'*

'This boy is not listening, Vinay. Why is he competing with a $70,000 car!' I yelled at everyone.

'This is madness,' Vinay exclaimed.

'Gosh! How am I going to face his parents? They must be watching it live,' I was distraught.

## Lap 41

*'We can call the podium positions; the American machine will take the ultimate prize, the Indian Zila will finish second, and the third spot is still up for grabs, although Karl seems to be in control. Wait, what do we have here? Karl has just whizzed past Zila, which is now in third position, and now fourth, and fifth! Neel is retreating! What the hell is going on? Why is Neel slowing down? This is turning out to be an anti-climax. What the hell? This can't be happening.*

*'Looks like Zila has bailed out on Neel. He is driving back to his pit. Let me tell you, He is not going to have a good reception at the pit. He has let his team down and put the poor car through*

*unrelenting torture for two hours, driving more than 200 kmph for over five minutes at a stretch!*

*'What a shame!'*

'Not so much, Neel. What is wrong with you?' Vinay yelled at Neel on the radio.

'I don't know. The car's not responding to acceleration,' he sounded scared and helpless.

'Of course it isn't!'

'What should I do?'

'You know what, Neel? Fuck yourself. You piece of crap!' Vinay almost slammed the $250 walkie-talkie radio on the ground.

Neel entered the pit, but no one was willing to serve him. He parked the car all by himself, and the others just cleared the way while Vinay and I saw him coming. It was just a matter of nine more laps, and we could have finished the race. The media and Shantanu were going to have a field day. But worst of all, after three years of sweat, back-breaking stress, and creating the perfect car, the dream came crashing in full public view.

'*Chal*, let's pack up. We will finish the presentation and then see what's next.' I tried to hold my composure. I didn't want to look at Neel, who perhaps knew this and still had his helmet and shades on.

'You idiot! Watch where you are sitting. It's a $600 kit on rent!' Vinay yelled, and Neel immediately stood up like a foot soldier at the sight of a general. 'Now get inside and dare you to talk to anyone from the press, you moron,' Vinay yelled.

We assembled inside and brought down the shutters to block trespassers, especially Shantanu. Aman, Vinay, and I were waiting for the someone to begin. I had to collect myself so I didn't break down in front of my team. I needed coffee, maybe somewhere to hide, I hinted to Vinay to lead.

'Are you on some substance? What the hell was that? I don't even know why I am still talking to you,' Vinay ranted while pacing around with rage and frustration.

Neel sat in silence.

'I am talking to you, you bloody joker! What were you thinking? You wanted to be an international star by beating the Americans on debut?'

'I know. I am sorry! I can't tell you how well it drove. It was soaring like an F-16. I still think we could have won. It was only a matter of another fifteen minutes,' he began explaining earnestly.

'But my innocent little boy, we agreed that we are not here to win. We told you we could come back to win next year. It means you didn't care what we had to say. You had made up your mind when we arrived here,' Vinay kept going.

'I am sorry, Vinay. I wasn't planning to do any of this. I accelerated exactly as we did in the practice run, but when Karl almost choked trying to barely keep up, I suddenly felt we could win this one,' Neel answered, holding back his tears.

'You should have listened to me, Neel,' Vinay didn't sound angry, just heart-broken, helpless, and dejected.

'Now, stop! And listen …' I stepped in finally!

'Honestly … all is not lost, okay? If we think of it, what we achieved was nothing short of extraordinary.'

'Had we finished the race, it would have been magical, but never mind. Till the time we were on the circuits, *we* dominated. So to everyone here, hold your head high when you walk out of this garage today.'

'The journalists and Shantanu are all expecting us to be disappointed. Let's deny them that pleasure and emerge from this shed like the champions that we are.'

'Even the best of the bests were sweating at the sight of Zila,' I claimed with conviction.

'Neel, you need to walk out of this door like a superstar racer. Is that clear?' I could see Neel nod with some relief.

'Grab some coffee, and let's go.'

'It's celebration time, boys and girls. Zila is on the world map!' Aman joined in, cheering everyone up as he held his arms around Neel and Vinay.

Everyone did feel better after my address. Although Neel was still being treated as an outcast and he deserved it. We stepped out, cheerful and falling over each other with joy. Finally, we stood at the edge of the circuit with Neel at the center. Many journalists charged at Neel while Aman blocked their access.

'Aman, was it an engineering failure or just poor driving?' one of them asked.

'Neither! Just lack of experience on the racetrack.'

'Did you not test enough?' came another one.

'You know the rules better. The federation issues a fitness certificate before allowing entry, so we had tested enough, and if you see, we dominated for forty-one laps. Zila was flying! This car is phenomenal. Did you see the speeds it clocked up?'

'But you couldn't even finish the race ...' pointed a French reporter.

'We could have, easily, but there was no point. It was too late to recover. We will finish and win next year.'

'Will it be Neel behind the wheel next time?' the reporter asked provocatively.

'After the show he put on today, is there any driver in the world who even comes close to this boy?'

Even though Aman and the rest of us managed the media quite skillfully, it was all unraveling slowly in our hearts. And no matter how hard we tried, it was impossible to look away from the blitz that was to follow.

Next, I remember getting together with everyone at the Marriot restaurant to catch up for a beer and laugh about the fiasco. Vinay kept going after Neel while Aman and I kept providing cover.

'Boss, the car drove like a dream. I can't tell you, but it just kept asking for more. You should have seen the expression on both Mark's and Karl's faces. I saw it in their eyes. They knew they were going to lose,' Neel spoke with suppressed passion, 'But why did it suddenly stop?' Neel questioned.

'This is why I asked you to learn the power dynamics inside a battery when we were training. Do you receive notification that a certain app is consuming more power than usual?' Neel was in for a lecture on electronics and design from Vinay and Jatin, our chief mentors.

'Yeah, often,' Neel replied.

'Does your phone suddenly dim the backlight to save power?'

'Yeah,' Neel kept nodding.

'That's the moment when you have to pay attention! You can't kill the motor by working it at high speeds for such a long period. Peak speed allowances are only to overtake during a close contest. After this, you are supposed to release and let it breathe. Otherwise, else the intelligence of the car believes that the driver is incapacitated, and auto deceleration gets invoked.'

Jatin Soni, our chief engineer, added, 'You were lucky it didn't catch fire because it was Zinc-air and not Lithium-ion.'

'Wow, auto deceleration!' Neel exclaimed while the entire team looked at him in utter disbelief at his ignorance of technology.

'Hey, boys. I thought I was part of the team too. Partying at my cost, and I am not even invited?' Shantanu crashed the party, determined to ruin it. I regretted not wrapping up fifteen minutes earlier.

'What the hell happened, Mr. CEO?' Shantanu stormed in and grabbed me by my collar.

I pushed him away just strongly enough to get him off.

'Easy boss, my team's here,' I tried avoiding embarrassment in public.

'Let them know what a clown their leader is,' he spoke with gritted teeth. The other guests around were now staring at this circus.

'Everyone can see who the clown is. Let go, Shantanu!' Vinay warned him in no uncertain terms. Shantanu let go of that. He then picked up a glass of beer from the table, splashed it on my face, and walked away, yelling, 'I will see you all in court!'

'That's the last we saw of him,' Bharat concluded.

'Looks like he can't wait to see you, either. Let's get going. It's Game Time!' I said.

# 2

# JUSTICE BANSAL

## NIVEDITA

We were up against another formidable lawyer, Satish Ranjan. Many considered him near invincible. While there is no such thing in a court of law, it simply implies a lawyer who can make even a loss land well for their clients; he charged a fortune, and Shantanu clearly had the pockets for him. We needed to bring out our 'A Game,' or else, Satish is more than competent to walk all over us.

We follow an unwritten code of ethics within the legal fraternity. No, it's not about being fair; no hearing is fair. It's just a code to keep everything decent and civil. Even though Satish committed to this code like every other lawyer, his word was no more than a line in the sand. We were in for an out-of-court mediation, hoping to arrive at a compromise that worked for both sides.

The mediation was being presided by a retired Supreme Court judge. Justice Bansal and I had practiced together when I used to intern under him. He was a man of impeccable integrity, although, many believed that he could go soft on celebrated lawyers like Satish. 'Let's see,' I told myself.

We drove proudly in the all-new Zila as we approached Justice Bansal's house. Adding to the line-up of parked cars cramping up the already narrow inner roads of Safdarjung Enclave was a Fortuner that stood next to Satish's semi-premium Toyota Innova.

Please make no mistake about his collection; his garage boasted far more exquisite cars. However, he drove for the occasion, and if this choice of the ride was anything to go by, he didn't think very much of this meeting. I couldn't be more pleased if that's indeed what he thought. A complacent or over-confident opponent is a battle half-won.

As we approached the doorstep of the meeting place, I looked at the boys, and they looked back at me one last time, and we gave a reassuring nod to each other. As soon as I walked in, I had my first real glimpse of Shantanu (the chief complainant), a fifty-something affluent man with an imposing personality. Imagine any rich man walking the corridors of a Gymkhana Club or warming the seats of a business class cabin, and that is exactly him. I don't know if Satish instructed him or if this was his natural persona. He projected a stone-cold and uptight demeanor. Nothing unusual there. Most clients use this to intimidate the other side. He was ill-mannered and couldn't care less to exchange pleasantries.

Bharat, Aman, and Vinay on this side of the table did everything they could to get under Shantanu's skin with their calm exterior and condescending smirks, almost mocking their former boss. They exchanged a handshake with Satish and his assistant, who sat behind him, ready to take notes. We took our places around the meeting room. I noticed there were tea and cookies neatly laid down in porcelain dishes that Justice Bansal had arranged for us.

Bharat sipped from the glass of water, silenced his phone, and placed it inverted on the top of the table. Everyone took a cue and followed.

'Hey, boss, good to see you. I thought we would never meet again,' Bharat couldn't hold back. Aman face-palmed in his subtle manner. Only it wasn't subtle enough, which everyone noticed.

'This was your last wish that came true. What else have I been doing all these years with you guys?' Shantanu remarked, as condescendingly as you would expect.

'Without a doubt, you have been a genie, been out of the bottle for too long now, you need a break, boss! Save yourself the embarrassment and go home.'

This was going nowhere, and I had to intervene now. Satish intently looked at me, suggesting it was time to honor our commitment to civility.

'Let's…' The meeting room door gently opened, and Justice Bansal made his way in, instantly drowsing the simmering emotions.

Justice Bansal, a former high court judge, was considered a man of good integrity with an intuitive sense of jurisprudence. He was the one person who had seen enough of Satish and his antics in the courtroom for decades now. Though I felt comfortable in his presence, I was prepared to protest if he showed any over-the-top courtesies towards Satish and his stature. I had seen him guilty of showing reverence for certain lawyers, even asking junior prosecutors to shut up. I wasn't going to tolerate any of that.

Even though this wasn't a courtroom, we stood up as the sixty-one-year-old sauntered in.

'Good morning, everyone. I see that tea has been served,' he began, his voice still firm, something that age hadn't taken a toll on. The last I heard him speak was some four years ago, and his voice didn't seem one bit frail, still as booming and commanding as it sounded then. We smiled and acknowledged the hospitality.

'Sir, the Vatican City painting still looks as good as new, just like your health and fitness,' Satish remarked. We turned around to observe the rather stunning landscape of the land of the Pope, signed by someone I presumed to be some celebrated European artist.

'Ha! Thanks, Mr. Ranjan. It is one of the rare gifts I have accepted in my career only because it came from you,' he paused momentarily and continued, 'You, too, seem to be in a great shape. We must catch up for a fair game of tennis someday. It's been a while,' he returned the compliment gracefully. I was already feeling uneasy with this male bonding and bromance.

'Most certainly, sir,' Satish responded, and both men enjoyed a stretched and hearty laugh, holding each other's hand firmly on the table. Aman, Bharat, and Vinay looked unamused, and Shantanu swelled in pride at the clout of his lawyer.

Justice Bansal wore his glasses, picked up his phone, and you could tell he was slowing down, especially watching how close the phone was to his pupil, despite his reading glasses.

He called his house help and asked him to pay a visit to the meeting room while checking if we needed anything else. Satish asked for a Diet Coke while the rest of us gestured that we were okay.

'Let's now quickly cut to the chase,' he stood up to set the tone.

'I hope you have copies of the legal notice and don't need me to read the charges. As you know, Mr. Shantanu Vashishta has pressed several accusations, including fraud, deceit, and misappropriation of funds. We will use this forum to reach an agreement that works for both sides. At the moment, Mr Vashishta has sought compensation of fifty crores for the financial, mental, and reputational trauma he has suffered due to the behavior of Bharat Kinetics' management team. The break-up of the demand notice has been provided in Annexure-4, for your reference,' he took a brief pause as the house help entered the room but waited at the entrance till Justice Bansal finished.

'Both parties must also be mindful that my recommendations will not be legally binding at the end of the mediation process. If either party still feels aggrieved, they are free to pursue a trial. My recommendations may or may not influence the outcome. However, it will be admissible in court. Both parties can begin recording this session if they so desire. I will also hold a copy for my reference,' he concluded and waited for questions.

'I would like to place it on record that my client categorically denies each one of these charges and further adds that these are malicious and vindictive,' I stood up to contest and dismiss the charges, looking at Shantanu and

Satish. Vinay's fist pumped in a silly display of confidence, and Bharat looked at him with wide eyes and nodded gently in disbelief.

'Very well! Now, give me a few moments before we begin,' Justice Bansal signaled towards his staff, who stood at the door, waiting for us to finish. 'Mahender, please remove this painting and place it carefully in Vaibhav's room,' Justice Bansal served the first blow to Satish's ego while also sending a strong message not to try such stunts again.

I was genuinely impressed with Justice Bansal, and I could see the team was about to break into a fit of subdued titter at this. I gave them both a stare while trying to suppress my emotions. Bharat took a deep breath to keep calm, still unable to get rid of the expressions on his face. Vinay hid his mouth behind the glass of water. It was pointless to give any advice to the two. Bharat was argumentative, and Vinay was, I don't know, just crazy. The only person who had any sway over the two was Aman, but he didn't make any attempt to discipline the two and just focused on the task at hand.

We all watched the helper. The driver left the room with the painting while Satish went red in the face. Along with the artwork, what left the room was any leverage Satish assumed he might have over Justice Bansal. All that was left now were pieces of the shattered ego of an entitled rich man, or rather two entitled and arrogant rich men.

'So, Mr. Vashishta, confirming we have covered all your charges, let us know if there is anything amiss,' Justice Bansal asked Shantanu to voice his views at the outset.

'Thank you, Justice Bansal. My list of charges is endless, and I can't begin to tell you how much trauma I have suffered by investing in this circus,' he lamented like some helpless peasant.

'You know what a circus is? This whole thing right here and you! You are the biggest joker who thinks he is a ringmaster. How stupid is a man who calls the world's greatest electric car project a circus?' Bharat replied in sheer impulse.

Although a little roughed up, Shantanu didn't go on the defensive. He collected his composure and continued, 'World's greatest electric car project! Pfft! It was no more than a failed science project for amateurs who couldn't handle the little success they got early in their careers.'

'Everything begins as a project. Your client, who has spent much of his life as a consultant, should be well aware, and please mind your tone, Mr. Vashishta. Your words are insulting and provocative,' I warned and took him back to our commitment.

'Duly noted, Ms. Das,' Satish acknowledged.

'Okay, so Ms. Das, if you are ok, can I offer the floor to Mr. Ranjan first?' Justice Bansal sought permission.

'Sure, sir,' I smiled.

'Sure,' Bharat confirmed.

'Okay, brilliant! Is it true that Mr. Vashishta provided you with early-stage funding of rupees five crores?' Satish began.

'Yes, that is correct,' Bharat replied calmly.

'Is it true that, but for his funding, your company could have gone bankrupt?'

'Totally incorrect! Anyone who believes this, is living in a fool's paradise,' Bharat responded, this time agitated, direct, and combative.

'Mr. Srinivasan, please only address the points. Don't add any color,' Satish advised, warned, and cautioned, all at the same time.

'I am sorry, but I wanted to place this on record that what Mr. Vashishta thinks to be a favor was a privilege extended to him to be a part of not just India's but the world's biggest EV (electric vehicle) revolution—The Zila series,' Bharat answered directly like he was asked.

'Mr. Vashishta, anything you would like to add?' He offered the floor to Shantanu.

'Of course, quite a lot, actually,' he exclaimed and began. 'I cannot curse my judgment enough to have invested five crores of my life savings with a bunch of manipulative jokers. At first, they were all very nice, as if I was a godfather incarnate to them. And then began the procrastination, the lies, deceit, and eventually, when the facade was demolished, all this man wanted was to kick me out of the company I seeded with hard-earned money.'

'Mr. Ranjan, for the last time, please ask your client to mind his tongue. This whole conversation is not going well,' I stepped in and warned.

'Sure, Ms. Das. Shantanuji, please,' Satish acknowledged and continued, 'Mr. Srinivasan, tell me one thing. Don't you think a seed investor has the right to know what's happening to his money?' Satish asked Bharat.

'Sir, I don't think I agree. Your client, our seed investor, was kept up to date with all the important developments. I couldn't give him the team's daily timesheet if that's what he expected,' Bharat clarified.

'Very well, if that is indeed the case, don't you think participating in a global racing championship was a big milestone worthy of an investor brief for a young company like yours?' Satish posted another elementary question.

'He was informed about everything! What was he not told?' Bharat responded emphatically.

'Mr. Srinivasan, did you participate in the event despite objections by my client?'

Satish got even more direct.

'Sir, now you are shifting goalposts. The investor had to be informed, and he was informed. If he starts to assume he is an approving authority, then that's a figment of his imagination with which we can't help,' Bharat clarified quite clearly.

A few more rounds of cross-examination ensued between Bharat and Satish. With Satish going back to the same argument of investor misinformation and improper treatment, Bharat held his ground. He remained on point and steered clear of confrontation with Satish quite cleverly.

'I now request the opportunity to re-examine some of the arguments with Shantanu.

'Mr. Vashishta, were you ever made to believe that you will be an approving authority?' I began.

Shantanu shifted uncomfortably in his chair, 'I was the only investor. The company was living and breathing on my money. What kind of question is that?' he replied patronizingly, 'I know my rights as an investor. I can't be expected to leave five crores of lifetime savings with three amateur boys and not have a say on how it's spent!' He almost shouted.

'Hold on, does your contract give you any executive powers on decision-making? Please only answer this point directly. Else we will be here all day,' I persisted.

'Your clients, especially this guy Bharat are the biggest manipulators you can find. I was made to believe that I would have an active role in the proceedings of Bharat Kinetics,' Shantanu served another personal blow.

'You don't seem to get it. You are an idiot, a bigot, a total nutcase. That's who you are. I told you a million times that you only need to be concerned about returns. At the same time, you will be informed about the important updates,' to everyone's surprise, Aman suddenly went ballistic. He continued, 'Apologies for my choice of words, but this was only to get you to mind your language because if we get foul-mouthed, you will have no place to hide. Your lawyer requested you. Even Nivedita ma'am warned you, but you don't seem to be listening. Get hold of yourself.'

Aman was still not done, 'Okay, just so we don't sidetrack, Mr. Vashishta was duly told on several occasions that he would have no approving rights. He was free to advise, and we would evaluate any advice on merit. The final call would always rest with the three of us,' Aman concluded quite powerfully.

'I can't believe this!' Shantanu exclaimed in disbelief; he didn't expect the usually calm Aman to explode this way. 'These two are the most ungrateful human beings I have ever encountered. I picked them up from a university campus as two sloppy trainees, who couldn't speak two sentences in English in front of a client, and in return, they decided to gang up and steal my life's savings!' Shantanu continued. 'But they don't know me well enough! I won't rest till I see them in prison, which is where they belong,' he swore, sounding like a resentful, nagging old man.

'A well-meaning man doesn't spy on his founders. Your client is a crooked, ego-centric man, trying to destroy a company he couldn't control,' I retorted vehemently.

The gloves were off now. The place turned toxic and stressful less than an hour into the meeting. We were going in circles, and no one was holding back. I blamed Satish's failure for not placating Shantanu. I didn't see how this would lead to anything fruitful, and it very clearly seemed like all of us were certain to land up in a court, burning through more time and money.

'You all need to bring down your volume. My grandson has his exams!' Justice Bansal interrupted.

'Seriously, Justice Bansal, I thought he was only four or something.'

'No, no, Mr. Ranjan, he is six now,' Justice Bansal clarified.

'Exams! At six?' I asked curiously.

'Oh… so we will spend time on my grandson's education. Well, be my guest, but let's head out to a café then,' Justice Bansal chided firmly, mostly directed towards me.

Everyone retreated.

'You both need to take it easy. How will we get anywhere if you, as lawyers, act like a bickering couple? This is not Indian parliament where everyone speaks over one another,' Justice Bansal continued.

'Let me tell you what I think. Mr. Vashishta overestimated his influence in the company. But at the same time, Ms. Das, how do you expect someone who has invested five crores not to have a say? This is impractical, and the promoter should have shown more respect.'

Justice Bansal gave his opinion and continued, 'I think we can call it a day for now. But you both need to work together and tutor your clients better for the next discussion.' He concluded the discussion for the day.

I had to reset and start from the very beginning all over again. How could a man who invested five crores suddenly turn against the very boys he hired and mentored? I wanted to believe Bharat, but something wasn't adding up. This didn't seem like a straightforward good vs. evil battle, both sides had skeletons, and I had to drag them out of the closets.

# THE ZILA PROJECT

## BHARAT

# 3

# ONCE UPON A TIME

*Present*

It would have been a different ballgame had Neel finished the race. But now, it was open to interpretation and opinions. The guys were going to be kind to themselves and call it a huge success, but for a rank outsider, this was nothing short of a disaster, especially from a legal point of view. Shantanu was within his rights to go hammer and tongs after the promoters of such adventurism. Fortunately, the way the meeting turned out today, Satish wasn't armed with anything too potent.

Bharat continued this time from day zero or even earlier.

* * *

2013

You might think of us as a bunch of men on the brink of collapse, but it wasn't like that always. It was as if Aman and I were living a dream. We were directors at a top management consulting firm before we were even thirty. Pubs, hotels, fine wines, and a regular seat on the table with the big boys of the top companies was our daily routine. A career many would kill for at that age. And the man who was making all this happen for us was none other than Shantanu.

He, too, was minting money big time. We were his sharpshooters on an extended leash. His age and family commitments meant he couldn't travel as much, so he needed some intelligent men who loved airports and hotels, men who could build business connections, get insider information, work tirelessly and on D-day, stand up, and blow everyone's mind. Men who would be forever indebted to him and never threaten his position. Aman and I checked all the boxes, and life couldn't have been better.

But things were rapidly changing. I was getting restless. The perks of the job no longer numbed the longing of the soul, and something had to give soon.

I think this was in early 2013. We were on this enormously taxing restructuring project with a company with a holiday business. They had their offices in a place called Plainview on the outskirts of New York.

The goal was to become one of them. The closer we got to them, the more information we could extract. But everything had to feel organic and not superficial. Once we had built a positive image in their minds as capable and well-meaning professionals, the support would follow.

During three weeks in this company, we were dropped home every evening by our colleague in finance, Jamie. He was the local finance director of our client and was genuinely impressed by our fancy PowerPoint and deeply analytical statistical models. Every evening he would drop us off in his new Tesla. He would occasionally use the charging stations that the Marriot hotel had installed in its parking.

One fine evening, the clients took us pub-hopping.

One after another, we checked out a few local joints till we found this unassuming little pub tucked away in the middle of nowhere with a board that read, 'The smallest pub in New York, with the biggest welcome on the planet!' It could seat no more than ten, yet had over twenty people inside.

'So, you guys heading back next week?' Jamie asked, almost yelling, to cut through the chatter and music.

'Yeah. Tuesday. We have our meeting on Monday before we leave,' Aman replied.

'You have plans for the weekend? I am taking my kids to the city if you want to join?' he offered quite graciously.

'That would be lovely, Jamie, but I quite love this side of New York. You know we are city kids from Delhi. What would I not give to stay away from the traffic and the crowd,' Aman politely declined.

'Sure! I get it. I can only imagine what Delhi traffic would be like. No problem. You guys take it easy here,' he smiled.

'So, how much did your Model S cost?' I asked.

'I knew you would ask. I see you noticing it all the time,' he jumped with pride.

'Haha, yeah! Guilty as charged! It drives like a dream,' I confessed.

'But isn't it too expensive? How do you justify buying a forty-grand mid-sized car to your accountant side?' I posed an accounting question to a finance guy. But in my mind, the proposition didn't add up.

The popular perception is that once you have bought an electric car, the upkeep of it is almost nil due to cheap charging, almost no maintenance cost, and many other benefits. The cost of owning one will not add up overall. It doesn't account for returns one could accrue if one were to invest the same amount of money elsewhere.

'It's for the love of Tesla. You're not supposed to do the math here,' he chuckled, and I lifted my mug to acknowledge this mindless explanation.

I played along in any case, 'Yeah, that's true. I would love to own one of them. I haven't been able to take my eyes off it.'

'So how is it back in India? You have like a Tata electric car coming up?' he enquired.

'I have heard a great deal about it, hopefully soon. In my limited view, this Lithium-ion combination is not the answer in the long run.' I clarified that it was a limited personal view and I could be wrong.

'Really? So what instead?' he enquired. I saw the others had already lost interest. I needed to be brief and move on to something more interesting, like perhaps Baseball, Game of Thrones, etc.

'A lot's been going on. There is Zinc, which seems most promising, and Aluminum, too, is making waves. Have you been to this little pub before, or have we discovered it together?' I shifted topics to get the others in.

'Never been here...the first time ... love the vibe and the price.

'It's two dollars for a pint. You must be kidding me. I am staying here!' Aaron, one of the business analysts and Aman's fan, spoke excitedly.

'Bharat!' I heard a familiar voice and felt a hand on my shoulder.

'Ankit *Bhaiyya*! Can't believe it's you!' Ankit was a senior from engineering college, and I had always held him in high regard, more like an elder brother he always tried to become.

'Likewise, Bharat, so thrilled! So do you live here in Plainview?' he asked.

'No, just here for a meeting.'

'So, in touch with Vinay? Where is he these days?' Ankit had a significant role to play in us becoming friends.

'Yeah! On and off. He dropped out of MIT. I think he got placed with TCS or someone, but I am not sure. Nowadays, he is just freelancing for the most part and coaching few entrance aspirants,' I informed.

'Wow! I thought you both would be up to something together after college,' he commented. I think the underlying message was, what the hell was I doing without him?

'That's what everyone from college says,' I replied with a wry smile.

He shrugged and nodded in a 'such is life' way. We stood there for a few awkward moments. The baggage from the past on both sides. Well, more on his side than mine. Either we had nothing to discuss or so much that no amount of time would be enough. Eventually, we just warmly embraced each other, and he went away to join his friends.

We spent another hour in the pub before calling it a night, and like always, Jamie was kind enough to drop us back at our hotel. We headed to my room and ordered some ice, glasses, and whiskey.

And just as we were getting in the groove, like always, Shantanu interrupted us with a phone call.

'Hi, boss,' Aman answered.

'Have you already got your weekend vibes going?' He taunted. Buzz-killing was his second nature.

'Yeah, Friday night. Just finished a hectic week, as you might know,' Aman explained politely.

'No, I don't know!' He continued to be curt.

'As in? We just won the implementation project. There is even a formal mail from Chris to you,' Aman was now slightly frustrated.

'Yeah, there is. But nothing from you or your project manager,' Shantanu threw the rule book at us.

'So, what new information were we supposed to give you? When the deal is won, what more could we update you on?' Aman argued.

'Really? Is that how it works? You have traded roles with the client?' He was stretching it like always.

'Boss, you know I didn't mean that. It's just that I couldn't add anything beyond what was already in the client's email,' Aman tried to reason with him again.

'Come on! This is the story on all your projects,' Shantanu hammered on. He conveniently ignored the number of deals we had handed him on platters, which got him his promotions, the DLF penthouse, and the new posh villa he was so obsessed with redesigning.

'Okay. I am sorry about this. We will share a formal update with you shortly,' Aman didn't want to keep doing this and gave in.

'Forget it. I don't want to spoil the rest of your day. But don't blame it on me. If you just stay consistent, I won't ruin your evenings.'

So, it wasn't him but us.

'That's fine, boss! The night is still young,' Aman replied, downplaying the episode.

'The sun is up and shining bright here! You guys have fun. Bye!'

'Bastard! Such a sadist,' Aman lamented.

'Of the highest order. Bloody moron!' I added.

SAME TO BOTH OF YOU ... IF THAT WAS MEANT FOR ME. We both received a text from him.

'Damn!' we said almost in chorus. That was Shantanu.

'How could he have heard?'Aman exclaimed. 'Oh, he's bluffing!' I responded.

This was nothing but his way of keeping us grounded each time we cracked something big. Just a reminder of who was in charge. Nothing seems to have changed.

'Let it go,' I reminded everyone before Shantanu hijacked another one of our evenings. 'Yeah.... anyway, so ... you remember the guy we met at the pub?' I began.

'Yeah, the tall guy. Ankit, right?'

'Right, him.'

'What about him?'

'I think I have an idea,' I attempted to take my first little step.

'You mean, related to the project or otherwise?' Aman's commitment to karma would make even Lord Krishna proud.

'Not the project, come on! A business idea, and idea to build something of our own.'

'Not today, please! I am tired,' he replied, worn out, and it was barely ten.

'Hear me out, at least!' I insisted.

'Hmm, what is it?' I was still unhappy with his enthusiasm, but I had little choice.

'Show me some energy! What's wrong with you? Let's head to the lobby,' I proposed.

'Forget it! Some other day maybe,' I said, calling it a night.' I knew it was pointless talking to Aman, he was so enamoured and drawn in with this job, he wouldn't engage, perhaps just hear me without listening. I let him be and headed back leaving the unfinished bottle of alcohol in his room.

Though I was trying to chill and watch some TV, the meeting with Ankit wouldn't leave my mind, it was like some old simmering emotions were suddenly brought to the boil.

Ankit was a final-year engineering student in my second year at college. He was highly regarded for his GPAs and knowledge, and in general, he was the template every mother would want her son to turn out to be. He was also the college's chief troubleshooter and the most scientifically gifted person I'd met of course till I came of age.

Each time a dignitary with deep pockets visited, Ankit would window-dress the campus into a miniature version of an ISRO, NASA or a DRDO. Semi-conductors, drones, little battery-operated cars, concept launch vehicles, and much more. While some would work, some would just be cosmetic versions, wall mounted, beyond the scope of any physical scrutiny. He was skilled in both science and marketing. So, naturally, he was the head of most student committees. Unless Ankit continued as an intern with the faculty, this would likely be his final year on campus.

For me, he was like an elder brother who helped with notes, coaching, and even supported my bid to be drafted for the college cricket team. After all the countless favors he showered on me, there was one that would make me indebted to him for life, which felt like a big humiliation back then. It was when he denied me the opportunity to lead the college in one of our most prestigious engineering and science events.

The Indian School of Mechanical and Electronic Sciences, or ISMES, was famous for hosting one of India's most prestigious science fairs. It must have been in the top ten in the country at that time. One, that was frequented by a marquee pedigree of industrialists, ministers, and scientists who were in attendance every year.

Of the several themes that were agreed upon, which included defense modernization, sanitation, public transport, and civic administration, Ankit was assigned 'Power: Its Management and Delivery through Technology.'

I was assigned to a project where we were given six weeks to build a 3D-printed power plant prototype. Everything was great till then, and I was told that the project would be led by a geeky, pompous, stout student from my batch, Vinay Aggarwal.

Everyone knew Vinay as someone who secured stellar grades and regularly contributed to the college magazine. Not that I had a problem with Vinay. Just that I thought I should have been considered to lead this project.

I protested with Ankit as much as possible, but he wouldn't relent. My respect for him meant there was no way I could defy him once he had made up his mind. At best, I could debate, and I tried.

I finally did as he commanded and showed up the following evening just like he had asked me to, at the E-block canteen.

Dressing up and grooming was a considerable pressure every time I had to pass the computer science department, which typically had the best dressed and best-looking kids on the campus. I decided to request to hold the meetings at C-block, the civil and mechanical block, where I could simply walk out in a run down t-shirt, shorts, and flip-flops.

I walked into the canteen where Vinay was already sitting with Ankit. Vinay was stout, about 5 feet 6 inches, with a waistline expanding like the Chinese border on all sides. His hair was unkempt, and he wore an oversized white knock off Levi's t-shirt (like everyone else on the campus).

I wore a smile and walked towards them.

'Hey, Vinay, congrats, man,' I started on the right foot and greeted Ankit Bhaiyya too.

'Thanks,' Vinay said.

'Alright, so Vinay, let's look at your plan,' Ankit began after getting us tea and samosa.

'Sure, Bhaiyya. I have made some points. I don't need more than three or four people. I will manage programming and 3D modeling. The other two guys can build the printer, wiring, and tooling. We will use FDM modeling, and in four weeks, we will have the working model ready,' Vinay explained, without mentioning my role in the program.

'Plus another two weeks for testing and fixes, then showtime,' Vinay explained with confidence.

'That's good. You and Bharat work on the programming together,' Ankit suggested, almost instructed.

'But does he know 3D programming?' he asked.

Ankit looked at me for a response.

'He asked you, Bhaiyya, you answer,' I replied with disdain.

'Okay, buddy. I am sorry. If you don't, we will lose time with you catching up.'

'We both attend the same class. Stop patronizing me if you want this to work,' I made my point with candor.

'Okay, we need to recruit some volunteers, and here are some posters I have designed,' he kept some posters on the table. He asked me to flood the campus corridors, library, canteens, basketball courts, and the cricket ground with his posters and application forms. Less than five seconds into reading the application form, I was aghast at the insanity of it.

'What nonsense is this? I will get lynched if I ask people to fill this out. What does it even have to do with the project? What are these questions?'

*What has been your most significant achievement in life? What's your view on the moon landing? Who would you date, a passionate engineer trying to change the world or a rich uneducated sportsman? Do you believe in Illuminati?*

Followed by some mechanical engineering questions. Thankfully Ankit Bhaiyya couldn't stop laughing.

'What? I need to be sure of who I am working with,' Vinay was unapologetic, and it was agreed there would be no change to the questions. If we did get into trouble, we would just say Ankit designed the questions.

'So, dude, we will need to head to the market tomorrow to buy some material; boards, wireframe, tin sheets, copper wires, reflectors, metal powder, etc. This is my list,' Vinay continued.

Let me know if I have missed anything,' he said, turning his laptop to me as Ankit left.

'A lot. Conductor material isn't here, such as bearings, nuts, bolts, and drilling equipment. I will add it tonight and share it with you,' I replied.

'Good! I was just testing,' he mocked, and I felt like wringing his neck.

We traveled the next few days all over Nagpur city, even made an odd trip to Bombay, looking for the material we needed. The rest of our time was spent distributing applications, sometimes fleeing the spot as the seniors read through the questions and, but mostly to my surprise, watching freshers responding to them like it was a Roadies or America's Got Talent application.

The HOD even summoned us for the nature of the application form, but like always, Ankit Bhaiyya came to our rescue.

After many tiring nights, we finally did have the power plant fully built and assembled. Not a big one, but enough to power up our library without the air conditioners.

Professor Sawney was truly impressed with what he saw, and our power plant had created quite a buzz around the college. The only other project that was close or slightly ahead was the artificial intelligence-powered traffic management system for cities by the computer science and electronics department. The campus was brimming with competitive yet positive nervous energy. Everyone was guarding their creation against sabotage like a fortress.

The big day was finally here, and I dressed in my best, rather the only suit I had, while Vinay wore just another oversized college T-shirt for the event.

We demonstrated our product with pride to everyone who visited our stall. Professor Sawney stood by our side, helping us wherever he could, quoting examples of how something like this would transform the lives of people in his village in Rajasthan. Everyone seemed impressed, private investors, professors from other colleges, including representatives from government institutions, but our big ministerial and bureaucratic visit was pending. We couldn't wait as we watched the contingent with armed bodyguards with machine guns alongside a casually dressed young minister and IAS officers make their way to our stall.

'This is quite good, boys. Well done,' the minister spoke calmly, we however, were expecting a more enthusiastic response. 'Boys, don't get me wrong, but I don't see how this solves a current problem for the government. Today we can make as many power plants as anyone in the world,' he explained his position.

'But sir, this technology will reduce the cost of building a powerplant by almost sixty percent. The best part is that locals can be employed for management and assembly,' I countered passionately.

'Low-quality jobs, bro! You want to be employed with NASA and Microsoft, but you make solutions that will turn locals into nothing more than rule-based robots,' he looked me in the eye as he spoke.

'You know, don't get me wrong. This is a great technology, but if we had this fifteen years ago, it would have been a big shot in the arm, but today, you might want to check with the private sector.'

'Sure, sir,' Vinay said in a subdued tone. The fact that we had been rejected was beginning to seep in. Vinay gave up.

'But sir, transporting the plant and setting it up has incredibly long lead times. This can be set up in twenty-four hours and commissioned in the next twenty-four or even less, and you can make so many changes on the go instead of having to release new tenders all the time,' I continued to argue our case.

'Let me do one thing. I will take note of this and put this down for another review with you boys. Let's see if we can fund this.'

We knew he was just trying to be polite and that we were done here.

'But honestly, you boys must be proud of this,' he said, leaving the place with his armed guards while Vinay and I stood there with arms around each other's shoulders.

We didn't wait for the closing ceremony and just left the place, not caring to pick up our model from the stall. We must have had at least three cups of tea and five odd cigarettes lamenting over the entitled minister lecturing us on engineering. If it was in our hands, I wouldn't hire him in any department except for maybe HR, that too because his English was good.

Before we knew it, our teacups were replaced with beer cans.

'We will go to the private sector,' I tried to be optimistic.

'Yeah! The private sector is where we should have gone. Bloody joker! He probably came with a memorized speech for every counter. This is such a waste of our time!' Vinay howled.

'But you know what? I was wrong about you, buddy. You weren't as dim as I thought you were,' he said.

'Likewise, my friend, feelings are mutual,' I retorted, and we laughed out loud and toasted again.

Ankit Bhaiyya kept calling on our cells, but we didn't care to answer.

'You know what I was most impressed with? You didn't let up, brother. You stood your ground. Respect!' Vinay complemented, now slurring.

'Forget it, bro! We will make something even bigger than this one day. Don't worry. We'll take it directly to the people!' I vowed.

Only this time, we promised not to tell anyone. It will be like a sleeper cell operation inside the college.

We woke up the next morning with twelve missed calls from Ankit Bhaiyya, who, after reprimanding us for our attitude, took us to Professor Sawney.

'I heard you boys had quite a party last night,' he quipped lightly, much to our relief. As he went on, we stayed silent, neither accepting nor denying our guilt.

'So, all is not lost, and I have some good news. We might get our grants after all. I have received some good feedback. Your project was even mentioned by the minister in his speech when you had both left,' we looked at Ankit Bhaiyya, and he nodded, confirming the professor's statement.

'So, what's next, sir?' I asked, unsure of what this would entail for us.

'Nothing, just email me the project documents. I will need you to come and present a few more times and let's see where we can go from there. Nothing is confirmed, but we might just have a chance.'

This was enough to charge us up and even feel slightly guilty about how we talked about the minister last night.

'Guys, this was so irresponsible! You need to learn to handle criticism better,' Ankit Bhaiyya said after we left Prof. Sawney's office.

* * *

Life resumed, and I think by now I could call Vinay a close friend. We were sitting in the canteen when a junior placed a pamphlet on our table. It sought volunteers for a battery-building project. Mechanical and electrical students only, from years one to three.

'What the hell?' Vinay exclaimed.

'Looks like the minister gave everyone the same speech,' I remarked.

'Now what?'

'Nothing, we build the best battery pack ever! Our underground mission…'

'Mission Minister!' Vinay coined it, and I facepalmed.

'What?' he exclaimed at my lack of amusement at the lousy project name.

We continued with our secret battery project and demoed the 3D power plant to whoever Prof. Sawney asked, sometimes in person and on other occasions on a Skype call. Almost six months had gone by with no news of any grant or incubation investments. Professor Sawney had also turned cold to our calls now.

We tried everything from Zinc to Aluminum to Iron. We tried building circuits that enabled transmission and recharging—sometimes with success, sometimes with holes in our lab coats and t-shirts. So many nights, we saw this to work out well, but it never worked long enough. Our bond, though, only got stronger. There was camaraderie brewing with trust and respect for each other's skills and tenacity.

We couldn't be hundred percent sure, but it did feel like we had this invention all wrapped around our fingers, and something told us that it was no longer about 'if' but about 'when,' just that one last trick before we built the prototype of the world's best non-lithium-ion battery combination ever.

Plus, we were also confident Prof. Sawney to get us funded on our other creation. Persistence was going to be the key, and we knew it.

But for now, it was time for Ankit Bhaiyya's farewell, and he called Vinay and me one last time.

'Okay, you both need to know something before I leave college…' We were intrigued but we were more interested in the stuff he was to leave behind that we could get our hands on, like the dumbbells, the punching bag, etc. I knew he wouldn't part with his PS2 though.

'Bharat!' he almost yelled with a sense of urgency to get my attention, and I was now all ears.

'Listen. Don't waste too much time on the power plant project. It's not going anywhere,' I could feel my heartbreak instantly. One project and two heartbreaks. Were we that jinxed?

'But why, Bhaiyya?' Vinay demanded.

'Forget why, what, and everything. Just focus on your exams and get on with life. I know you have big hopes for some incubation and funding. None of that is happening,' he now almost stamped and sealed it.

'But why? We need some feedback. We can improve! If someone can tell us what's wrong,' I strongly persisted.

'Nothing's wrong with the project. It's just a matter of ethics and stuff. You keep yourself out of it.'

Why was he being so tight-lipped? He was leaving anyway!

'Bhaiyya, you can tell us! We won't tell anyone,' Vinay promised.

Ankit Bhaiyya took a deep breath and lit a cigarette, 'Open the window and turn the washroom exhaust on,' he instructed.

'So ... Professor Sawney has traded almost all the projects from the science fair to some small-time companies around the world, mainly to China and Korea. Nothing can be done now.

'He has made his money and is now on the run. This is it, boys! I am sorry.'

# 4

# MID AIR

Our Monday morning meeting with the clients went smoothly, as expected since we were already awarded the implementation contract.

'Cheers,' Aman raised his glass, and we took a sip of our whiskey. We spent some time discussing random topics like comparing this business class to another airline, Jamie, his family, and eventually, like all our other conversations, we circled back to Shantanu and our last project.

'Solid trip! Shantanu will jump with joy with these rates and margins,' he remarked.

'Let's see, don't have high hopes,' I cautioned cynically.

'He will. I made sure of that. I sent an update too. He has nothing to complain about,' Aman assured.

'Aren't you a good boy!' I remarked.

'What is it? Something wrong between you and him again?' Aman knew I couldn't care less about how happy Shantanu was going to be.

'Boss! Till when will this whole business of sending updates continue?' I posed a rather existential question.

'Until we have a job, I don't see a problem. But sometimes, it can get to you. He is not wrong in asking for an update,' Aman continued, but I had switched off.'

'Okay. I am not arguing with that. Maybe you are right, but we need to think about starting on our own,' I said.

'That's an adventure we don't need.'

'I would rather retire at thirty-five than dabble with some start-up idea at this stage,' he replied with a straight face.

'But even at thirty-five, you will need something to do. What will it be? Advising people on their business without having set up one yourself?' I continued to challenge him.

'I will become an investor. Some of the stock options will mature by then. I know you like to keep things exciting, but I am not like *you*. I will invest in your start-up, promise!' he chuckled.

'I know you want to marry and settle down, which is why you are avoiding any drastic career shifts,' I tried to understand his point of view.

'What the hell! Don't make the bloody thing about my wedding,' he warned and walked away.

'Dude, listen! Who knows, a Gujju uncle might be looking for a gutsy businessman, not some bespectacled corporate slave like us? Make your community proud, start a business,' I continued to persuade him.

'Are you through?'

I shrugged and stopped briefly, allowing him to speak his mind.

'What's your idea? It better be solid,' he cautioned before I could begin.

'You remember Jamie's electric car?' I started with a relatively straightforward question.

'Of course!'

'Do you know how much it costs?'

'What's your point?' he asked disinterestedly.

'Wait, you need to understand this. Do you know why it's that expensive?'

'Yes, and you know how? Because you have told me a million times that it is made up of expensive lithium and cobalt batteries that make up for sixty percent of the car's cost.'

'Great! So glad you have been paying attention,' I said sheepishly.

'Keep going.'

'Sure, so here's the thing. You know Vinay, right? He and I came very close to building a Zinc powered battery pack.'

'Yeah, the one your professor conned you on?' He remarked pretty dismissively.

'So, you haven't been paying attention. That was a 3D-printed plant design.'

'You want to make batteries?' He instantly raised his question.

'No, why just batteries? Let's make the whole damn car! World's best electric car ever!' I announced excitedly.

'Bharat, my budding Elon Musk, this is not going to happen. You know that, right?' He kept his hand on my shoulder, hoping to talk me out of this.

'You are crazy. This will happen. We will make it happen. You don't know Vinay yet and haven't seen us in the workshop. We are a kickass duo.'

'Okay, wait! The thing with starting one's own business and everything is that it does *feel* liberating…' he paused and took a breath before he could launch into me, '…like an escape, like this new girl you met. It all looks magical till you decide to commit.'

Though the advice was relevant, what didn't land was something like this coming from a man who had been on a sum total of one date in the last four years.

'See, I am not your client, so don't "analogy" me. I can counter this in my sleep.'

'You tell me what's wrong with this idea?'

'For starters, it's not practical. WE CAN'T MAKE A CAR! What the hell are you talking about?'

The stewardess interrupted our discussion with her safety brief, and I began again from where we had left as the seat belt signs went off.

'How many moving parts do you think an electric car has?' I quizzed but didn't stop for a response.

'Only fifteen! Now compare this to the thousands in gas/petrol/diesel cars, also called internal combustion engines. Making a battery that is better and cheaper is the hardest part. Once we have the battery, we have the numbers for the lottery. Trust me. I could make a car in my second year of engineering.'

'Now tell me this. Why can't you just make the batteries and sell them?' Aman began.

'Will you agree then?' I countered.

'I might. But answer this. If you have made the battery case before, and that's the piece that will make all the difference …' he didn't complete, but I got his point.

'It will mean sucking up to big car makers and their conditions. If we sell to the public, it's down to quality and marketing,' I argued.

'Okay, so it's all down to answering to people and not your passion for the cause. Then you must not do it.'

'Aman, dude, you are stretching it!' I was getting impatient.

'When you have made eighty percent of the effort, why leave the value addition to someone else? Basic business fundamental! Value addition is where the big bucks are,' I could tell he was being drawn to this side.

'What will I do? You and Vinay are engineers. How am I going to add value?' he seemed a bit interested now, figuring out he would fit in this project.

I assured him how important he would be in securing funding, interfacing with bankers, investors, and employees, and keeping the whole thing on track, enough to give him a sense of self-worth and belief that he won't end up as some sidekick in the equation.

'Funding?'

'You think, with you and I present, we won't be able to secure funding? When apps selling vegetables and biscuits are getting funded, then imagine what our odds are! After all, we are making the world's best electric car.'

'They get funding because their idea is practical. It's like solving a problem,' he retorted.

'Solving a problem! You mean that? It's going to save the planet. The cost per kilometer will be as low as one-to-two rupees! What are you even talking about? We will have wait lists for our car. If we don't scale up fast enough…' I defended. 'People will fall all over themselves to buy it. The only possible failure is... building a bad car,' I think I was painting the vision quite alright, both for him and myself.

'Hmm. Will Vinay agree?' he enquired, almost implying he had agreed.

'Err... we will... we will have to get him to agree once we land,' I confessed. 'Whoa. Wait, wait, wait. You haven't even asked him?' I guess I spoke too soon.

He sighed, 'Why hasn't' this idea taken off yet? Why hasn't anyone else done this yet?'

'Long answer or short answer?' I checked.

'Whatever... '

'You already know the short answer. It's an underprepared technology,' I clarified without adding more color to my argument.

'Hmm...' He acknowledged.

The discussion continued until we landed in Delhi. By that time, I had pulled him to my side of the court, even if not entirely.

'Okay, listen, I was thinking...' Aman nudged as we walked out from duty-free counters towards the carrousel belts

'Speak up now...'I was curious to hear what he had on his mind this time.

'This whole thing is so convoluted,' he suddenly began sounding very confused.

'The current automakers have an established model, making decent petrol and diesel cars. The supplier network and everything else is also in order. At best, they will introduce some token EV models that are too exorbitantly priced that it will remain a non-starter.'

He kept explaining.

'Even in the US, the traditional automakers continue milking the petrol and diesel market. The closest they came to this was with some hybrid cars.'

'When did you get so smart?' I acknowledged his theory playfully.

'When you were still in school,' he shook his head, laughing.

'Haha! You are hired, Aman Trivedi,' I said and patted him on the back as we made our way out of the airport.

# 5

# BLUEWATER INC

Like any other workday at the sprawling office of Bluewater Partners in Gurgaon, Shantanu called for a meeting to brief us on a new project in a meeting room named Morrison.

'This is going to be huge, boys! We will need to get another office just to manage this one client,' announced Shantanu in the conference room on the twenty-fourth floor overlooking the massive national highway of Gurgaon.

Shantanu, Aman, and Abhishek Banerjee, the head of projects, were seated on the other side of the table while Aman and I sat next to each other. Imagine any disgruntled and resentful colleague who couldn't reconcile why the jet setting life Aman and I were bestowed with couldn't be his. That was Abhishek. If he was bold enough to ask me, I would have told him, 'Dude, you just don't want it enough.'

The members from our Middle East office in Abu Dhabi were on the video conference.

'Aman and Bharat! Get ready to travel to Dubai next week. Let's bring Al Grand home.'

Al Grand was among the top three energy companies in the Gulf, and we were bidding to manage the integration of some seven companies they had acquired worldwide. A deal that would earn the company several millions in profit. Another fat bonus for Shantanu and pretty decent leftovers for both Aman and myself.

The money that could seed our dream, for the moment just mine. Aman was still only playing along.

So, since the day we returned from New York, whatever time we could spare from our travel and routine office work, we made sure to use that to attend seminars, watch videos, learn new age battery technology, and chemical formulations, understand automotive software, battery management system, aerodynamics, and auto designs. I would drag Aman to most of my meetings, even though he had nothing to do with engineering. Once the meetings began, he immersed himself entirely, and no one could tell the accountant from the engineer.

We even visited some battery and spare part manufacturing factories and several motor and automakers. No one would entertain us if we told them what we were attempting to do. So we posed as YouTubers, journalists, research students, to documentary filmmakers just to get them to open up and take us through the drill. No detail was too small for us. From where they sourced raw materials to how they manufactured the parts, the landing cost, the margins, the durability, the approvals they needed, and even the kickbacks. Being trained as management consultants, we knew how to get deep inside an organization.

For now, though, we were still in the Morrison conference room, downloading the truckloads of documentation the client had sent using Bluewater's secure cloud.

'I need to eat something first,' Aman proposed. I could certainly use a break.

We had this plush mini cafeteria called Byte right in the middle of the shop floor. It used to be lovely. Their contemporary décor, amazing cappuccino, masala chai, veg patties, etc., had the entire office hooked. The seats were like little pods with noise-absorbent material where you could have an undisturbed chat, take your calls or just quietly work while you snack. That's one thing I really miss about Bluewaters.

'Legal entity, headcount, P&L, competition—we will need to prepare some slides. I will pick up the finance and HR side. You pick up the tech and systems. Let's review today evening so we have a peaceful weekend,' Aman began halfway through our snack.

'Let's do this on Monday. I am done for the week,' I knew he wouldn't like my attitude.

'Yeah, whatever. What can I say? I will sit with Abhishek and close it then.'

'Brilliant, like always. Keep going, but don't kill yourself. Meanwhile, I have a life beyond this.'

I returned to my office covered by glass offering no privacy, which was supposed to be the whole point of a private office. Only Shantanu was allowed privacy in this office. Aman and I were given offices to show that we were a notch above the rest and several notches below the king of the place.

While I wanted to pack up, Aman's panic rubbed off on me, and although reluctantly, I did examine everything the client had provided. I wrote some emails introducing us and seeking appointments with the client employees. I knew there was no running away from this mundane routine. But how much longer, we had been farming the Electric Vehicles market place for months now!

There was nothing new left to understand.

There was cause for skepticism, in all honesty. The fact of the matter is that while the technology for electric vehicles had already taken off in India it wasn't in form of fancy cars. It was still raw and was finding root in e-rikshaws—we had over twenty lakh battery-run rickshaws plying all over the country, especially in Delhi NCR.

The e-rikshaws didn't need the long-range an e-car would. In addition, the e-rickshaws could operate without charging their batteries but only by changing them at local lead-acid battery rentals, which was impractical for electric cars. So, the business model for e-rickshaws works perfectly for their requirement supported by an underdone, yet effective lead-acid battery ecosystem.

We had to build something robust, and there was no reference point in the country. The clock on my system blinked at four in the evening, just when Aman walked into my cabin.

'Dude, you still haven't opened a single file,' Aman rudely reminded me.

'I have. You have no idea. In fact, I have made some notes. Let me email them to you.'

'Okay. I am going to meet Abhishek. You can join us if you want to,' he offered, but I declined and asked him to carry on. I needed some time to think on my own.

'I am leaving now, but I need you to know that I am not happy with your indifference to our plan. If you don't want to do this, I will figure something out,' I warned as I packed up my stuff.

'Drive safe.' He didn't seem one bit bothered about my simmering frustration.

The drive back to Pitampura, was my final challenge everyday. Parking! I had to make several patrols to find a safe spot to park, and when I say it doesn't mean safe from being stolen, it just means a corner where it won't be struck by another vehicle. On a good day, I could find a spot in fifteen minutes, even though distant, but it was at least visible from my house if I stood on a stool, but today wasn't a good day.

I had to park some three lanes away in neutral gear, leaving the hand brakes down and, most importantly, leaving my phone number on the windscreen, so I could be contacted if someone had trouble removing my car out of the way. I got better with practice and I could manage the entire drill of finding a spot and parking sharply in about thirty minutes.

My dad opened the door for me, Vinothkumar Iyengar, a regular retired and highly educated, proud middle-class man. During the day, he was active in stocks. Evenings were spent well, watching IPL or some Tamil TV series.

He was proud of me for the most part. I had a good job, got my own house at twenty-four, and was traveling the world.

Another week, another weekend, and I had had enough of this. I called Aman. Since he wasn't forthcoming, I planned an evening booze session so he could come clean—one way or the other. We couldn't keep going on forever like some electric car enthusiasts. We knew the tech, we had the brains, and unless there was a lack of interest or self-doubt, there was no reason to defer this anymore.

With no patience for parking nightmares, I resorted to ordering a cab from my phone. My ride was there soon enough, and a man named Mohd. Aslam was my driver. It was such a filthy car. I felt like I was sitting inside someone's socks.

'Why don't you use some good car freshener?' I was foolish to expect an honest response. 'Sir, I usually have one, but I just ran out of it,' he replied with nonchalance. Clearly, he had enough practice.

'Let's stop at a shop and buy one. I can't sit like this for an hour.'

'Sir, I have one at home. The ones here are a rip-off,' he replied evasively.

'Yeah! But what do I do about the smell?' I continued protesting.

'Sir, I will earn Rs 300 from this ride, and if I spend Rs 250 on a perfume, what will I be left with?' So, I had to adjust.

'Aslam Bhai, the ride is one time, but the car freshener will last much longer.' I wasn't letting go, either.

'Sir, you can very well go ahead and cancel the ride. But I can't afford such costly fresheners.' He used the nuclear option, and I had to find a way out.

'How about we buy an incense stick, at least? It will be like ten bucks.'

This suggestion seemed to land well, and he agreed to buy one. We lit it up, and it made a world of difference.

Fifteen minutes in, I lit a cigarette, and he gave me a stern glare in the rearview mirror above him.

'The cigarette has done much more than the incense stick,' he remarked. He did not forgive me for the ten rupee incense stick investment.

'Hmm, next time the smell troubles me, I will remember to light another one.'

'So, do you own this vehicle or work for someone?' I tried lightening up the tension after a few moments of stressful silence.

'No, no, this is mine!' he replied with pride. 'I have two more. My brother drives one, and I have hired a driver for the other.'

I kept chatting just to learn their model, how much they make, and to get their perspective on the world outside.

'How much do you earn every month by driving a cab?'

'We usually invest about fourteen hours a day, which gives us thirty-five to forty thousand on each vehicle, excluding the salaries, CNG, EMIs, and maintenance.'

'So, about one lakh altogether!'

'Maybe not one lakh, but we manage about eighty to ninety thousand a month.'

'Great, another five years of this fourteen hours regime, and you would have paid off the car EMIs too! As it is, you don't care too much about maintenance,' I said with a tongue-in-cheek tone.

'My rating is 4.8 if you want to check. It's just one of those days today…' He countered my remark.

'Anyway, have you heard of electric vehicles?' Aman wasn't showing interest, so maybe a cabbie could be my partner.

'Yes, but very little, I would say. I know about the e-rikshaws we have here.' He seemed more aware than most of my colleagues.

'I meant a car, an electric car. Just invest once and then keep charging the battery as you do with your mobile phones. A relief for the next five years.'

'I am happy with this vehicle, sir. CNG is pretty reasonable too. All these electric parts.... what if they stop working? How will I get them fixed? Where will I find a mechanic? They import all the parts from China anyway.'

I kept listening. He had a point.

'Chinese phones do not work for more than six months. Their cars would work for about the same time. My business would come to a standstill.' His apprehensions were all valid.

'Hmm... You are not completely wrong. But just keep an eye on the latest launches in the market.' I couldn't resist my soul's calling to provide unsolicited advice to random strangers.

'Should I keep an eye on these morons who drive haphazardly or on the market for more big cars that take up the whole road, leaving no room for us?'

This was enough hint that I must shut up and let him figure out his business.

'Where are you from?' I tried changing the topic. But he resorted to making a phone call at the red light and ignored my question.

I mean, come on! So now, even a cabbie would snub me. Such were the days.

Fortunately, both for him and me, the drive ended in another thirty minutes and I was outside Aman's gate.

I finally reached Aman's house and rang the bell. Aunty let me in. I touched her feet, and she affectionately said, 'God bless you! It's been ages since I have seen you, Bharat.'

Aman's mom had spent most of her life as a feisty single mother working with the Central Bank of India as a teller. She refused promotions to attend to her boys, who were nine and four when her husband died in a road accident.

She would find solace in meditation, general community work, and freelance volunteering for the underprivileged, like occasionally teaching Maths and English.

'Hello, Aunty! How are you?' Aman's mom was family. The energy she radiated was magical. Never had I met a woman more stunning and confident.

'As fine as I can get! You guys are off to Dubai again next week?' she asked appreciatively. Frequent foreign travels were indicators of a healthy career.

'Coffee or tea? What would you like to have?' Before I could respond, she was up and about. I followed her to the kitchen to help but primarily to chit-chat.

'So, how is your meditation going on?' She believed her energy and strength were a result of her meditation regime. Maybe someday, I will try. If it helps me quit smoking.

'Perfectly fine and divine!' she replied and paused for a moment as she looked for a tea strainer.

'So, Aman was telling me you wanted to do something of your own?'

'Just plans so far, aunty.'

*Aman told her*? I thought to myself.

'What's wrong with what you have now? You are at the peak of your career. Everyone at the office gives you credit and appreciates your hard work. Is it a good idea to take up something like this?' she continued in a cautionary tone.

'We are financially stable at this point, aunty. This is why we felt that it is as good a time as any to at least try. It will be life-changing even if we fail,' I defended gently.

'But how will you make a car from scratch? You, at least, are an engineer. But this guy here only has a CA degree. How will he help you?' She had always been so direct with her words. I didn't know what to say.

'It is not as difficult as it sounds, Ma,' Aman jumped in.

'We have been learning and researching this for over six months and have already met many people from the industry to educate ourselves on every detail.'

'So, you understand what you are getting into?' she cautioned again.

'There is nothing much to understand. I, too, had science till twelfth grade, remember?' he reasoned, explaining this was no rocket science.

'I still am not comfortable with the whole idea. But if you decide to do it, my blessings are always with you. Just be careful. Young kids tend to dream of a career like this,' she concluded, realizing that it was no use to arguing further.

'We will leave our jobs only when we have something solid in our hands, aunty. Don't worry!' I tried to reassure them.

'Ah! This way, you won't be able to do anything independently,' Aman's twenty-one-year-old younger brother, Amit, spoke egging us on to just do it, just wish his eleder borther also had some of his bravado.

'Nothing is set in stone as of now, Ma. Trust us, and don't stress. Okay?' Aman continued reassuring, following her around the kitchen and dining area.

'Why will I worry? I am not quitting my job. I have my PF, pension, and my own house. You should be the one stressing.' Our light debate continued as she continued preparing ingredients for dinner.

'*Arre*, aunty, leave it now. You tell me how long your trip is this time?' I attempted to switch topics.

'I want to go to Nainital for a vacation or Ranthambore maybe. But Aman doesn't let me go anywhere,' she replied helplessly.

'We will take you out, aunty,' I offered.

'Why? I don't want to go with you. I have my social circle. I enjoy more with them.' A single woman who had picked up the pieces after a tragedy, built a life brick by brick, got her kids educated, could undoubtedly manage a vacation independently.

'My mom's a Rambo. Now unless you want to spend the rest of the evening chit-chatting, can we go?' Aman quipped.

I touched aunty's feet before leaving, and she affectionately blessed me again as any Indian mother would.

We checked into a BYOB, a.k.a Bring Your Own Booze restaurants that are all over Gurgaon now. These are perfect alternatives to expensive pubs. You can get your booze at MRP and just need to order snacks or food from them.

'Have you read Al Grand's documents?' Aman began. I didn't know if he did it to annoy me or if Bluewater meant that much to him.

'Of course, you were in the room when I briefed the team. We can talk about the rest in Dubai,' I remarked, downplaying his point.

'Come on, Bharat. We are flying on Tuesday and presenting on Friday,' Aman kept at it, and I was just done with him.

'You come on, Aman! Enough is enough. It's been six, almost seven months since we have been learning this. We know every nut, every bolt, and you can't seem to be getting over your obsession with office projects,' I replied in a raised tone, visibly upset.

'Bro, hold on a second before you take off! This is a big assignment, and you are messing around too much,' Aman stayed resolute, and the day I dreaded so much was here. This was going nowhere, and I had to start on my own. Maybe he will join when I get this off the ground with Vinay, and hopefully, he will behave better.

'Wait! Let's order first and get this guy off our backs,' I said, referring to the waiter with shoes of cement who wouldn't leave till we placed an order.

'Two glasses, one ice bucket, one veg platter, and some roasted peanuts,' I ordered.

'Sure, sir.'

I didn't want to start the conversation immediately and pretended to look through the food menu. There wasn't much to think about, especially if you were vegetarian. What options do you have outside of some paneer and soya?

But Aman didn't seem to get cue. He brought up his annoying Al Grand discussion like we were some interns dealing with our maiden assignment.

'See, I am controlling the ERP side of things and partly even your technology areas. All I want you to do is approve the content and supply the additional pages you had prepared.' I couldn't believe what was going on here.

'Yes, sir, let's make the deck. I see you have got your laptop too,' I retorted, but he stayed unfettered. Why did I even come here today?

'You don't get it, do you Bharat? I am not saying we won't do this … all I am saying is let's see this one through so I can focus on what you want.'

'Boss! Don't do this for me, okay?

'If you don't want to do this, by all means, you are free to walk out. Be my guest!'

'Just stop this project hype and everything. I have told you the deal will not slip, at least not because of me,' I asserted.

'No! Project after project, we get into this panic zone and then work through the night to scrape through. This can't be the story every time.'

I didn't know what to make of it, impressed by his commitment to work or aghast at his indifference to business.

'Okay, tell me what you want?'

'I will forward you the pages, but no matter how much you go over the plan, ultimately, we will be stuck in our hotel room working through the night on this,' I knew it was pointless.

He pulled out his laptop and a rough presentation. One of his top skills was to give structure to ideas. He started explaining, and I agreed to pay attention again!

He went on for some forty-five minutes. It was a helpful briefing. Honestly, it wasn't one I couldn't have done without. It was the same old same old. You spend so much. We will make you save so much. You will buy a new system, fire 1000 people from your rolls, then hire another 300 from us. Pressurizing people to do more work for the same pay to meet your budgets when the automation fails or, better still, buy some new company that keeps everyone busy in the name of integration. Whoever delivered this message better walked away with the dollars. What's the fuss all about?

'So, our pitch is ready. Let's see what Chatterjee brings,' he sounded confident of a good product, and I was done for the evening.

'Banerjee,' I corrected.

'Yeah, yeah! Banerjee. Let's see what he brings. Phew! Now … tell me when is our EV going to be ready?' he mocked, and I was almost ready to splash the whiskey on his face.

'Forget it. Finish your drink. I am done. I will see you on Monday,'

He could tell I was now on edge, and any needling could result in an ugly turn for the evening, which might be hard to repair. He acted with subtlety and quietly lit up a cigarette and allowed me to cool off a little. I, too, lit up my own and asked the nearby table for a lighter to avoid conversation with Aman.

I looked around the BYOB business that was being run. The place was packed with people sitting almost elbow to elbow. They had a transparent kitchen, a new theme adopted by most of these BYOBs to dispel all doubts about their hygiene and quality, a ploy that seemed to be working and could be evidenced by crowds frequenting, which included women and families too.

'Okay…you tell me your plan. I am listening, I promise. For starters, we know it is a killer idea by a mastermind,' he tried to lighten the vibe.

'Boss, bill please,' I called out.

'No, no! Wait. Please. I mean it. I will listen with focus. Tell me about the plan,' he attempted to salvage the situation and get me talking.

'I will, but to someone more than an armchair enthusiast. I am booking my losses with you,' I remarked.

'Swear to god, and I am serious. Tell me what's on your mind,' he pressed further.

'You sure? You make one off-color remark, this whole thing will be in your face,' I pointed to my drink.

'Done. I will splash it on my face myself, I promise,' he assured, and I began.

'See, we have researched enough, and what we need to solve for cracking this project is the battery science. I mean, that's the foremost,' I continued, and he nodded, suggesting that he was tuned in, so I kept going.

'You know all about the cost of the battery as a proportion of the overall build costs of the car, which makes the whole thing impractical from an upfront cost perspective. The second thing is the time the battery takes to charge and where can you charge it.'

I paused to check if he was still with me. This was nothing new anyway, so I continued.

'Larger corporations are deploying large battery units to reduce cost through scale, but we can't build factories of the size of a city. We need to pull off a Mangalyaan-like feat, and it will be the Zinc battery formula we used during college.'

He kept nodding.

'There is no point discussing Lithium (LI) batteries. Most people are trying it out already. Plus, for India, it's not even an option, given the low Lithium reserves. We will just end up replacing our petrol import bill with lithium imports. We need something in abundance for India and get it to work better than LI. Zinc or Aluminium, perhaps. We have the world's seventh-highest reserves of Zinc and the sixth-largest Bauxite or Aluminum. I have my votes for Zinc.' I paused to see if we were on the same page. He took another sip of whisky and ate a piece of onion. I, too, sipped from my glass, waiting for his reaction.

'So, what are we making? A car or a battery?' he asked, and I stood up to leave.

'What the hell! Sit down! Are you crazy? What did I say?' He held my arm as I turned to go.

'I am sorry, but I asked you about the plan, and you are telling me things I already know. If you don't remember, I, too, was in all these master classes,' he reasoned.

'I am leaving, bro. I have no more patience left. Let's do this some other day.' I replied, now exhausted.

'But you tell me, what is the plan? Where do we go from here?' he repeated.

'What plan? We decided to agree on a "go or no go." You didn't let me complete,' I lamented.

'Honestly, I think I am going to do it myself. This is too stressful. We will stay friends. But I don't think we can do business together,' I concluded.

'That's your call, but I have some fundamental questions.'

'Okay, let's park this for a while… come on!' He requested. It was hard to tell if it was even sincere or if this whole thing was some grand circus for him.

'Go on. I am listening. What do you want me to say?'

'Order something,' I replied. I had already refused dinner at home.

'If you don't mind, *bhai*. I need your input on another deck we need to finish.'

Hell! This was unbelievably audacious, and I couldn't believe I hadn't left the place.

He took out his laptop again, to my utter shock. Assuming I would contribute to the discussion, he turned the screen so it was visible to both of us and clicked on a PowerPoint file named 'ZILA.'

The first slide was titled 'Bharat Kinetics,' and then he went on to the next slide of an electric car as the background theme. I was confused and surprised, but inadvertently, a slight smile emerged on my face.

'My very own Elon Srinivasan! This is my understanding and an initial plan,' he announced.

'There are six big areas we need to understand. And this is not Bharat as in you. This is ' Bhaarat' as in India,' Aman clarified.

'First, it's the motor. This transfers power from the battery pack and, with the help of a DC convertor, spreads to the car's various components, exactly how the heart pumps blood to our organs. Basic so far? Clear till here?' he asked, and I nodded.

Aman continued, 'Second is a reducer. Assume this to be like a regulator to control revolutions per minute (RPM) or torque.

'Third is your battery. These are like carbs that degenerate and inject energy into the body. Fourth is the Battery Management System. This is the center of your brain. It regulates how much power the components get. This will need to be controlled through sophisticated automotive software.

'Fifth is your Onboard Charger. This converts AC to DC, which is like converting indisciplined sea waves or choppy water supply into a shower or a more efficient tap or like transforming Bharat's broad vision into Aman's usable insight,' he said and looked up for a reaction. By this point, he had more than atoned for all the delay and mockery, and honestly… he had me on slide one! And how cliché I was!

He continued, 'Sixth, and the most important is the software that will orchestrate, control, repair, and power the entire machine, always online, connected to a central server, unless the driver decides otherwise.

'And finally, the entire automotive hardware, the chassis, the axle, the wheels, and other parts.

'Almost all of this, except for the chips, are made in India by companies like Motherson Sumi, Kirloskar, and several others. Still, I am not sure how much they will entertain us, given our size, value, experience, etc.'

He continued flipping through slides; so far, it was all in line, just all well-structured information and plan.

'So, what options do we have?' he flipped to the next slide with the same title.

'Option 1: Fly to China, Korea, Taiwan, and Vietnam to find suppliers.

'Option 2: Assemble a diverse team right here and build from scratch.

'I suggest we build from scratch because most of these are electrical components. It will be challenging, but at least we will have total control and will be able to make changes in the process. I will leave that to you.'

'For the chips, we can repurpose some from existing vehicles for the launch vehicle and figure out a long-term plan as we get closer to the launch,' the Aman I knew, always thorough, detailed, and meticulous. That's why I now wanted to hug him and celebrate! But I held back for him to maintain his train of thought.

'So, who do we need?

'One battery expert, even if he is from a college or a lab. One solid automobile engineer who can build the physical car, a team of software developers to create the operating system, and another team of developers who specialize in 3D auto designs. We also need a top-quality team to design the battery management application for Zila.'

'Why Zila?' I inquired.

'I don't know. Let's see. Zinc Inside Literally Awesome,' he said and chuckled, and I laughed out loud.

'What if it turns out to be Aluminum? Will it be 'AILA'? We both cracked up at that. 'Cheers!' We both said in unison.

'Now the next question is where will we get the money from?' He flipped to the next slide.

'So, your savings plus mine, all of it will add up to some thirty lakh. If we do this next project well, add another ten to this. It'll be forty, and if we liquidate our provident funds, that will be fifteen more, so we are at fifty-five.' The slide read (5,00,000) in the accounting format, indicating a shortfall.

'Now, wait,' he could tell I was itching to pose my next question.

A fifteen-member team with an average pay of fifty thousand will need at least sixty lakh for eight months, including expenses for renting, equipment, laptops, and travels. To sustain, we need to find an investor after eight months with a minimum viable product.

'I can raise more money by applying for a loan against property. Thirty or forty lakh or so against my house,' I added, which could take our opening balance to about a crore.

'Wait, not yet, dude! We need to get the model car out in less than twelve months from the day we start,' he advised, and I heeded, but we knew.

'I, too, can ask mummy for a loan, so we can figure this out. I don't think money will be a problem,' he said, and I acknowledged.

'We just need to get it right ... So, what next then?' I looked up for a cue.

'In a country of 120 crore people, if we can't make a car with fifteen moving parts, then we can't make anything!' He announced.

'*Wallah Habibi,*' I replied. 'Wallah Habibi!' We both yelled in chorus.

# 6

# WHEN IN DUBAI

It was a rather dull flight, and I got through it by watching *Ben-Hur*.

We landed at the Emirates terminal at the Dubai airport and proceeded to immigration.

'I am going to crash,' Aman announced as soon as we were in the cab.

'Yeah. Me too. Just need to clear a few emails and inform the clients and Shantanu we are here,' I replied in a routine tone.

Check-in took fifteen minutes at a sixty-story hotel tower. I got a 1 BHK suite while Aman got a three-bedroom with a view on the thirty-fifth floor. The living room was spacious with a leather couch, LED, chandelier, carpet, and dining table. The kitchen was equipped with an induction stove and fridge. The king-size bedroom had a closet and a private balcony. We had four days to work before our pitch on Sunday.

We walked into the Al Grand office. Their wallpapers were full of pictures of massive refineries, Dubai locations, UAE,

Bahrain, and Saudi rulers inaugurating and inspecting their plants and processes.

Our meetings were all booked, and we diligently went about our business of extracting as much information as possible.

It was about the end of our first day in Dubai when Alan Wooding, their British CFO, walked into our meeting room to size us both before we presented to him and his courtiers on Sunday.

'Hey… Alan Wooding.' A tall white British man in his mid or late forties greeted us. He was our main client and our sponsor.

'Good evening, Alan. Bharat.' I stood up from my chair and greeted him.

'Hello, Alan. Aman.'

Alan then walked all the way in and shook hands with us both.

'So, when did you guys get here?' he enquired in his thick British accent.

'We got here yesterday evening,' Aman responded.

'Hope you've rested well? Get ready with your sports gear. There's going to be a lot of running around. I have been here one whole year, and I am still getting familiar,' he smiled.

'Oh, this is now a way of life for us. Please don't go by our suits,' Aman added, suggesting that we weren't expecting things to be easy.

'Alright, so you are fighting fit then. Good to know!'

We gave him a detailed account of our day and our plan going forward, and at the end of it, he offered to take us both out for drinks in the evening. We didn't complain. He wished us luck and left the room, and we continued working to gather intel and validate our assumptions and inputs.

It was about six in the evening, and Alan located us sitting next to his finance manager.

'I will be done in thirty minutes,' he spoke softly, signaling that we wrap up quickly.

I gave a thumbs-up in confirmation. He drove to this place we had been to many times before, a pub called Trader Vic's, a trendy pub in Dubai.

'So, have you been here before?' Alan opened the conversation.

'Yeah, quite a few times, our favorite whenever we're here,' I replied.

'I, too, started just like you guys, living off a suitcase, providing financial advice to companies around the world,' he continued, sounding much like Indian bosses with their teams at BYOBs in Gurgaon.

'Always Oil and Gas or beyond?' I got the conversation going with some small talk.

'I have oil instead of blood running through my veins,' he said. No wonder there was blood all over middle eastern oil.

We went on for a while, engaging in small talks about Dubai, his life, and our lives back in India, essentially getting a measure of each other before he could trust us with something more substantive. Such profiling was a routine affair for us. We stayed careful and confident, going light on drinks, expressing our view of what we had seen so far, balanced criticism of their organization, praise for his vision, our points of view on areas within our pay grade, sometimes slightly beyond, staying mindful of not encroaching his territory. Flattery does get you some distance, even if not all the way.

Then, he started to open up about his motives for getting us here. It certainly wasn't to make us feel comfortable.

'Okay, so I need you guys to know one thing. You might want to note this down too. This is some real intel. But first, I need your phones on the table, please, if you don't mind,' he was professional, and there was no awkwardness in his tone.

We followed instructions, unlocked our phones, cleared all applications, and placed them on the table, assuring him that nothing was being recorded. Aman even switched his off. I followed his lead. Alan smiled, acknowledging our familiarity with customs.

Once he was sure, he immediately cut to the chase, unambiguously explaining what he wanted to see in the proposal—the timelines, the systems, even the suppliers he wanted us to partner with, and the cost. We bargained tactfully and eventually agreed upon a range he would consider.

He ordered more drinks and food and drifted away to other topics like his experience from other assignments, why he thought we both had a bright future and how we went about business. We stayed attentive like sincere schoolboys, and soon he asked us to feel free to use our phones. He asked us to pull up our LinkedIn accounts.

He typed some names and told us to consider hiring these people as part of the core project team, all of whom he had worked with in the past—some leaders always travel with their flock, and he was one of them. We concurred as one would expect, and more cocktails followed.

Everything was fine till the drinks began kicking in, to the point that I was blacking out. I went to the restroom several times, but with every passing moment, my mind spun more rapidly, and I knew I was losing it. Alan was a hardcore corporate politician, and he was putting us both to the test.

He began asking more open-ended questions compared to his earlier long-drawn-out speeches. He asked us about our interests, if we invested in stocks, our ambitions, and so on.

'So... Alan... what's *your* view on this whole electric vehicle revolution?' I asked in a moment of indecision. The urge to discuss EVs had gotten the better of me.

'Everything these days is a revolution!' He mocked.

'But if you were to invest, won't this be among your top bets?' I continued and could vaguely tell Aman was livid without even looking at him.

'I doubt it. EV is a work of an electrician, a real car is a work of an engineer,' Alan mocked again.

'In interesting quote,' I remarked. I was almost slurring now.

'But you guys are the new generation. So, what am I missing?' He pressed, looking into my eyes the whole time. He either thought I was the weak link or the bright light.

'Oh, nothing. We just watched this Tesla documentary on the flight, so it got us thinking how this will play out,' Aman stepped into downplay.

'Seventy-five grand on a car? That's madness,' Alan remarked.

'Not seventy-five, it's about forty,' I clarified, like a dumbass.

'Are you guys up to something here?' He was now looking at me with greater intent.

'Err... I so wish, Alan. As bo... boring as it may sound, we are in love with what we do,' I replied, gathering all my faculties.

'No, sure! You do have quite a job. Keep in touch, boys, if you ever decide to start on your own.'

Now, this was a surprise coming from a guy like Alan.

'Of course, Alan, we will,' I wasn't shutting up.

He wrote down his personal email address and phone number on a tissue and handed it to me. We didn't know what to make of it. Was it a trap, or was luck smiling on us? Did I just pull off an investment without even trying to? He drove us back home, and I almost immediately dozed off in the car.

The following day at the breakfast table, when my head was still spinning, Aman began to have a go at me.

'You were such a wreck yesterday. You almost blew everything up!' he grumbled, applying butter to his bread while. I feasted on some Cheerios. I loved the quality we got here.

'Now, don't blow it up so much. I was drunk! He got me drunk!' I defended casually.

'Why don't you call him up and share with him the Zinc-air formula too? It was a lot to take while defying a hangover.

'Okay, now! Come on! Alright! I was just getting a sense of what these guys with deep pockets think of concepts like these.'

'We could have compromised the deal and, more so, our dream with this one reckless act,' he continued with anger. I knew he wouldn't stop till I apologized.

'So, what do you want me to do now? I told you I would be careful,' I assured him. He was spoiling the morning. I hated such stressful conversations. It's like how my mom does it.

'Thanks! Please grow up! I can't be babysitting you all the time, for god's sake!'

'But nothing happened! Relax!' I reacted.

'Nothing happened because I cooked up the Tesla documentary story.'

'Why do you think he wasn't looking into my eyes? But he saw through you, you idiot! I can't believe this. He is a Brit, Bharat. An old generation Brit.

'He can size you up without even uttering a word! Another ten minutes of your drunken banter and you would have given away the entire plan!' He went on.

'Okay, now you are grossly underestimating me. Second, I am not a gullible kid, alright?' I was practically screaming now, 'Thanks for saving me, but don't forget there have been times I have come to your rescue too. It's called looking out for a friend.'

I got back to my breakfast. We had to leave in ten minutes, and I still had not gotten to my fruits, black coffee, and morning smoke. Ugh!

He didn't say much after that. Aman didn't see that we had Alan's personal email. He wasn't the kind to be handing over his personal info unless he saw a genuine spark. Plus, so much intel for the deal. It was a great meeting!

We spent the rest of the day, till about one in the night, putting together our proposal, in line with the cues Alan gave us, packed with our observations, recommendations, implementation plan, etc. We had to get a high-quality working draft ready before Shantanu arrived the next day, and I think we did an excellent job of it. In the process, Aman had also loosened up.

We woke up late the next day to a message from Shantanu confirming that he had landed and would get to the hotel by about two in the afternoon, while we were supposed to meet him at the café by five.

We continued perfecting the material for the presentation with Abhishek's team in India before heading to the café. Shantanu arrived looking relaxed in his black Guns and Roses t-shirt with shorts and a pair of Crocs.

'What's up, boys? How's it going?' He greeted and gave us both a hug before settling in.

'What's this? Sandwiches? When did you both become so polite? Let's order some beers!' He sounded pretty upbeat.

'*Arre* sir, we have a lot of beers in the apartment. It's exorbitantly priced here,' Aman advised.

'My boy! Go ahead and have a good one. Don't worry about the price. It's my treat!' He offered magnanimously even though he would bill the company.

'Okay, spend if you want to', but I explained that we have two crates stacked up in the fridge. He hated to waste time on such mundane decisions.

'Let's order one each, at least. It doesn't look nice. After that, we will head to your room.' This was sensible, and we agreed.

'So, boss, we gave you a full lowdown of what Alan wants to see. This is how the pack looks. We can make some changes through the day, get Abhishek's team to proofread, and wrap it up in gold tonight,' Aman said, and we started going through the proposal in detail.

'How do you think Alan will react to this?' Shantanu asked.

'We can find out,' I replied.

'Really? Bharat, I don't have time for your sarcasm. I need to know from you,' he replied, already a little riled up. Such was the threshold of his patience, and I loved testing it.

'That's what I am saying. We can find out from him tomorrow informally, at some Starbucks,' I announced, and he looked at me suspiciously.

'You can do that?' he asked in disbelief.

'I think so,' Aman confirmed.

'Not bad. You have been here for less than a week. I am impressed,' he remarked.

'All it takes is that one magical evening,' I added, and Aman nodded with an unimpressed smile.

After about fifteen minutes of texting, Aman pulled off the meeting over a cup of coffee with Alan for Saturday at four. This also meant that today was going to be another long unhealthy night—both, for us and the teams back in India helping us.

We worked till two in the morning, knowing we had a great proposal. It was one of our best works—sharp and crisp.

* * *

We printed four color sets of the presentation and drove to Starbucks in Shantanu's 4x4 rental Range Rover.

After another couple of hours with Alan, debating numbers and strategy, we finally agreed.

'You guys are in business. Best of luck!' Alan remarked. We saw Shantanu's eyes light up just a little bit.

We walked Alan to his car and wished him a good day.

'See you guys. Take it easy,' he said and drove away in his Porsche Cayenne.

'You both are the real deal at Bluewaters. I feel so proud watching you both come of age,' Shantanu remarked. His promotion had drawn closer with this deal. Our humble ten lakh felt at arm's reach.

It was the day of the meeting, and we were all suited-booted and ready to roll to the Al Grand office.

We convinced most of their executives in the room and concluded on a high. Shantanu thanked them for their time and support. He finally invited them for a wine and dine session in the evening.

Shantanu played a gracious host at a plush restaurant in downtown Dubai, after which we walked everyone out to their cars. Everyone appeared to be in high spirits and full of praise. We both could tell how excited Shantanu was feeling.

'Shantanu, you are lucky to have these boys on your team. I am truly impressed,' Alan remarked, now almost ready to hop into his car.

'Thanks, Alan. That means a lot coming from you. They are indeed the best I have,' Shantanu acknowledged.

'And boys, if you do decide to pursue something bigger and better, you know whom to call,' he concluded as he drove away in his car.

Aman and I exchanged pleasant looks.

Shantanu looked at us and smiled suspiciously, recognizing the connection we had established in virtually no time. He didn't say much. He lit a cigarette and pulled out his phone as we waited for our car.

Aman quickly hopped onto the rear seat, leaving me with him in the front.

'So, what do you think,' he asked quietly after a few minutes of driving.

'I think it's ours to lose from this point,' I replied.

'Yes… And what spell did you cast over Alan? I have known him for a while now and never seen him this vocal in his praise.'

'We don't know, honestly. I am surprised too,' Aman added from the rear seat.

'Hope there is nothing I need to know. What was it about "bigger, better things"?' he enquired.

'No idea. He has been saying this since our first evening with him at Trader's Vic,' Aman replied nonchalantly.

'You better keep me in the loop…' he said, issuing a veiled threat.

'But that's between him and us, boss,' I said, fanning the flames of his imagination.

'Bharat, this is not funny,' he warned, getting impatient.

'I know you both better than you know yourselves. You know, I have seen you since you were these sloppy management trainees taking notes,' he added, reminding us that he alone was our true master. We better hail!

We nodded.

'So, Bharat, you have your European holiday sorted if this goes through?' he started again. 'Your private beach villa must be on its way, too. Right?' I responded.

'Oh, sweetheart! Don't be jealous of other people's success! I am twenty years your senior. The way you guys are going … at my age, you will have weekend yacht parties. When I was your age, all I could afford was Kerala.'

'Kerala is not bad, actually,' I replied.

'Yeah? Why don't I cancel your bonus you seem to have seen enough of Europe.'

'Up to you, boss. But please give my total share to Aman.'

'*Yaar* Aman, tell your friend to grow up. How has he come this far? I sometimes wonder.'

'With your mentorship. How else?'

'Even though you try to be sarcastic, you know deep within how true that is.'

'I am being honest, how much have I learnt from the master,' I played along knowing I was flirting with a lot of danger here.

Our hotel was, thankfully, a fifteen-minute drive, so this ordeal got over pretty quickly.

Soon it was time to head back home, and we were waiting for our ride to the airport the next day.

'So, what do you think? Our ten lakh now sealed?' I asked Aman.

'Who knows? Maybe we are destined for something "bigger and better" than ten lakh. Perhaps your little drunken stunt might fetch us a lot more if we are in luck,' he exclaimed, smiling freely now after weeks of stress.

# 7

# PROFESSOR VINAY

We landed in the pollution-filled air of the city that I have called home all my life. It was time to finally make the one call I had wanted to make for months.

'Haan bhai, what's up, Mr. Director?' He sounded alright

'Awesome bhai, you tell me…' I replied.

'Brilliant, like always. Doing some random jobs, rather, odd jobs. But all is good,' Vinay had been unable to secure a steady career for himself, and you could tell. Behind this funny exterior, he was bitter watching his friends he once considered quite ordinary having raced well ahead of him.'

'Yeah, not bad, but it doesn't sound like a career. Are you happy?' I checked.

'I think so. It's great to be with these bright young kids, plus I can stay in touch with the subject,' I was unsure of pushing him further on what felt like a raw nerve, presumably, one he had managed to numb.

'We can talk, right?' I checked if he was in that frame of mind or not.

'Of course!'

'Now, remember I sent you a text about the project idea I had in mind?'

'Of course! Took you a while. I thought you had given up on it AGAIN!'

'Yeah, I know. I was just combing the field before coming to you. So, what is it? Our battery, right?' He knew where this was going.

'More than that actually … a full car!' I replied and waited for a reaction. 'Wow!' he said and went silent.

I waited for him to say more: good, bad, ugly… something, but he didn't

'Hello? What happened? You don't sound convinced,' I probed.

'I was convinced even back then. Just don't know if we will be able to pull this off, that's all.'

'As in?' I probed further.

'As in… a number of things: the money, the making, setting up a company, doing this commercially, assembling a team, plus we know just the design and battery angle of the things.

'Besides, will you fight for it if something similar happens again?' he never stopped taunting me about what happened. To both of us. But to him, it was all my fault. That's been his problem. I didn't want to go there, just keep it focused.

'You are listening?' He checked.

'Yeah, go on, I am with you,' I acknowledged.

'How convinced are you?' He spun the whole thing back on me.

'Zila,' as we plan to call it, will run in the next twelve to eighteen months. That's how convinced I am,' I replied, adding further, 'I will pledge my life to this. That's how far I will go to fight for this.'

'Not bad, Mr. Bharat Srinivasan! So, who all? You, me, and ...?'

'You, me, Aman, and several others we'll find during the next few months. But I cannot do it without you ... no way in hell,' I announced emphatically while also making a humble plea.

'Oh, Aman! Hmm ... he is a good guy, but this whole thing of creating a company, having employees, and setting up a factory means putting in a lot of money. Let's meet someday. These are the kind of things best discussed face to face,' he said, and I had bagged what I wanted.

'What someday? Tomorrow afternoon at one, Starbucks, Ambience mall,' I confirmed.

'See, this bossy attitude? You better lock it up if you want this to work.'

'Coming from the most humble human I have met, I will see you at Ambience,' I reconfirmed.

* * *

Aman and I reached slightly before time and occupied the only couch in the café. It wasn't long before I sighted Vinay from a distance making his way in.

The Vinay who walked in was in sharp contrast to the one from college; the extra inches had made way for an athletic body with well-defined biceps. He was dressed up casually yet smartly in a round-neck t-shirt in dual shades of blue, denims, and white sneakers.

I had seen some of his Facebook posts, but I never really took much notice, assuming he must have used some filters and Photoshop, but now that it was all here and real, I was genuinely impressed and frankly crossed with myself for resisting the gym.

'Hey, Tiger! How is it going?' He asked as he hugged me tightly. 'Awesome, bro. You look like an aging stud.'

'Ah well, this is all I have to do now. I never wanted a regular corporate job, so I invested that time in myself. Gym and swimming is a way of life for me now,' he replied, acting like a star trying to be humble.

He also shook hands with Aman. After the initial greetings, I ordered three large Americanos and went straight to business.

'So, you know the concept. We are building the world's best electric car, a real one, not like the token boxes we have currently,' I started.

'We need to get a team on the ground, and I want you to lead the entire engineering module,' I proposed.

'Who else do you have on the team?' Vinay asked again. 'For now, I am hoping Aman, you, and me.'

'So, will you guys quit your jobs?' He was still in inquiry mode.

'Oh! Without a doubt. This will require us to do much more than that,' Aman said.

'You need me to quit too?' Vinay enquired.

'But you need to have a job to quit,' I mocked.

'F.O. (fuck off) This amounts to workplace bullying … Okay. So, I will also need to give up on my flourishing career. It's going to be hard, but I will think about it,' he replied in a self-deprecating tone.

'See, we know the idea is phenomenal, but no one has been able to crack this battery and charge problem,' Vinay posed his first serious reservation.

'Except us,' I corrected him and continued, 'In fact, some people have. I have read enough on this. Israelis have cracked it with Aluminum; Koreans, Chinese, and Europeans are making tremendous headway with Zinc …'

'We did crack it … in a way … but it wasn't tested, so let's not overstate this,' Vinay attempted to ground my exuberance. He should have known better. Nothing could!

'Okay, be that as it may, but I know you, we *can* crack this. All I need is two years of our life.'

'You tell me what's there to lose?' I asked.

'Crores of rupees, careers, friendships, self-confidence,' he answered.

'Which of these can you not earn back? I asked again.

'I forgot to add health.'

'Try yoga for that. Come on now! You know it's worth pursuing!' I stressed.

'I don't know. This is similar to telling your alter ego, you know life is great, let's add some stress!' he was playing the devil's advocate, and I was okay. I had enough practice with Aman already.

'Good argument, but just not true. We know life is not going to be the same forever.' I warned that we are all just one bad boss away from turmoil, compulsions, frustration, and stress, which will cause more damage to your health, confidence, and career. 'Now, just think of it. We build the world's best electric car that runs not just in India but all over Europe and America. We will never have this opportunity ever again!' I said with firm conviction.

They both heard me silently.

'And you know the best part is we have the competence, confidence, and credentials to crack this … So, what are you scared of?' I asked.

'I am not scared. This is going to be really tough. I am telling you now,' Vinay cautioned.

'I know, but that's the problem with most people, immediately after thinking of a brilliant idea, they switch to only considering fallouts and risks, losing sight of the big prize, the big dream!' As usual, I didn't realize I had again switched to my prophetic side.

'Bharat, we need to test each other's resolve and vision,' Aman butted in.

'Boss! You hold on. All you have been doing for the last six months is testing me. Now I can't spend the next six months with Vinay,' I snapped and shut down Aman before he could turn this into some committee discussion.

'We can't just swim at the shores forever. I've had enough!'

'Let's not quarrel, please. Now tell me what the team will be like?' Vinay tried forging a truce, and Aman pulled up his grand PowerPoint and took him through our plan, team, and funding.

'We will need a lab to experiment. I can arrange that. I am, you know, kind of a professor now,' Vinay announced.

'You have an MPhil, Vinay?' I questioned.

'I am an ex-MIT. That's hot property. Even if *you* don't see it that way,' he defended quite meekly, though, for his standards.

'Ex-MIT drop-out! What was it? Six months?' I challenged.

'One year! You bloody Indian! Ah, well ... I will speak to a few colleges and get working laboratories to perfect our formulation,' Vinay agreed to organize the lab.

'Next question. Who will be the CEO? Let's address this here and now,' Vinay raised a rather uncomfortable question without any awkwardness.

'I am not in the race,' Aman announced almost instantly.

'Me neither,' Vinay followed.

'So, then it is decided. Bharat becomes our CEO, and we both will be his defiant subordinates. Let's give him a taste of his own medicine. Maybe he will realize how Shantanu feels,' Aman said and laughed. It was further decided that Aman would be CFO and Vinay will be the COO.

'That Shantanu guy is still your boss?' Vinay chuckled.

We got down to work almost immediately, shortlisting contacts, listing suppliers, and planning our trip, and before we knew it was dark and time to call it an evening.

'Dude, listen, now don't start to gloat,' Vinay paused as we left the mall.

'I missed you! Only Bharat Srinivasan can pull this off. Unless you abandon this, I am going nowhere.'

'Hell, I should have called earlier, bro. I am sorry,' we hugged tight.

'Now be on time every day,' I quipped.

He flipped the middle finger at me and playfully choked my neck around his arms.

# 8

# READY… STEADY… NO! WAIT!

'Hi, boss,' I greeted Shantanu as I walked into his office.

He didn't respond right away and looked engrossed in typing a long email, something he wasn't known for. I sat there opposite him, just observing his office and in between fiddling with my phone. I had just made my Instagram account which proved good company. I checked the latest news on Zinc-air through Google alerts to find inspiration and stay ahead of competitors.

'Can you look at this once?' Shantanu asked me to go over the email he had just finished writing.

It was almost a page-and-a-half update on the consulting practice for the board newsletter. I took a closer look and suggested a few points; he dismissed them, except for a few commas and full stops.

'Okay, now tell me. Coffee?' He asked, and I nodded in agreement.

'Boss, I need to work from home for a few days. Won't be an issue, no client escalations, I guarantee,' I assured and requested.

'You, as it is, work from home half the week. What's new here?' He didn't see any point to my request.

'I mean a couple of weeks, or most of the time, when not onsite,' I tried explaining cautiously.

'I'm okay with it. Just don't blow the trumpet. Someone asks you, say you are on client sites or working night shifts. But no escalations, and your team needs to step up in your absence,' he gave the permission and the warning together, 'We should meet more often when you are in,' he remarked as the office boy arrived with his coffee.

'I think that's the point. You and I both travel so much,' I defended, but he didn't seem to care.

'One more request, boss,' I added.

'Yeah, go on!'

'Aman will also need to work from home during this time,' I politely added.

'What nonsense? Now come on! Not happening. I don't own this place.'

'Only a few weeks, boss. This is personal. Otherwise, I wouldn't have asked. Please, sir,' I implored.

'Bharat, you, Aman, and Abhishek are my three next-in-line leaders. I can't let both of you be missing,' he continued to resist.

'Boss, but that's happening as it is when we are on client assignments? There won't be an issue, just a few weeks. We will just tell everyone that we are on the US project working overnight,' I stood my ground and now almost prodded him to relent.

'What is it?' He asked, just as we had expected.

'Something personal, I promise I will tell you. Don't want to jinx it,' I assured, hoping he wouldn't doubt.

'Hmm... hope nothing underhand,' he enquired suspiciously but fortunately, on a different train.

'Not at all, boss! If we had the guts, we would have been millionaires,' I chuckled using humor to underplay it.

'I don't want any rude reminders. Nothing that is out of line,' he warned again.

'Take it easy, boss! We aren't going to Iraq on some spy assignment,' I played it down again.

'I hope that is indeed the case. I don't have a good feeling about this, so leave the room before I change my mind,' he ordered, and I complied.

'Take your coffee. I am leaving early today. See you around whenever next,' he added as I got up and left his room. Phew!

With Shantanu placated for the moment, we had to quickly begin our meeting routine with everyone who had agreed to spare some time for us. The focus was on two critical skills. Firstly, to find someone to work with us and build a rechargeable and highly efficient battery using a Zinc combination. Second, to find a software genius who could write an automotive operating system worthy of the world's best electric car.

One of the several meetings I distinctly remember was with an engineering professor in Patna, Dr. Rabil Haroon. She had worked for the government in the past with the Ministry of Heavy Industries, had a degree in Mechanical engineering, an MPhil, and a Ph.D., and her thesis was on friendly energy with almost two chapters dedicated to the electric vehicle where she had discussed the perils of Lithium-ion batteries.

After much follow-up, she agreed to meet us in Patna. The flight tickets on such short notice cost a bomb almost 40,000 rupees. There was no way we could spend that kind of money on one meeting, so we logged on to IRCTC, and we were shown a waitlist of 45 for AC classes and 116 for sleeper classes implying that we could forget about this.

While Vinay and I had almost convinced ourselves to burn money on air tickets, Aman was a pro with railway bookings. Thanks to aunty's frequent travels from Surat to Delhi. He logged into *tatkal* the next morning and got us three tickets on a sleeper class coach.

We were at the station on time, and surprisingly the New Delhi railway station looked clean. I had seen Tube stations look much worse. We spent time judging and commenting on how if we had the chance, we could change the face of everything wrong with this nation.

Our fellow passengers were a family; the patriarch of the family appeared a little uncomfortable at the sight of three twenty-something high-octane boys around the women accompanying him. The man of the house gave us a stone-cold expression. Which in hindsight wasn't such a smart thing to do to three well built men.

There was one thing he could thank us for; the three of us just had one carry-on bag compared to his seven or eight suitcases that occupied every inch of storage. Seemed like they were moving to Patna or to wherever they were headed.

We didn't have much to do. We hung out at the door, smoking and chatting, finishing countless cups of railway tea.

We had booked rooms in a hotel advised by Dr. Haroon. The hotel arranged a cab, and we were well rested before meeting at a CCD, some 500 paces from the hotel.

Dr. Haroon arrived on time as she had promised. She double-checked with her immobilizer that her Ford EcoSport was locked. I always do it in Gurgaon, and this was Patna. One has to be careful.

Dr. Haroon was as white as milk. Dressed up in a regular salwar suit and semi-framed large glasses that she wore to read from the menu. At forty-something, 5 foot 3 or 4, she was a graceful presence.

We ordered some samosas, sandwiches, and cappuccinos. Vinay finally began.

'So, ma'am, why did you leave a government job, if I may ask?' Vinay took off on the most awkward note one could imagine. I managed to hold back my sense of embarrassment by looking at the skies.

'I had my kids growing up, and the posting was mostly in Delhi. It was a paper-pushing job, and with family, I couldn't get into the research side of things, so I took up voluntary retirement once I got my Ph.D.'

Such a waste of a job, I thought to myself, but then it dawned that's what every second Indian wants, take up a job, take a VRS, and take up another job. This is like a citizen scam.

'So, just to bring our focus onto what we are here for,' Aman tried getting us all back on track.

'Sure,' she replied.

'As you know, we are trying to build an all home-grown, "Made in India Electric Car",' Aman was setting the context, but I hated when he used "trying." We were not trying.

'Yes, of course! I was even trying to search for Bharat Kinetics but couldn't find your company website,' she commented.

'We are just starting up. Web presence is still in progress,' Aman defended.

'Okay, so how may I help you?' she was way more to the point than any of us.

'So, we need you to guide us in building a battery with

a combination other than Lithium-ion,' Vinay was such a wreck. He spoke as if we had already hired her.

'If you don't mind me asking, what are your qualifications?' Now, that was quite a badass response by Dr. Haroon.

'Sure, Bharat and I are mechanical engineers from NIT, and Aman is a CA,' Vinay answered with pride.

'Okay, you both being engineers helps. So, what are the other combinations you are seeking to build?' She had a distinct sense of poise in her questioning.

'As we told you on the phone, Zinc-air is what encourages us the most,' Vinay promptly answered the professor's question just like he used to in college.

'Why don't you try to improve Lithium-ion's efficiency?' she probed.

'Tesla has already improved it to the limits, and they still can't sell even their cheapest car for under 49,000 dollars. That's almost thirty-two lakh Indian rupees,' I intervened.

'But that's the only technology that works. No one has succeeded with other combinations. Experiments are going on everywhere on Hydrogen cells, Zinc-ion, and so much else.'

'Ma'am, with due respect, you need to read more. Israelis have succeeded with the Aluminum-air concept already. They will be in the market in a few years. The Zinc-air formulation is so much more viable,' I contested.

'These are things that only work in labs. Try Lithium-ion,' she insisted.

'We will set the lab for you right here in Patna if you want. Let's try to make it work!' I almost pleaded.

'Honestly, I don't think you understand what I am saying. This concept won't work,' she declared with utter disdain and contempt for our competence.

'But, ma'am, your thesis advocates using Zinc and Aluminium, and you have called Lithium-ion the biggest peril to solid waste disposal and a drag on countries like India,' I paused for a moment.'

'Dump the thesis, I am telling you right here, only Lithium-ion will work, don't waste more time and money', she refused to reason.

'Ma'am, either you were insincere in your thesis, or your research was wrong. But our research, unlike yours, is both sincere and thorough. You and I know the only way this can take off in India on a large scale is if we change the battery technology.'

'Mr... what did you say your name was again?'

'Bharat,' Vinay answered in a silly way.

'Yeah, so Mr. Bharat, I am not being personal, but you and your friend, being engineers, should have known better. Zinc and Aluminium are not rechargeable, even a tenth standard kid would know this. You don't have a company website, have no idea of technology, and no business plan. You come here with a bunch of PowerPoint slides, and think you can comment on my credentials. How dare you?'

'I can because, unlike you, we have not wasted a government job, using it as insurance for a permanent secondary source of income. Vinay and I have been eight-pointers, and Aman is an all-India seventh rank holder in his CA. We are trying to create something in India by aggregating some of the finest minds from around the country, and we thought you were one of them. I must say it was a total waste of time.'

'Good luck with your car, if ever there is one. This is for the coffee,' she left some two hundred bucks on the table and left.

I promised myself that I would send her a Zila video one day.

At some level, she had given me a reality check I didn't need at this stage. I was still very confident about my technology understanding. If there were any issues, Vinay would have pointed them out already.

This was certainly a setback, one I wasn't ready for, I didn't know how to react and all I could think off was some time alone. I didn't say much to either of them till we got home.

I didn't know what to say, I got home and all I remember is locking myself up in my room only stepping out for food, glued into my gaming laptop gifted by my parents, who assumed I was preparing for some certifications. I knew Vinay and Aman were getting paranoid with my sudden dissaperance, but that's all I could think off, their phones rang, followed by texts, I didn't respond to any.

* * *

The Al Grand assignment was moving in full steam. I had to spend over ten hours each day, jumping from call to call to iron out pending issues so the contract could be signed. I smoked like a chimney more than I ever had, drinking more coffee than water, but I didn't flinch even for a second.

Two weeks into this madness, I knew this couldn't go any longer, and I finally called them both to my home.

'Namaste, aunty,' Vinay said.

'Namaste. Where have you been all these years?' I was surprised mummy recognized him. He looked nothing like college.

'The same old, aunty. Got busy with work,' Vinay responded.

'So now this is a gang of three. Aman, how is mummy?' Mom went on.

'All good, aunty,' Aman responded politely.

'So, another late-night party plan?' Mummy continued her inquiries.

'No, Aunty, I am here for your coffee and *murukku*,' Aman responded and cleverly sending her to the kitchen.

We got into my room. Vinay locked the door from inside, and they both raged towards me. I told them to back off, but they picked me up, kicked my ass red, and flung me on my bed.

'What the hell,' I screamed in pain.

'What the hell? You tell us,' Vinay demanded.

'Just one bad meeting and you go into this self-isolation! Aman continued, 'What were you doing? *Vipassana*?'

'Yeah, kind of,' I responded, still recovering from the pain and the jerk my back had suffered. I was waiting till my wedding to change the mattress. I really should have done it earlier.

'Now speak up. What is it?' One of them said I don't quite recall which one.

'You have wasted two full weeks. We had to meet that Chennai guy,' they both kept going at me.

'Meet them for what?' I asked like I was done meeting people.

They looked at me like what was I talking about?

'So now look here,' I drew their attention as I limped back to my laptop.

I typed "BharatKinetics in" and I could see the curiosity build up in their eyes.

I designed the landing page using Flash and some dot net code I learned on the internet, plus some material I downloaded and printed for ready reference.

The page took a couple of seconds to load up and showed lightning bolt graphics depicting a charging. It went from 2% to 98% and then to the first graphic, which had sketch-like animation outlined with LED like theme starting with a Hatchback outline, turning to a Sedan and then to an SUV, and finally, all three lined up against one another left to right in their order of entry as though they we plugged to the charging point.

I glanced to see their expression, and they both looked stunned.

'Welcome the Studio Zila, High on Power, High on Design, and Low on Pocket. An electric car for everyone,' appeared a line of text with a wash effect, immediately followed by a red colored "start" like a car ignition prompting the user to click.

I could see their amusement growing, their eyes lit up, and their smile getting wider.

Vinay clicked on it, and a blue layer with sixty percent transparency and a lightning bolt watermark in the background covered the screen page. On the left, it had slots that read Username and Password, and on the right, it read, 'Just moments to go.'

I typed 'Let's do this!' in the user's name and 'Hell! Yeah!' in the password box, and it took us to the access-controlled landing page.

There came a knock on the door. It was mummy indeed with some *pakoras* and filter coffee and *murrukus*.

'Why have you locked the door?' she asked.

'Mummy, we are working here. You want to come inside and check?'

'But what's there to lock? No one is coming inside,' she responded.

'Okay, we won't lock it. Now I am swamped. Love you. Bye.' I took the tray from her in a hurry and came right back in.

'What the…' Aman almost yelled but held back, realizing mummy was still around.

They read through the content of the website. The animation was comparatively more subtle, with a greater focus on content.

The Site Map had basic options, like who we are, our Models, and our Technology. Aman clicked "Our Models" and viewed three vehicles (Zila Seed, Zila Air, and Zila Max) with accompanying icons (Hatchback, Sedan, and SUV, respectively). He then selected "Compare side by side," and the vehicles appeared on a blue background with sixty percent transparent borders.

### Zila Seed

- Type – Hatchback
- Horsepower - 150 HP
- 0 -60 KMPH – 6 Seconds
- Range – 300 KM
- Transmission – Automatic
- Battery Type - This is the big one … you will find out soon!
- Expected price – 5 to 7 lakh

### Zila Air

- Type – Sedan
- Horsepower - 350 HP
- 0-100KMH – 8 Seconds
- Range – 450 KM
- Transmission – Automatic
- Battery Type - This is the big one ... you will find out soon!
- Expected Price – 8 to 10 lakh

### Zila Max

- Type – SUV
- Horsepower - 450 HP
- 0-100KMH – 5 Seconds
- Range – 450 KM
- Transmission – Automatic
- Battery - This is the big one ... you will find out soon!
- Expected price – 10 to 15 lakh

He now clicked on 'Who we are,' and the section opened with a bounce effect.

'You are a crazy character! And this is just fantastic. Even Tesla would be proud of a website like this. I bet,' Vinay complimented, smiling in utter admiration before he gave me a tight hug and lifted me off the ground in his typical way.

'I have something more to show you.' I walked towards my bed, pulled out a delivery package from the side table drawer, and flung it to Aman, who couldn't catch it.

He picked it up to open, and there were three smaller boxes. He unpacked the 1st one and read the contents through the transparent holding case, 'Vinay Aggarwal, Co-Founder, and Chief of Engineering, Bharat Kinetics.' After seeing the website, he handed the box to Vinay, who was already on steroids.

'So, Mr. CEO, why didn't you tell us, though? I still don't understand,' Vinay asked.

'That lady made me feel like some frivolous salesman, I pledged that I will never walk in to another meeting so unprepared,' I knew they felt the same way.

'Anyways, there were some lessons, and I wanted some time off. I didn't have the plan to discuss it. I am sorry. I know, it could unnerve anyone. But I knew I could take such liberties with you both,' my eyes welled up.

'Now shut up. It's her loss. We will show her, not just her but to everyone who has been patronizing us. And you, if anything, deserve a big reward for this,' Vinay announced.

'How about treating me to some beers?' I suggested still slightly emotional, which was strange for an other wise collected personality like me.

'Sure, but before that…,' he said. Both of them looked at each other when one lifted my feet and the other held my arms. Countless kicks on my butt followed before I was tossed up on my cot again. I made up my mind to order a new mattress right away.

'You are both fired! Security!…' I yelled.

# 9

# TAMIL NADU EXPRESS

Our next meeting took us to a Chennai man named Govindan Rajashekaran. If all went well, he would help us build our operating system. He had worked for Delphi for twenty years.

He was a regular speaker at several events we attended during our research and was working as a consultant for organizations like Fujitsu and even SAP. So he knew automotive and circuits and was widely respected as a software wizard.

We were on the Tamil Nadu Express to Chennai. Another long cross-country train journey while running my office on board. I had to finish a few calls en route and review multiple presentations on the train before they could be cleared for final submission. Aman had his projects, so it was just Vinay who could entirely focus on the points for discussion with Govindan. He had strongly suggested that we do this on the phone, but somehow, I felt, at such an early stage of our company, we had to look people in the eye if we were going to work with them.

Govindan asked us to show up at the Amethyst Café in Nungambakkam. It was a beautiful setting for a romantic date to escape the chaos of the busy and noisy city of Chennai. No screeching sound of autos, no incessant honking, no random yelling of hawkers and other worked-up Indian men. Although the cafe was located right in the middle of the city, they had done well to insulate the place from all outside stress. The moment you stepped in, a whole other countryside experience awaited.

We walked through at least a fifty-meter walkway leading up to the restaurant and could only spot mushy couples around us. A Starbucks would have been more appropriate for a meeting like this.

We called Govindan to check where he was, and he told us he was stuck in traffic and will need fifteen more minutes. He then instructed me to order something since the café takes a lot of time. I complied awkwardly.

The place had an easy and lazy vibe to it. No waiters were hounding to note down orders. It wasn't for guys like us who had aged before time. We walked up to the counter and ordered some coffee. The barista returned with the coffee and the light snacks we ordered for Govindan.

Aman and Vinay warned me not to blow it up even if the guy said anything out of line and I assured them I would be as patient as possible. We also agreed that if any one of us places the next order, the other two see it as a sign of approval.

We sipped coffee and lit our cigarettes in the smoking area, waiting for him, and he showed up in about another ten minutes.

A slightly obese guy, some 5 feet 8 inches, maybe with a whitish complexion, walked towards us. He was dressed in a plain brown shirt and black comfort-fit denims pulled to his hip. He had a *Naaman*, a trident-shaped red outline, on his forehead, typically a sign of Iyengar Brahmins. I, too, was one of them. Just not fully practicing

'Hi, Aman.'

'Bharat.'

'Vinay.'

We introduced ourselves and handed over our shiny new business cards.

'Very hot today,' he started as he wiped away the sweat from his face with a handkerchief.

'Yeah, thankfully, these guys have good indoor seating, too,' Vinay added.

He looked around the place and uncomfortably moved in his seat, 'We have ordered,' I kind of second-guessed.

'Oh, okay. No, these people take a lot of time, that is why I said, so we don't sit and waste time by waiting,' I wasn't having a good feeling about this. I had warned Aman after our first phone call with this guy.

'So Govindan, just to save time, it will be good if you can give us a brief about your experience in automotive software?' I began in a lose moment of impatience.

'Yes, before that, if you don't mind, can you apply this?' He passed on a Fogg pocket body spray to us.

'I am really allergic to the smell of smoke,' he explained, so we don't take offense.

'Oh, of course, we didn't know. By all means,' I agreed, and we took turns spraying it on.

'Now, I have twenty years of experience designing automotive software. I have worked extensively with General Motors, Subaru, and even for Mahindra & Mahindra,' he began.

'Brilliant,' I added and continued.

'If you could give details about the modules, it would be very useful,' I asked him to get more specific politely with a plastic smile.

'I have worked on all layers, from applications to microcontrollers. I started with testing in 1999 on a main frame system and then moved to Houston for two years. I even completed my master's in Embedded Systems while I was there. So from door opening to ignition to sensory functions, I have done it all. I am a certified AUTOSAR coach and a design guide. Nowadays, I provide coaching on MATLAB online to Chinese students,' he said and continued explaining his exploits.

Vinay and I kept asking and learning at the same time about several other nuances he faced while working in China, Japan, and any country of relevance; he was just the kind of guy we wanted. He was absolutely thorough with his trade.

We took him through our vision, and he seemed pretty interested.

'I think it will be great if we understand your expectations,' Aman addressed the next elephant in the café.

'I know you people are just starting. Do you have funding?' he checked.

'We are bootstrapping as we explained,' Aman responded.

'Why are you using your own money? You can easily get money at the ideation stage itself,' he advised.

'We know, but we want greater control to begin and seek funding during the MVP stage. But we have strong connections, so that won't be a problem,' Aman clarified.

'You are a Chartered Accountant. I know you understand finance better than any of us. I make some two lakh just by spending three to four hours a day,' he continued.

'So, unless you have funding, you won't be able to afford to pay for this. It will be a big burden,' this was an insult served cold but rang true.

'We can work on an equity basis, Govindan,' Aman made another proposal.

'Yes, the equity model works, but I will have to devote a lot of time to this, and I also have responsibilities as a visiting priest at Parthasarathy temple,' this was going to fail. I really wanted him to be on our team.

'I can devote four hours a day maximum,' he explained, very politely, statesman-like as he had been throughout the conversation. This is all we expected of Rabil.

'Then why did you agree to meet us?' I asked politely.

'I did not know that you don't have funding. Since you have come this far, I will give you one promise...' He said in his typical plain-speaking manner.

We heard intently.

'You build a team, and I will give you mentoring for free, and if you get your operating system to a beta version stage,' he continued, 'use me as your critic and reviewer. Don't waste money on me now; focus on building the MVP instead.'

'You really mean that Govindan? Or you want us off your back,' Aman quipped.

'You know this is the problem with people from the North, especially from Delhi. Everything is profit and loss,' he remarked directly yet politely.

'I want Indian start-ups to succeed. You just get a competent software engineer. In fact, I will give you a few references. You speak to them, get them to work fourteen hours a day, and then come to me. I will show you some magic.'

We couldn't stop smiling at his generosity. He had dwarfed us in knowledge and character.

'Well, I mean, thank you so much, really,' Aman's expressions depicted our collective and absolute gratitude.

'No problem, best of luck. I am, in fact, sorry that I am unable to join this team right now,' he continued explaining.

'No, no. absolutely, we understand,' I added.

He assured us that he would share references in a week, and we gave him a sense of our budget. He validated that our range wasn't bad. Most start-ups were paying much less, so we had a good chance of attracting high-quality, impatient talent.

He signaled to the waiter so he could get the bill. We insisted that we pay, and finally, he gave in. I paid 3,500 which I thought was a steal for the two hours we got from this hugely talented yet humble genius. We finally met someone who taught us technical skills and valuable life lessons, most importantly, to never judge a book by its cover. Govindan was a powerhouse, a pocket dynamite of knowledge, competence and character.

These trips were more than just finding people. They were a source of new perspectives and insights. We realized there was a wealth of skill and talent in the country. Our luck continued when we stumbled upon another brilliant mind, this time from the heartland.

'Look here,' Aman took us to a YouTube channel on battery making, anchored by a YouTuber Professor, with 150 videos on battery technologies. We watched all his fifteen videos on Zinc-air formulation on our phones for the next couple of hours before it got tiring. He also had more on Lead-Acid, Hydrogen Cell, Aluminum, Iron, and many other circuits and electrochemistry.

The videos had average production quality with fluctuating audio, but leave that aside for a moment. He had put out a wealth of ultimate science in the public domain and all for free. The best part was that even a sixth grader interested in physics and chemistry could start making batteries after watching his videos. The irony was where crass and abusive videos fetch millions or even billions of views, such steroids of knowledge had no more than 15,000 views on any of them. Some had as low as seventy-five views.

His name was Animesh Mishra. His bio read that he was a professor during the day and a scientist at night.

'Call him?' I asked Aman.

'What do I say?' He replied nervously

'Just say *Ram, Ram,* and start,' I advised and almost prodded him to make the call.

He resisted for a bit, hoping one of us would, but he had the best record of scoring meetings. After bickering for a few more minutes, he relented and agreed to make the call. The thing about making a call in a moving train is you can't be on speaker, so the best technique we figured out was to be at a conference.

Aman called him and put him on speaker so we could all hear the *Swag Se Swagat* caller tune, nothing much one could judge except him possibly being a Bhai fan. But the Bhai fan is a scientist ...? Really?

Luckily, he answered, 'Hello?'

'Am I speaking with *Akhilesh Mishra Ji?*' Aman began and took the call off the speaker.

'Animesh Mishra. Who is this?' He voiced his offense at being addressed wrongly.

'Extremely sorry, Animesh Ji. I am Aman from Bharat Kinetics. We are planning to venture into Electric Vehicle space, and we wanted to build our core battery and design team.'

'You mean Electric Space Rocket... Tesla and SpaceX in one company,' he could be genius scientist but his sense of humor seemed awful.

'No, Sir, I did not mean the real space...' Aman clarified in a lighter tone.

'Yes, sir, I know. Please tell me how I may help you,' he said in a tone that suggested he was willing to talk business.

'So, Animesh *Ji*, we need to talk to you about building a new-age battery system. We saw your videos and found them informative,' Aman began making a buttery start.

'Oh great, I am so glad you watched my video. How did you even find them?' we could see a spark in his tone hearing someone watch his videos.

'They were brilliant,' Aman responded with sincerity.

'Thank you so much. Can I ask your name one more time, please?' This appreciation from Aman got him going. At least it sounded so from his voice.

'Sure, I am Aman.'

'Yes. So, Aman *Ji*, where is your company?'

'We are in *Gurgaon,*' Aman replied tentatively.

'But I am in *Varanasi*. How will I help?'

'We have a few options, Coimbatore, Jalandhar, Manesar, or Ludhiana,' Aman was now sounding like a credit card caller desperate to keep the prospect on the phone.

'Why don't you also explore Varanasi?' His questions kept getting weirder and weirder.

'Animesh ji, hi! I am Bharat. Why don't we meet? Maybe you can show us something that will make us consider what you are suggesting,' I said, entering the conversation.

'I am telling you, making an EV is very easy. You can do it anywhere. You don't need any major supplier ecosystem, especially with 3D printing, and make anything from anywhere,' we could tell he would insist we set up our shop in Varanasi.

'But we need you to help us with a kit that's cheaper, more effective than Lithium-ion,' I pointed out. I think slightly curt. When will I learn to be polite?

'*Arre* Lithium-ion is a talk of the past. You come over, and we can talk,' he agreed.

God! He agreed!

'Brilliant! So when can we meet?' I checked.

'I can meet whenever you want after five in the evening. Before that, I am sending you some links to my videos on making Zinc-air batteries,' he offered, assuming he was going to ask for our mail addresses at some point.

'Will we be able to recharge them?' Now Vinay butted in.

'Bharat ji, if you are going to challenge me with the basis of your knowledge from Wikipedia, then you are calling the wrong person,' Vinay had dented my credibility. I stared at him in dismay.

Animesh continued, 'You, please come over and believe in Indian research and engineers too. Just because Google says it cannot be recharged as per MIT, and you take it as final,' he sounded highly confident of his invention.

'No, that's not the case, even if we want to go the Zinc-air route,' I tried to damage control.

'Boss, but if you are doubtful, how will you convince your investors, employees, and customers,' Animesh remarked, and I didn't like it.

'Animesh ji, hold on, I have no doubt. I have made enough batteries with my own hands. I want to know if your batteries are rechargeable,' I said assertively and emphatically to shut him down.

'Now, if you could please tell us when we can meet, we will plan a trip,' I added.

'I would recommend you watch the video to understand the battery process, especially Zinc-air and Zinc metal batteries. I am free after five-thirty or six in the evening. So, you can drive or take a train and call me when you are here.'

'We have seen all your videos twice at least, and they are brilliant,' I replied. He was so stuck up.

'So even after watching, you have doubts. I have given the demo for the recharge process, too,' he answered with contempt for my intellect.

'My dear sir, many things look good on a video. I was just confirming,' I said again. Vinay shrugged his shoulders.

'That's completely okay.' Really? I thought to myself while Animesh continued, 'No problem, sir, it's always good to confirm. You just tell me one day before you arrive. I will make my plans accordingly,' he finally climbed down from his high horse.

'That's excellent, Animesh! We will try and meet you sometime this week,' Aman confirmed.

'Animesh ji to Animesh in ten minutes, ominous traits for being a true businessman,' he remarked. Shantanu once called me sardonic. I would so love for the two to meet one day.

Animesh was going to be challenging to work with. He had a gift of science, and he knew it. He was a proud man and desperate for recognition; what would our lever be to get him on this side? But first, we had to confirm he knew what he was talking about.

While all of this was going on, Abhishek had upped his political game at Bluewaters. Shantanu was constantly being fed about how I had slipped on a few projects, by being unreachable, growing discord about their boss missing in action. To compound what Abhishek was cooking up, I even had some really ugly showdowns on the phone with Shantanu. I knew this hide-and-seek charade was now on borrowed time, and I could no longer dodge Shantanu's command to see us both back in office.

Guess it was time to return to the office...

# 10

# WORK FROM OFFICE?

There was little doubt in our minds about how the day at the office will play out. I knew how Shantanu was going to probe, and we were going just dodge, dodge, and dodge. No confrontation; just repeat, 'We will tell you, boss. We don't want to jinx it!'

Abhishek was thrilled to find us in the office, hoping for an epic takedown of us both, perhaps, secretly imagining us being fired. Sometimes it's hard to fathom how a father of two, could get kicks with such petty acts. I hope his children turn out differently. The world needs less of such men. I waived and winked at him, appearing relaxed and my usual confident self. He nodded spitefully.

It was almost ten minutes in, and Shantanu hadn't arrived, so Aman left a sticky note in his office stating that we were there and could call us whenever he was ready.

My eyes were already burning. Everything was okay about the sleeper coach except for the seat cushioning. The people approving this quality, the big guys, the ministers, and officers must be made to travel in these at least once a month, if not more. The only way I see this improve ever.

'We can meet now,' my messenger blinked. Shantanu was here.

I stood up and could see across the floor that Aman was also getting up from his chair. Talk about privacy at workplace!

'Hi boss,' Aman and I said in chorus.

'Good morning,' he replied, surprisingly relaxed.

We stood next to the couch in his office, checking if he wanted to discuss on the sofa or if we should walk to his work desk another ten paces away. He stood up, indicating this would be long drawn and the sofas would work better, also a sign that he wanted us to open up more. He was in for some more disappointment.

'Have you booked your flight?' He asked me even before he could get to the couch, referring to me traveling back to Plainview, an assignment I had been pushing out.

'I don't think we need to. We can discuss,' I replied.

'Since when did you start deciding on your own?'

'Boss, the billing is already at 120 percent. We don't have people to meet current requirements. I will travel. I promise. We just don't need to do it right now.'

'Bharat, I don't want to debate this anymore. Please talk to Jamie and plan for an IT meeting. Take some IT guys with you. Let them deliver it.'

'Let's park it, boss. Please don't stretch it.'

'Excuse me?' he said, sounding riled up.

'What else is it? You want me to travel, so I must travel? You and I both know this Middle-East deal will need three times the number of people in this building to deliver on. Our current billing is also surplus,' I reasoned.

'You know how many people in the market would give an arm and a leg to be on that plane?' This was such a beaten-down premise.

'I am sure there would be a few, can't say exactly,' I replied coldly.

'That's the problem. If you don't value what you have, you won't have it. I will send Aman and Abhishek then,' he announced.

'I don't value it. I worship it. The work I do is sacred to me. Tired of explaining this. The choice is yours. Whatever you decide, I'm fine with it. Who am I to say anything?' I bowed to his decision. I got what I wanted, but he still didn't.

Aman kept silent through this so far. It was the right thing to do. At least someone should serve as a bridge if things go wrong.

'Okay, very well, then. No more work from home starting this minute. If you need to travel, please apply for the leaves accordingly.'

'Sure, works for us. It's the right thing to do,' I replied.

'There will be many leaves without pay then, and don't expect us to work on leaves and weekends,' I added.

'So you really want to do this?' He looked me in the eyes, daring me.

'About?' I acted dumb.

'Boy, I know what you are trying to do. You won't be allowed to resign,' he declared, almost like I was here to resign.

'I wasn't thinking of it, honestly. I have been training my teams since morning. What are you talking about, boss?' I played it down.

'You have been missing from work, traveling across India. I don't even know if you are in dual employment or starting a parallel company. I am serving you with a show-cause notice,' he announced.

'To both of us or just to me?' I asked and looked at Aman's aghast expression, which got me to crack up slightly at Shantanu's horror. I tried calming myself down, sipped some. coffee, took some deep breaths, and apologized.

'Sorry boss, but now enough, please. I mean, who gets fired after winning a 150 million deal and 120 percent billing.'

'You wanted to scare us. We are scared,' I tried restoring sanity while suppressing my funny bones, which I think helped greatly in lightening up the mood in the room.

'Why Aman? I'm only talking about you, but I have a way out for you if you agree to play ball.'

'Boss! We can tell you nothing. There is honestly nothing to even share. It's all work in progress,' I explained.

'But if you stop us from working on this, there will be nothing except just news of new wins, demos, and conferences,' Aman now finally entered the conversation and quite directly.

'I can't let you travel across the country on work-from-home without knowing what you are up to. You must consider my position too,' Shantanu was willing to dialogue suddenly.

'Does your lapdog have no work other than keeping track of our whereabouts?' I added referring to Abhishek.

'I couldn't care less about petty office politics. Now tell me what you are working on. You want me to trust you. It's time you showed some, too,' he said.

'There is nothing, boss. We are just looking for a girl to get Aman settled. It is taking us around the country…' I cracked up so loud before I could even finish, and I was such a terrible liar.

He warned, 'Don't push your luck too far, Bharat,' though I could see him smile too.

'Will you invest?' Aman dropped a bomb out of nowhere.

Shantanu was caught off guard when Aman teased about unleashing the big secret.

'Well, err …if… if… I like it, I might. I can arrange for funds and investors.'

'No, we can bring in funds too. I want to know, will *you* invest?

We will need about five crores,' Aman tabled a proposition out of thin air. This was all out of the script! When did he even do the math?

I was quiet now, observing them both with bated breath.

'All at once?' Shantanu's response was an even bigger shock. It wasn't 'if.' It was 'when.'

'Yes. This will be bigger than you can think, and we are going to pull it off,' Aman was now tearing into his resolve, and I was simply an onlooker.

'What is it?' Bam! This was just unbelievable, Aman turned the whole thing on its head. Shantanu was talking business.

Shantanu, investing in a company we were creating! Could life get any more dramatic? This was a match made in hell!

'Boss, honestly, if you are a general enthusiast, let's not waste time. This idea is legit, and we alone can pull it off,' Aman was building more suspense.

'Go on, try me,' he assured.

'We are making the world's best electric car, forty percent cheaper with fifty percent faster charging time, and only we know how to do it,' Aman made his elevator pitch on the couch, and there was stunned silence.

Shantanu paused and spoke after a moment of thought, 'Can I think about it for a while?'

'Sure, but you know how it is, boss, though you are among the first ones, but not the only one,' Aman explained politely.

'Who else have you spoken to?' Shantanu enquired.

'Just a few guys who got interested during our initial discussions. We haven't gone back to them yet,' Aman was such a smooth liar but just so amazing

'Is there something you can send me?' He asked for literature.

'Boss, come on! Do you doubt our ability to create an impressive presentation? I have told you the crux. Anything beyond this will be privileged information. Honestly, I am so desperate to tell you myself, but you know, the time is not right,' Aman kept him in the hunt without ever allowing him to get within striking distance.

'We are leaving for Varanasi tomorrow. We will be back in a couple of days. We can discuss it then,' I butted in with a timeline for him to make up his mind.

'What the hell?' He reacted. The only way he would anytime I spoke.

'Boss, we need to meet people. You know, we can't lose the tempo,' Aman pacified,

'But what are you going to tell the clients? I have told them you will be there,' he asked me.

'Leave that with me. I will handle it. I will copy you in the final response.' He so wanted to disagree, but he was now an interested party. He nodded and told us to carry on.

'Wait… Since you're going to Varanasi … here…' He handed me some 2000 rupees. Please, offer this in my name when you visit Kashi Vishwanath,' he said.

*Har Har Mahadev…* Aman exploded as we walked towards the elevator.

# 11

# THE LANGUAGE OF THE GODS

Vinay suggested we take an auto-rickshaw to experience the streets of Varanasi from the railway station, an idea Aman found a little dodgy, but we agreed.

The auto ride wasn't very different from the streets of West Delhi. Dusty roads, the same cars, bikes and tempos, and scooters with their stifled horns. There were more cycles and more cows, almost the same number of street dogs, and more temples than ATMs or petrol pumps.

We checked into The Taj, got our Wi-Fi password, and went to our rooms. We gave Vinay a room to himself while Aman and I shared one.

We freshened up in about fifteen minutes, and Vinay joined us in our room.

'Boys! Let's have some tea,' Vinay proposed, notwithstanding the heat.'

Yeah, I will make some,' I said.

'No, I don't want this instant English breakfast tea made in this electric kettle. Let's go out and have *Kaashi's* authentic street side tea!' Vinay was a freak and sounded like some tourist from LA.

'I think I need to remind you that we traveled from Gurgaon, not New York! That too, Manesar,' I responded, shutting him down.

'Come on! Animesh won't see us before evening,' Aman joined Vinay as he started to call Animesh to inform him we were there.

'Hi, Animesh ji, Aman here.'

'*Ram, Ram, Aman ji.* A warm welcome to our little *Dev Bhoomi.*'

'Thank you, *maalik.* So, let's meet once you are free?' Aman sucked at his rural accent.

'*Arre,* I am free for you at all times of the day. Let's meet at five in the evening,' Animesh sounded delighted that we had followed through and made it.

'*Ji bilkul,* we are staying at Taj Ganges. Let's meet here.'

'*Arre, Taj Waaj* is great, but let's meet at *Assi Ghaat*. There are many cafés that you would like, trust me,' he insisted.

'Sure, no problem. Whatever you advise. You're the local hero,' Aman added.

'*Theek hai, fir.* I will send you the address. Do you have a car or something?'

'Don't worry. We will manage.'

'No problem, get an auto or an e-rikshaw. Don't pay more than fifty rupees,' Animesh cautioned.

'That's fine. We will be there. You just send us the location of the place.'

'Wow! This should be fun. I wanted to see the famous aarti, *#aartipecharcha*,' said Vinay. 'Seriously?' I said and glared unamused.

'Come on, Mr. CEO! Ease up! Connect with your team. Let's feel the vibe, *#varanasivibes!*' 'Yeah, whatever. Let's get out and get our *#suttaandsugarshots*.'

'Pathetic!' One of the two remarked on my hashtag-ing skills.

'*Chotte bhai*, *teen chai*, please. *Jaldi*,' Aman attempted local lingo again.

'*Abhi to banegi*,' responded an unconcerned boy at the stall glued to a video on his phone.

'How much time will it take?'

'*Ab jitna time lagega, utna lagega. Banayein*?' With little choice available to us, we complied and agreed to wait.

We lit up our cigarettes as soon as the tea arrived. I couldn't go beyond a couple of sips as the sugar got to me. I tossed it in a nearby bin and stood there gazing at the supposedly mystical streets of this holy city, considered the oldest in human civilization.

After the tea, Vinay made us walk more to satiate his touristy senses to explore the city on foot. The streets were filled with really tiny stores employing more people than they could even seat, some selling statues of deities, some flowers, and religious ritual material, and some selling sports equipment. Between them were cyber cafes, hardware stores, and sweet shops.

There were temples right in the middle of a commercial lane. For all you know, they must be the only ones turning in some cash in the lane. We sought divine blessings for our venture before soaking in some more #varanasivibes.

We strolled around and bought a few souvenirs. We saw dilapidated yet functional mosques, some with walls adjoining a temple. One such building had a mosque on the ground floor and a coaching center on the first floor.

We also met some *sadhus* who showered their blessings on us, granting us riches, a pretty bride, and great health. This was clearly the oldest city in the world.

'Yaar. So, what do we think will be a satisfactory outcome from our meeting?' Vinay finally got back to business.

'We need to examine his battery technology and convince him to come on board at the absolute minimum. We need to make this visit count,' I commanded.

'We will make an impression, don't worry. You got me to agree. I don't think this will be a problem,' Vinay spoke as he sipped from his glass of lassi when a spirited monkey jumped right in front of him and bullied him into handing over his glass of lassi without protest. Vinay screamed, but the monkey went on to sip away the entire glass of lassi from the straw, completely undeterred.

Aman and I almost died laughing.

Vinay was furious and terrified in equal measure and sat there stupified with his bulging biceps, which the monkey couldn't give two hoots about.

'#varanasivibes,' I added as Aman, and I broke into laughter.

Another hard to ignore visuals were the random abstract paintings on almost every other wall, paintings of meditating sadhus in blue background and saffron robes, sadhus enjoying their marijuana, young boys diving into the Ganges, vintage textile power looms in action, and paintings of the Kashi Vishwanath temple. We were supposed to go this joint called the Aum Café, near Assi Ghat.

We hired an auto and reached five minutes ahead of time. The café seemed to be in some sort of identity crisis. The décor, the walls, and even the seating were given a European bohemian feel. However, sitting in the lap of Ma Ganga, their menu was more Indian than even a Sagar Ratna or Haldirams. It had *samosa*, *kachori*, *chole bhatoore*, *masala chai*, and *masala dosa*. I am a sucker for Indian food, so I didn't complain.

Soon we saw Animesh walk in.

Animesh was wearing a Polo Tommy t-shirt and regular blue denims. He stood at about five feet six, with a wheatish complexion, and looked in good shape.

'Animesh ji,' Vinay waived from the table.

'Hi, I am Vinay.'

'I am Bharat. Good to see you, Animesh Ji. I must say your videos are truly impressive,' I could see his eyes swell with some pride at the mention of his videos.

'Thank you, sir. I am glad someone finally paid attention,' he responded.

'It's the world's loss, our gain; you get what you seek from life. I am Aman.'

I waved at the waiter, and we placed our initial orders for some samosas and tea. Aman then took over and began explaining our concept, vision, and plan.

We continued discussing our business vision and even our personal lives to some extent. We could tell he was keen to learn the pedigree of the people he would be working with, and he seemed pretty convinced and impressed with our grades and global exposure.

He worked as an assistant professor at a university, some days filling in for an electro-physics professor, some days for mathematics or mechanics, depending on who absented himself.

On days when all professors showed up, he spent his day checking assignments or manning the library.

It was clear as day why the videos meant so much to him. They were his escape and gave him a sense of redemption he so desperately craved.

He heaved a sigh and began explaining how he had converted the 240 sq yard plot he had inherited from his father into a five-storied boys' hostel. The first four floors were up for rent, while the fifth floor and the terrace were turned into a makeshift laboratory.

He agreed to take us to his lab and give a live demonstration of his Zinc-air battery invention. And we couldn't be happier. In a flash, we cleared the bills and drove with him in his Hyundai i10 to a place outside the general city limits. He parked his car outside a building that read Ganges Residencies, and we couldn't help but notice the security guard who stood up in rapt attention at the sight of the modest i10.

'How is it going?' Animesh enquired.

'All good. But this lift has stopped working again. I have been calling the mechanics for three days, but no one has shown up. They are saying that we haven't paid the maintenance due,' Animesh didn't say much to the guard. He just looked at us with a tinge of embarrassment.

'No problem, it happens all the time,' Vinay assured; it was no big deal, and we could take the stairs to the fifth floor.

We could see a corridor-style design with two rooms on either side of each floor. It was evident the place was poorly maintained. Even the arm rails and the stairs had a thick coating of dust.

The fifth floor, however, was more like an apartment with a generous balcony. He let us in and asked us to wait in the foyer—if we could call it that.

What caught my eye were the appliances in the mini kitchen visible to us from where we were standing, with the mini-fridge and the induction cooktop all powered by battery packs.

'Okay, let us go,' he turned around after locking both the doors at the entrance. One wooden and one steel, and we walked into this large open hall-like area. There we no rooms, just a big apartment hall surrounded by a running balcony on all sides. I am not great at measuring floor area, but it must have been at least 2,000 square feet of rectangular space. There was so much going on there, but one couldn't miss this big poster on the main wall facing us that read, 'Science is the mind of God, and Maths is his language.'

'Okay, so welcome to my little underground laboratory,' the pride in his voice radiated to all of us.

It was almost a fully equipped research lab. We saw some five working slabs made of concrete constructed like aisles in a supermarket about four feet apart from each other. Each one had a little basin, focus lights, and large drawers carved out from the concrete structure. My hunch was this allowed the place to be more fire-resistant.

The walls on one side had large glass windows covered by modern-day window panes. These allowed ample natural light during the day. The opposite walls were painted grey with blackboards to record the outcome of experiments or instructions before an experiment.

Then my eyes were drawn to the floor with a waste bin made of gypsum or plaster. They were painted in different shades, blue for general waste and red for chemical waste. This man was not some amateur science freak. He was a thorough, thoughtful, and intuitive scientist.

We also noticed hundreds of AA batteries dumped in one of the bins. It was clear they were put through extreme torture and had finally met their fate. We could tell it was not limited to just a battery workshop. We could see some miniature robots and battery-operated mechanical cars.

'Really impressive! Our college lab assistants could take notes,' Vinay complimented, and we could see Animesh's face swell with pride again.

'Now, before we leave today, we need to build a Zinc-air battery pack, use it to power up devices, fully discharge it and then recharge to 100 percent, alright?'

'That would be just brilliant,' I replied with enthusiasm.

'Safety is foremost,' he said and brought us some PPE suits, visors, surgical gloves, and shower caps.

We complied and dawned our costumes with no questions, 'I am quite reluctant to let people into my little secret space, so just a request, whatever you see and learn today, please keep it to yourself,' he implored.

'Certainly, you can count on us,' I acknowledged.

'You know, some of these may need a government permit. But in this country, people even get away with drugs and murder, while for people like us, even minor transgressions can prove quite costly,' he opined, and it totally resonated with us.

'I don't have the temperament for paperwork and permits. It's a slippery slope process—you seek a license, then there will be inspections followed by harassment. If it wasn't for this, I would have filed several patents by now.'

'Don't worry. We can help you procure patents. It is not so difficult. We will need to register our patent before getting it into the market,' Aman clarified.

'That will be great!' He sounded grateful and began our guided tour.

'So, do you know when the Zinc-air battery was made?' He was back to being a professor.

'1800s,' Vinay had to attempt. Nothing had changed since college

'Forget it. No one knows; we believe what the West documents. But yes, you aren't way off,' he said and continued, 'Do you know the cost per unit of electricity produced by a Zinc battery is ten times cheaper than Lithium?'

'We shouldn't be here if we don't know this,' I reacted, maybe somewhat combative.

'Of course! Don't get me wrong ... But the problem with these batteries was that they couldn't be recharged. It's like burning a piece of wood that releases high amounts of energy when set on fire, but can it ever become wood again? No, just ashes! The same was the problem with these battery combinations.

'The trick to recharge was bringing the electron back to the anode. This is like a battle; the soldier who sets out to take on the enemy must return at the end. That's what you call recharging. You keep losing soldiers… soon there won't be an army.'

He continued, and we we remained tuned in.

'Look around this setup. We can make batteries four times more efficient than the most efficient Lithium-ion combination anywhere in the world. So, let's begin making your first Zinc-air battery pack! But first, let's understand the stages of making a battery pack.'

Vinay and I could run lessons on these but we allowed him to continue so he doesn't lose his train of thought.

'So, on the first aisle, we will create 4 x 4 feet strips from these Zinc sheets,' he pointed towards the store where he had a stalk of some fine metal sheets.

'These will serve as the anode material from where the electrons, our soldiers, will proceed for battle. We will also create a sheet of separator layers and cathode using semi-permeable material that will allow the air to pass and trigger a reaction and, consequently, allow the flow of current.'

'Let's discuss when you are back,' Aman and I received a message from Shantanu. I looked at Aman.

'*Sure, boss, the day after will be great,*' Aman replied.

'*Works. Don't forget my offer to Kashi Vishwanath. All the best,*' he replied.

'*Done, boss! Har Har Mahadev!*' Aman replied as Animesh continued with his tour passionately.

We heard him explain other finer aspects like cutting the batteries, mixing the electrolyte liquid, drying, and testing voltage.

'The electrolyte formula is the secret sauce to this technology. Arranging metal sheets together is the work of a skilled mechanic, and preparing the electrolyte needs a passionate scientist.'

That's exactly what we had come looking for—the recipe and the chef.

'Remember, before we assemble our cells to a battery pack, we will need to test each of the cells for voltage. A healthy cell will give us a reading of 1.5, but we will work even with 1.4. Anything below this threshold will be rejected. So, alright then, best of luck, let's begin!'

The general ordered and we were on our way, and about six hours into the process, we had built forty-five cells, of which he approved thirty-six based on the voltage and other readings from a multimeter.

These thirty-six cells were now assembled in a rack that essentially was the collection of multiple grooves, also known as spacers. You could add as many spacers as you like depending on the power and scale you need. The more the cells, more the spacers, and the final battery pack is nothing but a collection of several kinds of cells stacked up together with the help of spacers, wires, and other useful technologies.

He asked me to pass the tester so he could dip-check the current. He inserted the sharp end of the tester in one of the sockets connected to the battery. The metal felt the current, and the tester lit up brilliantly, and so did Aman's eyes.

Aman almost immediately broke into applause, while Vinay and I, though impressed, had been this far several times.

'Alright! Congratulations here is your first battery pack, the Zila battery pack, beta version. How about that?' He exclaimed with confidence and an indistinct sense of pride.

'What you see here on the table can power up that little mini fridge for over two days!'

Animesh proclaimed.

'But remember, in reality, for this to be industry grade, we will need better equipment; for better drying and cutting.'

'No, we get it. Leave that to us. We can get this equipment from Coimbatore. I know at least half a dozen suppliers,' Vinay suggested.

'Brilliant. In the real world, we need at least 2,500 of these cells loaded into a power pack. The Zila Power Pack,' Animesh sounded like it was a done deal.

'Let's begin our tests,' I recommended.

First on the list was the mini-fridge, followed by a miniature car, a washing machine, an LED TV, an electric iron, and our cell phones. None of them discriminated against the technology. All they wanted was power, and our pack delivered it with competence.

I could see Aman and Animesh impatient to declare victory, but we had so far only cleared the prelims, the mains were still pending, and that was going to be the real test. Vinay and I both knew this.

So, will the soldiers return to the base? Will this be able to recharge itself? Or will this be another science project that will throw up a number of caveats?

I connected a voltmeter to gauge the level of the current charge, and it read eight percent.

Animesh then asked Vinay to connect our battery pack to a charging point while keeping the voltmeter connected, and Vinay proceeded as advised. Then we turned towards the voltmeter. It took some time to show progress, but in about a minute, which seemed longer, it was at eleven percent and from there to forty-five percent in about four minutes. I could feel my heart race slightly with every jump in the reading. The formula we were betting on was not a figment of our imagination. It was here, alive and kicking, and within eleven minutes, the meter had reached ninety-six percent.

'*Har Har Mahadev!*' Vinay chanted as loud as one could imagine. It was heartfelt, like a battle cry!

'*Har, Har Mahadev*!' Aman and I joined in, and Animesh looked on with his eyes full of spark and pride. Kashi was called mystical for many reasons, and we had found ours. Only our first celestial experience was not inside a temple!

'Science is the mind of God, and maths is his language.' These words suddenly rang so true and profound. It turned out Animesh was no ordinary man.

The struggling YouTuber professor held the keys to the kingdom! The Zila battery pack, the beta version, was ready!

'We are in business here, Animesh boss,' Vinay announced.

'You must call this Animesh's first law of Zinc-air conductivity,' he added, and everyone chuckled.

'Let's call it "Animeshan," defined as the process through which Zinc electrons swim through a cocktail of electrolyte waters and return to their anode base!' Vinay continued his charm offense keeping everyone's batteries charged.

'Animesh, in these nine hours, we have accomplished 1000 times more than we have in the last nine months,' I spoke with sincerity and gratitude.

'I always tell my students, even though they don't care, that knowledge always finds its seeker. You have been ardent seekers.

'Thank you so much, Animesh ji. So when do we meet next?' I asked.

'When is your train?'

'Tomorrow afternoon,' I replied.

'But we need to visit Kashi Vishwanath and offer our prayers,' Aman reminded us.

'Reach by seven in the morning latest. You will be done by about eight or so. We can meet at around ten in the morning, and then I will drop you at the station,' Animesh advised, and I looked at the time on the phone, which read 1:00 a.m. Another night with a truncated nap.

We helped him clean up the place, and then after locking both doors, he dropped us at the hotel. The next morning, we woke up by six and made our way to the holy shrine without any delay. Vinay insisted that we take a holy dip in the Ganga, but I convinced him that this wouldn't be the last of our visits to this amazing, life-changing city. I was just way too exhausted for a dip, and I could tell they were too.

Though reluctant, he gave in, and by about nine, we were back in our rooms. Animesh arrived at ten to meet us at the hotel café.

'Four Americanos?' Vinay checked with everyone.

'I will have regular coffee or cold coffee if it's available,' Animesh responded.

'Sure, by all means, *Gurudev*,' Vinay walked up to the counter to place the order.

'I have heard people of Varanasi love their *meetha*. So, I have also ordered a muffin, especially for you,' Vinay was just being Vinay.

'Thank you, Vinay ji,' Animesh acknowledged.

'So, Animesh ji, we were quite blown away with what we witnessed last evening, and now there are no two ways about using this technology and further polishing, so it becomes unbeatable,' I started.

'Well, that will be one of my biggest dreams coming true,' he replied with humility. 'Likewise, Animesh ji.'

'We just wanted to understand what your expectations were... you know, in terms of compensation, partnership, equity, and other things,' Aman began the real discussion.

'Bharat ji, I had a proposition in mind from the day we spoke. If you are okay, I will lay it out for you to consider,' he addressed his response to me.

'Sure, please go on,' I offered him the floor, and we were all ears.

'In my mind, this battery pack is central to this car and its biggest differentiator. So, I would like a twenty percent stake in return for my services and total autonomy over the design and build process. I live for this composition and don't want anyone to spoil it during its application,' he laid it all out, and there was a brief moment of silence.

'If you don't mind, can Aman and I take a break? Vinay is a great company,' I checked politely.

'Of course. In fact, you can respond after you reach Delhi. There is no hurry,' he said.

'Sure, but let's see if we can close it right here, or else, you are right, we can always decide later on,' I said, and we got up, appearing unfazed, despite what we thought was a ridiculous demand.

'One more thing, I also would like the entire production line to be set up here in Varanasi,' he added like he hadn't demanded enough already.

I gently smiled in acknowledgment, and we walked out with our cups of coffee in our hands, concealing all emotion, till we were outside the café.

'He is a bloody wolf in sheep's disguise!' I exclaimed to Aman.

'But… there is no car without him,' Aman defended.

'Really? What makes you think so?' I challenged Aman's assertion. 'So, who will prepare the battery?'

'Well… I will. He trained us. I know the electrolyte formula. I read some of the equations he had written down in that register of his,' I said, and Aman's eyes grew bigger.

'Now, don't get me wrong. I am not saying we will plagiarize. All I am saying is we can't be strong-armed this way,' I argued.

'No, that's exactly what you are saying. To copy his IP,' Aman was now in Anna Hazare mode.

'Hear me out. Think about it. We will proceed to build our own solution. I won't even tell Vinay that I know the formula. I am just telling you that Animesh no longer has unlimited leverage over us.'

'I didn't know this side of you, Bharat…'

'Yaar! Okay, let's walk in and give him a twenty percent stake, total autonomy, and a production line in Varanasi.

Let him run the company! We already report to Shantanu in the office. We sure can report to him as the new boss of Bharat Kinetics because that's where this is heading…' I held my ground.

'So, what are you suggesting we do?' I knew Aman didn't have a better plan.

'Ten percent stake—five now, five two years from now—no voting rights, the patent will be in his name sold to us for a period of ninety-nine years with exclusivity rights. The location of the production line will be decided after the team is constituted post wider consultation,' I made my proposal.

'Ninety-nine years is not permissible under the IP law,' Aman was missing the woods for the trees.

'Okay, so the maximum that is permitted, come on!' I insisted he stays on the main argument.

'We'll need to go up to 12.5 percent when he bargains.'

'Even this ten percent is hurting me. When this becomes a billion-dollar company, even this five percent will be a massive fortune,' I negotiated, but Aman didn't think Animesh would agree.

'Let's go back to the final offer of 12.5 percent, but no autonomy, etc., and no commitment for the production line,' I summarized.

We were now back on the table, both literally and metaphorically, and I laid out our proposal to him, which was followed by another brief period of silence.

'Is it okay if I borrow a cigarette?' Animesh requested.

'Absolutely. By all means, Animesh ji,' I gave him the packet and the lighter.

'I told you, take a dip in the Ganga!!!' Vinay spoke after a few moments of silence among us

'So, this is on me?' I protested.

'100 percent. You should not leave your visit incomplete. Partial devotion, partial results,' he argued.

'Science is the mind of God, and Maths is his language, my boy. You were not paying attention,' Aman came to my defense, and we bickered harmlessly till Animesh returned.

'Bharat ji, when I met you all at the café, I saw three honest young men trying to make a difference,' he began, and this was looking good, 'Today, I am talking to some corporate hotshots trying to arm-twist a naïve scientist from a small town,' I don't know if he was genuinely feeling this way or was this some kind of a trick.

'Sir, I am only asking you to be reasonable, please,' I implored.

'You do know there won't be a car without my battery,' from playing the victim, he had moved on to threats now.

'Animesh ji, you are a stunning scientist, and I hate to negotiate with you but look at your demands; complete autonomy, a production line in Varanasi, and what not. This is dictating for us. Not fair!'

'What is not fair? You have a dream to make it in India. I dream of making it in Varanasi.'

'Sir, all we are saying is, in due course, other senior members will also join. We need to take their opinion also.'

'I know the value of my work, and we will see if you can get a real car on the road with your fancy presentations and website.'

'Sir, maybe your students don't pay attention, but I did. We are seekers of knowledge, and, as you said, knowledge can't evade us for long. So if not this, then, you know, there could be other formulas too. Perhaps even better or at least as good,' I fell for his provocation.

Wrong move Bharat, I said to myself.

'Bharat ji, whether or not you make a good car, you will make a good businessman. You can look a person in the eye and manipulate him,' I heard these personal comments patiently.

'And I know why that is because now you know the recipe. I was such a fool to have given you the tour before we had talked numbers.'

'I… don't think that is… correct. I don't think you would be speaking this way if you were dealing with a TATA or a Tesla,' I said and continued, 'Sir, I have great respect for you, but our final offer will be 12.5 percent. Please join us and guide us,' I concluded.

'Not before you make a commitment that we will make in Varanasi,' he demanded perhaps implying he had agreed to our shareholding offer. I was kicking myself for letting up so soon. I could have struck a better deal.

'That's beyond me, sir. I need to wait for the team to take shape.'

'You guys must be getting late. Let me drop you at the station. I'll just be back,' he got up and went to the restroom.

We looked at each other in despair.

'Well, that didn't go to plan,' Vinay said. 'Bugger didn't even have the muffin. Let me have it then!' Vinay dug in, and we waited for Animesh to return.

We told him that we would manage, but he insisted that he drops us—an indication he didn't want to sever the relationship completely.

Vinay sat in the front, Aman and I occupied the rear seats, and we were on our way. No one spoke a word for a while.

'You see those young boys? They must be from engineering or a commerce college,' Animesh broke the silence and pointed out to a bunch of teenagers leaning on their bikes and chit-chatting outside a café.

'Possibly,' Vinay responded.

'Bharat ji, you know, all they want is a government job, UPSC, Bank PO, railways, SSC, anything,' I knew where this was going.

'I need them to feel the power of the industry by bringing this clean technology to Varanasi. For you, it's a made-in-India great electric car, profits, valuation, etc., but for me, it's more than that. This factory will change the face of this city,' I was so done with this beaten-down argument.

'I want my city to be known for more than Ma Ganga, Kashi Vishwanath, or…'

'Animesh ji, don't mind. This argument will hold true for any tier 2, 3, or 4 cities in this country,' I finally said.

'I am not *Mahadev*. I cannot solve everything, but I want to change what I can, where I can.'

'Then let's leave it to Mahadev, Animesh ji. Only his wish will prevail.

*Maybe we should have taken a dip in the Ganga after all.*

# 12

# DEAL WITH THE DEVIL

'I told you last time. We are making the world's best electric car; forty percent cheaper, fifty percent faster charging time, hundred percent more range than any in the market right now, totally biodegradable, hundred percent made in India, minimum forty percent margin per unit sold, cash positive in fifteen months, and only we know how to do it,' Aman was back in his elements as I watched the master in action.

'Let's go out and talk. I have a few calls, but let me cancel them. I suggest you do the same,' Shantanu announced.

Did it imply he was in?

'Abhishek, we are going out with Shantanu. You are the boss today, buddy,' I quipped childishly before leaving as both Aman and Shantanu shook their heads in disbelief.

We drove with Shantanu to a pub in Gurgaon. It was afternoon, so it was almost empty, the perfect setting to resume our discussion.

Aman continued leading the dialogue. He explained how we had been meeting people from all corners of the country, professors, mechanics, scientists, software engineers, accountants, lawyers, and anyone who could either be part of our journey in any capacity.

In a couple of hours, Vinay joined us too.

We showed Shantanu the website, and though he didn't jump with joy, his eyes couldn't conceal the awe and thrill he felt. Aman, who by now was a semi-engineer himself, explained the technology in detail.

'How long do you think you guys will take?' he enquired.

Aman explained we would need two years at least, a response Shantanu wasn't comfortable with. Then Vinay and I explained that building the software and the battery is one big part. The real deal is to put it through rigorous testing.

'Zila will be for everyone, from the guy driving a CNG car today to the delivery companies, the everyday Joe, the upper middle class, the middle class, everyone. The car won't always be parked in complexes with manicured lawns and dedicated charging infrastructure. People will charge at home. Some will even use counterfeit charging cables from China, Taiwan, and Vietnam. Fluctuating voltages in remote areas, heat, dust, pollution, everything will take a toll on the battery life and performance. So, we need to build a product that can brave this all and still deliver for decades.'

'What are the odds that you will crack this?'

'If this was a suited-booted investor meeting and we knew the money wasn't coming from their pockets, we would have said ninety-nine percent, but since it's you, we will be honest. It's fifty-fifty,' Aman replied.

'It's my life's savings, boys.' He tried overstating the lengths he was going to for us. I knew about at least four properties he owned that added up to over fifteen crores, and these were just the ones I knew. But to be fair, a person investing would add pressure.

'Then you don't invest. We don't want you to lose sleep over this every night, boss,' Aman advised.

'I won't lose sleep. If anyone will, it will be you,' Shantanu reacted sharply at the first possibility of being vulnerable.

'No, boss, what I mean is it's not even a million dollars. We are also talking to private equity investors. It will be nothing for them. Even if it goes wrong, they can stomach it. For you, these are your life savings.'

*And Animesh was calling me a manipulator!*

'Don't be a fool and fall in the web of foreign investors,' Shantanu advised. Vinay and I wanted to celebrate already. Aman had tamed him like nobody's business.

Aman looked at us, wearing a perplexed expression.

'What are you thinking? Talk to me,' Shantanu commanded.

'Nothing, just thinking. Hoping it doesn't ruin our equation,' Aman replied, looking sincere.

'Do a good job, get a high-quality car on the road, and leave the rest to me,' he reassured.

'Sure, boss. Your belief in us has always meant so much. Your guidance has been the key, always. I am sure, this time, we will be able to reach even bigger heights.'

'Hmm … So, let's assume, if we even convert one percent of cars on the Indian roads for the first three years, we still sell some 30k units a year even at one lakh per car in profit… I see where this is going…' Shantanu was doing the math out loud.

'When do you need the money? I will need some time.'

I was exploding in disbelief.

'In six months. We have funds till then, in fact, beyond that too, but six months will be perfect,' Aman said.

'Okay, that's reasonable, but I need a solid stake in this,' he was direct and meant business this time. I was now looking at Aman.

'Like, how much?' Aman replied, shrugging his shoulders.

'Fifty percent,' Shantanu said, and Aman just smiled.

'Even the three of us don't have that kind of stake, boss,' Aman said, and Shantanu smiled at his own obscene demand.

'I know, just kidding. But nothing less than twenty percent though,' he made a revised demand.

'Boss, not possible. You know, this is why I didn't want to involve you. I can't negotiate with a person I call my mentor. Let it be, boss, we will figure it out,' Aman issued a veiled threat to withdraw.

The discussions went on for another three weeks. We made our offer of a five percent stake, and he remained fixated on nothing less than fifteen. We took this time to also register our company so we could formalize his commitment. Eventually, after much back and forth, we agreed to a ten percent stake, five now and five after two years.

'We have a deal. Let's meet in my office,' I received a message on my Skype of business.

'Sure, will be there in a moment,' I replied. I moved my office chair back to see if Aman was walking out of his cabin. I stood up when he did, and we walked into his office.

'Okay, boys. So, best of luck. Make me proud,' he hugged us both.

'Thanks, boss, means a lot,' Aman added. Shantanu looked at me for a reaction. I nodded like, 'Yeah, me too.'

'So, when are you planning to put in your papers?' he asked on a serious note.

'Boss, when the Dubai bonus is credited,' Aman replied with honesty.

'Don't worry about that. It will happen with this month's salary, but there is a problem,' he said.

'I think Vinay will need to do the heavy lifting on the ground till I find a replacement.

'The contract is very sensitive, and there are big penalties for missing timelines. Resign today with a four-month notice, spend the next month or so putting your team together, and get ready to travel to Dubai,' he concluded.

'Boss, this will slow us down tremendously,' I exclaimed.

'I know, make trips on weekends and stuff. I will approve travel. But I need to get your replacement first. Alan will cancel the deal if he doesn't see the whites of your eyes on Day 1,' he explained his position, and we could see he had strong grounds.

'Hmm, please get someone in quick. We can't be missing at such formative stages,' I stated our position.

'So, where to next?' He asked, looking at me.

Not sure. But certainly, marching ahead!

# 13

# THE GARAGE BAND

Jatin Soni, a fifty-something businessman who ran a car modification and a general service workshop in Ludhiana under the name of Soni Motors, was the new person of interest.

His company's Instagram was full of 'before and after' photos. He could turn a regular Swift Desire into a rally car, old Honda City into a Ferrari! These guys could transform everything from the body to the engine.

I met him during a wedding I attended in 2013. My resident welfare society's president, Sachdeva Uncle, introduced me to him, and if my assessment was right, I think I hit it off quite well with him. I recall him as a man with a majestic presence, the kind who would stand out in any congregation. Despite this, he didn't seem one bit pompous during our interactions.

'*Abbe*, Sachdeva Uncle *ka poora naam kya hai* …?' [Hey, What is Sachdeva Uncle's full name?] There will be a million Sachdeva uncles in *Dilli* and Punjab,' Aman was developing cold feet moments before the call like always.

'I don't know, umm... Pitampura *waale* Sachdeva Uncle? Don't think too much and call,' I pushed.

*'Dhyaan rakhchi bhagwaan!'* [Please help, God!] He prayed in Gujarati and made the call on speakerphone as the three of us sat around the phone placed on Aman's bed.

'Hello,' we heard a squeaky voice on the other side. I could tell it wasn't Jatin Soni. '*Satsriakal, Soni sahab*,' Aman tried connecting in Punjabi.

'*Satsriakal ji, kide naal gal karni e?*' [Who do you want to speak with?]

The person on the phone replied in pure Punjabi, while Aman's Punjabi was done at *Satsriakal* itself.

'Jatin Soni ji *se.*'

*'O hai nai halle,'* [He's not here.] came the response. This was indeed too much for Aman, but he made another brave attempt.

*'Kabo avenge ode?'* Aman had barely finished, but Vinay and I were in splits and fell to the floor laughing at his butchering of the language.

*'Hain, ji?'* [What?] said the voice on the other side as though Aman had spoken Zulu.

'*Ji... matlab kab aenge*?' [When will he be back?] Aman responded, holding his composure, despite the commotion Vinay and I were creating.

*'Tuhanu ki kam si ode naal?'* [What do you want from him?]

*'Ji business ki baat karni thi kuch,'* [I have to discuss some business work with him.] Aman recovered, and we tried holding back ourselves.

'*Do mint mein ohnaanu laban ha*,' [He'll be here in two minutes] we thumbs-upped to him, and he flashed the middle finger to us in response.

'Hello? Jatin Soni,' Soni Uncle spoke in his baritone from the other side.

'Hi, Mr. Soni. I am Bharat from Delhi. Not sure if you remember, we met during Mr. Sachdeva's daughter's wedding in Pitampura in 2013.

'Hmm... Delhi, right?' He confirmed.

'Yes, sir, in Delhi. Pitampura. 2012. Remember, during the wedding, you and I spoke about your automotive business in Jalandhar?' Aman did a phenomenal job of impersonation.

'Oh yes, yes, of course! I remember. How are you, young man? Is it your wedding now?' He asked excitedly, to our relief and some validation to me that I was, after all, not such a forgettable acquaintance.

He had a polished accent like that of a high-ranking army officer.

'Ha ha, no sir, not so soon. We were working on a business idea, just wanted to talk to you about that,' Aman spoke smoothly. I so wish I had this gift, too, like him. He always managed to get past situations without fuss.

'Oh, that's brilliant. Tell me, how can I help? I have no money to invest, though,' he said and laughed gently.

'No sir, you have something way more important, the experience of making cars. We just need your guidance.'

'Okay, keep going.'

'Sir, we are trying to make an electric car, one made fully in India. We understand the tech side of it, like battery and software, but we need advice and support on the actual building process.'

'I don't know much about this electric vehicle business, though.'

'That part, we understand. We need your support in building a car, of which you are an expert. We have seen your Instagram pictures. They are just incredible.'

'Don't go by them. Everyone in Ludhiana has the same photos,' he said and laughed out so loud that even the iPhone trembled.

Aman waited for him to finish, 'Sir if you don't mind, we would like to come to Ludhiana this weekend to meet you.'

'Well! Are you doing this alone, or do you have someone working with you?' Mr. Soni sounded serious now.

'Sir, it's me and my friends Bha… err… Aman and Vinay as partners.'

'Okay, I need to know how many people you are planning to bring. Will your engineers also be with you? I don't want to unnecessarily create a buzz in the neighborhood. This is Ludhiana, and news spreads very quickly here.'

'Mr. Soni, don't worry. It will just be us,' Aman reassured.

'Okay, so no more than two people?' He checked politely.
'Yes, 100% just the two of us.'

'Alright, young man, how much time will you need from me?'

'Honestly, a lot, I think,' Aman responded directly.

'Honesty is good. The most important trait in an entrepreneur.'

'Thank you, sir,' Aman replied.

'Okay then, so come over this weekend, and let's see what we can do together. I will send you the location.'

'Thanks, Mr. Soni.'

'You are welcome. See you, Bharat.'

'Sir, one request. Please don't tell Sachdeva Uncle. Even in Pitampura, news spreads very fast,' Aman added on my behalf.

'Ha, Ha, Ha… don't worry. You have a good day,' he said, and we hung up. Aman had secured yet another meeting.

* * *

As we headed towards Ludhiana's Pavilion Mall, we couldn't help but notice the numerous Audis and car accessory shops. The city's roads were filled with *Vikram Autos*, cycle rickshaws, and poorly maintained buses. The further we traveled, the wider the roads became and the greener the surroundings. The mall was quite impressive, housing stores like Shoppers Stop and Apple Resellers, with even more Audis on display. Ludhiana had a completely different vibe from Varanasi, as the city was eager to embrace the new, both in its people and structures. Our meeting with Jatin was supposed to take place at a quiet, purely vegetarian restaurant called Bikano in the food court named Food Capital.

'Quite a loaded mall,' I remarked as we walked towards a table.

'Yeah, man, the city has everything and more,' Aman added.

'Hey. I have reached Bikano,' Aman received a text from Mr. Soni. 'Yes, Bikano,' he responded.

'Don't call him "sir",' Aman advised.

'I won't if you don't speak Punjabi.'

'Even my fractured Punjabi is giving better results than… you know… let it be,' he retorted promptly.

'It's called beginner's luck.'

A fifty-year-old man, about 5 feet 11 inches, with salt and pepper hair, looking like an immaculate painting, walked towards us.

'Hey, Bharat! How are you? Good to see you,' he recognized and greeted me.

'Good to see you, Mr. Soni,' I replied, not sure if I should have called him that. I shook his hand, and we took our places. He greeted Aman and took a seat next to him, opposite me.

'First time in Punjab?' He began.

'Yeah, the closest we have been to Punjab has been our trips to Moorthal for white butter paranthas,' Aman responded.

'Haha... that's good. Hope this is the first of your many trips,' his larger-than-life persona appeared to be perfectly warm.

'They actually serve great chole bhature here, but I wouldn't advise that before an intense discussion,' he advised. Jatin Soni embodied the chivalry of an ex-serviceman.

'So, boys, what's the dream?' He asked.

'An ambition, sir. We are trying to make the world's best electric car, and we need some solid guidance along the way,' Aman explained.

'You have started?' He asked.

'Oh yes, way past that. We know the battery formula, raised some funding, too, and we know our design. All we need now is to build a crack team,' Aman replied confidently.

'Go on, tell me more.'

'So, we have a team that understands batteries. Bharat is a mechanical engineer, and so is our other friend and partner,

Vinay. Both of them have cracked the battery and also the car design,' Aman elaborated.

'How much do you think it will cost?' Jatin asked.

'We don't know yet. No point giving you a meaningless number,' Aman replied, and we could tell Jatin wasn't happy with this.

'But you must have made some projections,' Jatin probed further,

'See, we are solving four primary areas; foremost is the battery technology, this is the soul of everything. This goes wrong. There is no car,' I jumped in.

'The second is building a car that runs from wheels to steering, axle to chassis. Third, the operating system or the nerve center of our car, which will control everything from acceleration to the battery, to navigation, touch interface, updates, everything, soup to nuts. And finally, the paperwork; company registration, GST, ARAI, patents, approvals before the rubber hits the road,' I explained further, still not giving any numbers away.

'Okay, this helps. And where are you on this journey?' Jatin's behavior wasn't much different from Bluewater's client's.

We spoke for about an hour or maybe more over a plate of dhokla, samosa, and tea before he asked us to come with him to his workshop, where we could resume the rest of our conversation.

We drove with Jatin to this workshop, who surprisingly was driving a Maruti Ertiga and not an Audi.

'Okay, boys, so this is my little workshop. We do a number of things here, from assembling e-rikshaws to modifying cars,' so our tour had begun. He continued, 'You see that Ford Ikon that's being refitted with a Nissan engine. We extracted it from some unclaimed vehicles confiscated by the police and scrappage buys.

'How about RC and the engine number?' I asked.

'We get it changed legally. Make no mistake, everything here is lawful. It's not some underground factory,' he sounded like he had taken offense to my question.

'Sorry, I didn't mean that; I just wanted to understand if modified cars are allowed to run without hassle. Then we should be okay when we launch,' I clarified.

'Yes, good point. We will talk about that. We live in a funny nation, you know,' he retorted, 'this is our front office. Everything we do here, be it repair, new assembly, or modification, all of it is recorded on this CRM for billing and taxes.'

He then took us to the shop floor.

'This is the A-Wing of our workshop. Those hydraulic jacks are all industry-scale. The senior engineers are given a black uniform while the more entry-level mechanics wear blue and yellow jumpsuits.'

Jatin Soni's car workshop was a mixed bag. On the one hand, the shop floor was impressive and well-organized, with high-end machinery. On the other hand, the staff didn't seem busy. The front office staff was busy chatting, the CAD programmers were watching YouTube videos, and the spray paint station's robotic painting arms had no cars to paint. The workshop's capabilities were showcased in an advert video, which oversold the place and didn't align with the in-person experience. Despite these issues, Jatin Soni was hospitable and welcomed our visit. And this kind of explained why a man like Jatin Soni would be entertaining someone like us.

Mr. Soni came back and signaled something to his housekeeping staff.

'So how did you find the place?' He asked.

'Very impressive, this video even more so,' I responded.

'There is a lot going on in that,' Aman added.

'Not as much if we decide to go ahead with your idea. This place will be on fire,' Wow! That was quite encouraging, I thought, coming from Jatin.

'So, when are you planning to build the car?' He asked quite directly.

Then it struck us that the time for research and groundwork was over, and we had to get on with it.

'Now, that's what we wanted advice on. You clearly have a pretty neat setup, but could you tell us now in what capacity you could participate in our project?' Aman asked.

'Participate?' Jatin didn't seem to take that well.

'I mean… partner,' Aman was quick to clarify.

'*Beta*! Advice number one! The first ten people will be the most critical. Treat all of them as equals, and don't worry. You will still be the first among equals. So be respectful and careful about the words you choose'.

'Sure, sir,' Aman replied, fumbling just a little.

'Okay, so let's see, I have a limited agenda. Before meeting you guys, I didn't have very high hopes, but after our discussion on your team composition, other plans, and the whole battery revolution, it makes me believe we are onto something. What do you call it?'

'Transformative?' Aman tried guessing.

'No, no, there is a word for that?'

'Earth-shattering,' I said this time.

'Oh… *kake*… wait!! Forget it, I will tell you when I recall,' he said and continued. 'The entire heavy lifting and the car building process can be run from here. For our concept car or the first car we built, we will use refurbished metals and fiber from scrapped vehicles. I have enough people who can help with this. We will run some stress tests to check endurance, and everything should be fine.

'Third is your IT team for building the EV software. I don't think you have anyone recruited yet. You can get new blood from the market, plus we can use our guys here as supplements.

'What you have totally missed out on is a solid test driver. We won't find anyone here in the north, so we will need to go down to Chennai or Coimbatore. That's where they have a car-worthy racetracks. We can get a good test driver for three hours a day for a period of two to three months. I don't know how much they charge for using their tracks, and we will need to find out,' he said.

I could almost picture Zila on a racetrack. The thought alone was enough to give me goosebumps, and the smile I was trying to suppress gave it away.

'Yeah, I know, watching a car we've built together run on the tracks will be an otherworldly experience,' Jatin commented, looking at me.

'MOONSHOT IDEA,' he announced quite loudly. That's the word. You guys have a Moonshot Idea!' To him and his staff, this exuberance seemed par, of course, but we were both certainly staggered as we smiled along while raising our hands for a high five.

'Boss, we get this right. This will go down in history as one of the greatest moments in Indian automotive history. That's the opportunity, this is that moment, young fellows,' he commanded resoundingly.

'Yes sir,' I replied like an energized foot soldier, and Aman nodded vehemently.

'Okay, now coming back,' Jatin brought us back.

'We also need help in clearances, approvals from ARAI, and patents, but leave that to me,' he assured.

'Thanks, that will be brilliant. Now, Mr. Soni, we would like to know what your expectations will be,' Aman asked. Frankly, it was now happening too quickly for us. Last month had been the most significant in our lives so far.

'Okay, so let's see... what do I bring to the table? Experience in car building, ready staff, understanding of regulation, and a place we can call our factory. I will use this space and deploy four to five members from my team to work on this almost exclusively for the next twelve months, at no cost to the company.'

I couldn't believe my ears, the biggest elephant in the room had been addressed. We had secured a shop floor. Nothing was sinking in yet. God! It better not be some cruel joke, I prayed to myself.

'In return, I want the following, a ten percent stake and national dealership rights when we launch,' he concluded.

'No, no, no, you will have international rights. This product is for the entire world', I replied with total conviction.

Jatin seemed impressed with the vision.

'We are actually okay with the ten percent stake too, but we would just want to distribute it into two, five percent now five percent end of the second year, and of course, we will create a formal contract to that effect,' Aman offered.

'Hmm… I am okay with this model of yours,' he confirmed after a pause. 'Wonderful. So how long will it take to build this?' I asked.

'What do you think?'

'Well, three months for the proof of concept, which is fitting our battery pack and converting an IC (internal combustion) car to an EV?' I replied, 'And another six to nine months for our first ready-for-the-road car. So about twelve months from the time we start, we should be ready to take it to market. What do you think?'

'That sounds about right…'

The next few hours were spent mostly discussing modalities and finer aspects like the earliest date we can start, the team's base location, etc. We took him through some of the designs we had in mind from the websites and sketches Vinay and I had put together. He handed them over to his CAD developers.

And so, it was decided that we will begin forty-five days from today. Our production base will, of course, be Ludhiana. Jatin will help us find apartments, and Soni Motors will serve as both the office space and the workshop.

He then introduced some of his team members, a body shop engineer Aditya Dixit, a.k.a Pandit ji, a tooling specialist, and a test driver, Ajay Bindra. We greeted them and welcomed them to the fold, and within forty-eight hours of being three men with a battery formula. We were now a team of nine with an office space and a state-of-the-art production facility.

It was around six in the evening, and Jatin offered to drop us back at the Pavilion Mall.

We drove through the same by-lanes of Ludhiana when Aman got chatty again, 'So Jatin ji, I wanted to ask you, have you served in the armed forces?'

'Hahaha, yeah, that wasn't hard to figure, was it?' He burst into another loud laughter.

'No, it wasn't. If you don't mind me saying… you must have spent a fortune on setting up this facility here in Ludhiana… Does it make commercial sense to invest this kind of money in a car modification unit? It doesn't quite add up for me,' Aman asked.

'I would have been very disappointed if you had left without asking me this,' he paused for a moment as the signal turned green and then continued.

'So, I set this up around ten years ago. Two years after retiring from the Air Force. During my time in service, I had seen some breath-taking car design studios all over Europe—cleverly constructed in spaces much smaller than what you guys saw today,' he began. 'And frankly, I wasn't the only one. Car modification was becoming huge, especially in cities like Delhi, Punjab, and Haryana. But despite that, ninety-nine percent of the guys in the business were just doing basics like music systems, car graphics, alloy wheels, adding spoilers, and some basic spray painting at best.

'Only a handful of people dared to or had the resources to go the whole nine yards and set up full-scale facilities that could take a car apart and bring it back to life with renewed body and soul—we became one of them after I hired the best engineers from around the country. In any case, you can't be an air force fighter pilot if you can't assemble a regular car.

'We designed cars that looked like Batmobiles. Although they're common nowadays among rich kids, back in the day, it was nothing short of a spectacle. We even designed a car that looked like a shoe as a marketing gimmick for a large footwear brand in Delhi. There was a time when people would drive all the way from Mumbai, Bangalore, Chennai, Jaipur, Delhi, you name it, even from Kochi, just to get their car designed at Soni Motors.

'But then, foreign cars came almost fully fitted with everything one may need, with full-service packages and new rules for safety and modification. Plus, this business also lost its novelty value significantly, and since 2010, it has been in a steady decline. At the peak of work, I did three workshops with almost seventy-five people!'

'Wow! That's quite a story, Mr. Soni... So, you don't modify cars anymore?' He asked.

'Of course, we do, but much less. See, even before, full-scale transformation orders were not many. Now we get most of our orders from wealthy Gulf kids. Even if we get two such orders in a year, we are through. We make about twenty-five lakh profit per car. Only the other subtle requests have stopped. People don't like to fiddle much with their cars anymore. We are now also into bikes, so we keep ourselves busy as possible,' he concluded.

'What makes you think we can compete now?'

'Because we are not competing on their turf. What we are doing now is creating a new arena. Here we are writing the rules and contesting on our terms,' from the get-go, he sounded like someone who could see the true potential in our idea in the way only we could so far.

'It feels you are prying into my mind. That's exactly what I was hoping to hear,' I exclaimed.

'You have to keep yourself open to new ideas, and life is very unpredictable... the armed forces teach you that, among other things.'

Another heavy and massively productive day, I thought to myself as we dropped our bags at a budget B&B when we called Vinay and shared the events of the day. Vinay was over the moon, as if he wanted to jump out of the phone to hug and kiss us both.

Despite the excitement, we had very little energy left and crashed without having dinner as soon as we reached our room.

In the morning, we had a sumptuous breakfast of three paneer parathas, each with generous portions of curd and an overdose of pickles, especially for me.

We began our trip back to Delhi at eight in the morning, and Aman took to the steering. An hour into the drive, my pickles and rajma were now making Aman extremely uncomfortable, to the point that he threatened to throw me out if I didn't stop the release of foul gases. We stopped over to get some digestives, including a bottle of *Hajmola*, which worsened the equation further.

'Yaar, what the hell! This is so disgusting!' He yelled at me.

'Okay, okay. I am rolling down the windows,' I tried not to laugh.

'I am taking a cab!'

'Their cabs are even worse. At least here we have this little Ambi Pur. car freshner!' I tried to reason.

'Why don't you drink some of it? Maybe that will help!'

We were back in the office the next day, and the chaos was unrelenting. I was severely behind on my project and emails. One day of missing emails, I felt overwhelmed by how much I had to catch up with.

Meanwhile, Vinay was getting frustrated with not being able to close development positions. Although the frustration was not limited to him, he was the one who was pursuing the recruitment process most actively.

Within the clutter of applicants, we found our first ray of hope. A girl name Arunima Banerjee, referred by none other than Govindan, the Chennai professor, who was true to his word and kept in touch on and off to check on our progress.

Arunima was a Bengali based in Bangalore and had over ten years of experience working on automotive software. She had started as a developer but swiftly progressed to other areas and was now a tech lead with a global automotive software company working on the operating system platform for a large electric vehicle maker. What made her candidature even sweeter was that she had resigned after a fallout with her boss and could join us straight away.

Govindan had given us rave reviews about her intellect and commitment. After a couple of phone calls and google hangout meetings, we decided to go meet her.

I couldn't excuse myself from work, so Vinay and Aman had to see this meeting through. This was our third trip to Bangalore in the last three months.

It was eight in the evening when Vinay finally called.

'Yo! How did it go?' I asked.

'She's not on, yaar. This won't work,' Vinay replied.

'What the hell? Why? She seemed okay on the phone. What's wrong?' I exclaimed, wandering into the office and looking for a vacant meeting room.

'She is asking for 75K, plus a 2% stake.'

'So, this is within budget. What's the problem?'

'So, you're okay?'

'Of course, what kind of a question is this?' I was now getting impatient.

'Okay, if you are okay, we are okay too. She's already hired. *Wohooo*,' he announced, and I knew they were going to pick on me for the rest of the conversation.

'Whatever, man!'

'So, how was she?'

'She was good. 5 feet 6 inches tall, seemed in shape, fair-ish, depending on the direction of the light,' Vinay was at it again.

'You planning to ask her out?' I responded.

'She doesn't want to get married, as she told us.'

'Nothing seems to have changed your luck with women, not even your biceps,' I mocked.

'Anything else you want to tell me?' I tried getting things back on track.

'Such is the impression we create! See, only one meeting, and the deal is sealed. Aman and I are a great team, you know. We are just getting things done! Wherever we go.'

'Keep going,' I knew Vinay was down a couple of drinks.

'She was actually quite brilliant! I got her to work on some minor tasks to get a full measure of her range. She was able to simulate a dummy operating system and even tested some of the code on a Jupiter notebook. I found her thorough with her work. In fact, I even picked up a few things myself. She is going to set the software wing on fire!'

'This is amazing! Glad my persona is rubbing off on you.' I closed as we hung up.

Now with Arunima on the team, we had at least one specialist across disciplines, Vinay and me for batteries and design, Jatin and his team for physical manufacturing and regulatory approval, and Arunima and her team for the operating system.

But before that, we had to find safe and suitable accommodation for Arunima and the rest of the crack team that would join us at our headquarters in Ludhiana.

* * *

Vinay joined us for his first trip to Ludhiana, and I promised them both to remain on a salad and green tea diet throughout the drive.

As we drove closer to Jatin's residence, it appeared as if he lived in an upper-middle-class township built for members of the military. Jatin's double-storied house must have been around 200 sq ft, compliant with the local peach color theme for the exteriors.

We parked our car next to his Ertiga, which was parked right outside the pedestrian sidewalk, as had the others in the neighborhood. This minor act of encroachment notwithstanding, the residents appeared to be well-behaved. At least the cleanliness of the roads seemed to vouch for it. There was almost no litter, and it seemed the roads were regularly cleaned by the municipal authoritics. Surprisingly, there were no posters of political leaders or campaigns on the walls either. The whole locality spread out over 200 acres and was among one of the most peaceful patches of residential space you are likely to find anywhere in India.

The living room door opened soon after we rang the doorbell, and Mr. Soni came out gazing at his phone. As he stepped out onto the porch, he looked up, and instantly an ingenuous smile appeared on his face at the sight of us.

We were all betting on each other at that stage and searching for reasons to trust one another.

Aman and I gently hugged Jatin, but Vinay didn't know what 'gentle' meant and, after touching his feet, gave Jatin a big bear hug!

'Paaji! Big fan. Can't tell you how happy I am to see you face to face,' he began.

'Oh, likewise, ji! Glad to see all of you return as a bigger lot than last time,' Jatin replied, setting a positive vibe at the outset.

'So… I have looked for localities for you to stay that are at less than a ten minute drive from our workshop,' Jatin announced, and we were glad he had a planned lineup. We knew we had to hurry up if we had to make this day count.

The rest of the evening was spent in house hunting, and after some confusion with the property agents, we finalized two apartments with two beds and baths, one for the boys and one for the girls, we knew we will need more as we progress.

Jatin invited us to his home for dinner and drinks, and we found ourselves in his living room surrounded by family achievements, including photos with politicians and his own picture in his air force uniform. The atmosphere was warm and inviting, with the aroma of cooking filling the air. He also introduced us to his two sons, who were bright and enthusiastic about their father's plan to build India's best electric car. Their energy inspired us, and we felt fortunate to know Jatin, who was not only a successful businessman but also a role model for living a wonderful personal life. He was a gracious host, offering us whisky on his terrace with its contemporary patio furniture. Our visit reminded us of the importance of maintaining passion for our work, even in the face of routine tasks.

'Beautiful house Jatin ji. I hope to own a place like this one day,' Vinay began the evening with compliments.

'You will have a lot more than this, Vinay, trust me,' Jatin replied, optimistic as always.

'Jatin ji, I think we should quickly close the lease agreement on both these apartments,' I reiterated, though we had already agreed on our drive back.

'I think so too; otherwise, we will just keep looking. It's a matter of one year or so. Then you guys can buy your bungalows and farmhouses here,' Jatin replied and laughed merrily.

'The agreement will be in the name of Soni Motors, so we will be okay,' he had it all under control. We continued drinking and chatting.

'Sir, I have always wanted to ask…' Vinay tested the waters with Jatin.

'Sure, don't be so formal. Go for it,' Jatin replied.

'Sir, you have everything, a decent business, a pension from the air force, your own house. Why do you want to take this chance with us?' He began.

Jatin smiled pensively.

'I could ask you the same. You also have a flourishing career, your own homes, families, and youth, then why work with a fifty-year-old like me?' He gave us a question in response to a the question, but I didn't wait for a response.

'It's the urge to go further, do more with life…' he paused for a moment and continued, 'Emotions aside, we do really have a phenomenal concept, and I trust you boys and myself to pull off something my kids will be proud of. Is that reason enough?'

Vinany didn't say much. Just nodded quietly as he had partially understood,

'Cheers, *Brraaaaaa*,' I rejoiced, and everyone followed.

# 14

# REPORTING TO BASE CAMP!

The next few days went by quickly applying for GST, formalizing more offers, getting a bank account and all of this without raising any suspicion with Alan and his team, and, more importantly, the mole in-house, Abhishek Chatterjee.

Meanwhile, Shantanu, the investor, dialed up the pressure. He wanted to see our designs, profiles of team members, finances, and everything we told him he would not have a say in. I had already started to wonder if Aman indeed pulled off such a smart stunt after all, or were we now going to pay a lot more than we had bargained for.

But at the time, we had switched gears with no room to pause and take stock, and finally, our next destination was our Base Camp, under commander Jatin Soni.

It was early December, and the three of us reached Ludhiana by two in the afternoon. We picked up Jatin and headed to our apartment.

Arunima was to arrive the next evening along with three new members of the development team.

Jatin took the kind liberty of making some basic arrangements such as beds in all the rooms, a mini-fridge, some basic cookware, an induction cooktop, a set of plastic chairs, a table for the living room, a Wi-Fi connection, an inverter for power back up. He had also arranged for some elementary grocery supplies like milk, bread, butter, Maggi, tea, etc. We put some of it to use straight away, helped ourselves to some tea, and began soaking in the new space.

'Pretty decent, actually, for the price,' I said, and everyone seemed to agree.

'Yeah, plus I am glad we didn't end up spending too much time on this,' Jatin added.

'So, it's day one!' Vinay announced.

'Indeed, my boy. May God bless us all!' Jatin Ji began with a short prayer.

'Now, let's get down to some art and craft. *Ganpati Bappa*... Vinay gave the call.

'*Maurya*,' we responded with aplomb.

'Here,' I passed an easy chart roll to Vinay.

Vinay pulled out some charts that would stick to the wall and serve as whiteboards.

He signaled to me for help, and we started cutting the easy chart rolls neatly. We placed them all over the walls, some horizontal, some vertical, of different sizes, to serve varied purposes.

We only had two adjoining walls in the living room on which to install flipcharts to record running points. The other two walls made way for the kitchen and the balcony, leaving little space. Soon we covered the remaining wall space on these as well with white charts, carving out the annoying switchboards on them that blocked our flow. With both walls ready to be scribbled on, Aman and I got down to getting our Zila designs from paper onto the walls for everyone's reference.

Vinay picked up markers of different colors and began sketching the wheels, the curves, the bumpers, the bonnet, the body, the doors, the powertrain, and every little component we would need to build or buy as we progress in our manufacturing journey. Initially, we were sketching together till it became a coordination nightmare, so I stepped back and followed his lead.

Vinay cleared the board a few times before nailing a technique to replicate the sketch from paper to the wall. This went on till late in the night, and by about the afternoon next day, we had what we had imagined.

After everyone gave the final image a thumbs-up, each component was colored. Yellow stickers indicated parts, pink programming, red market-sourced components, and green battery packs.

He kneeled down again and drew the ground line, counted five and a half wheels in between, and drew a rocker line with some clearance from the ground like an SUV should have. This went on till the rest of the team arrived; there were multiple attempts, many cups of tea, and the room was stinking of smoke from our cigarettes. What we now had on the wall was a stunning X-ray-like image of how Zila was going to look, both from inside and outside. Every part, every component, was etched out now: the bumpers, the wheels, the DC converter, transmission, battery pack, electric motors, and the powertrain running through the car.

Once everyone thumbs-upped the final image, a color code was assigned to each component. A yellow sticky note for component, pink one for programming items, red denoted components we will need to source from the market, and green meant the physical parts we had to build.

The room was now divided into two major parts: the big sketch of the Zila on one wall and, on the wall opposite to this, the listing of the parts that had to be either built, bought, or stolen. It had a listing of everything that was on the big wall as well as the stuff that wasn't. The next month was going to be devoted to putting dates to these and kicking off whatever we could.

'What do you think, Captain?' Vinay asked Jatin ji in anticipation of grand applause, 'You need to get better, but a good start nonetheless,' Jatin chuckled. We could tell he wasn't disappointed at all.

An ex-air force pilot like Jatin could, in no time, separate the chaff from the rice. He had spent the best part of his service inside high-intensity and high-focus planning rooms, where even the tiniest of lapses meant paying with life or a lifetime of disability.

'Jatin ji, you are just jealous! This is a masterpiece,' Vinay replied, and we smiled, surrounded by the blueprint of the cause we were all here off. This was our mission office, and it certainly looked like one.

How many mountains of impossibilities had we crossed to get to this point? Less than two years from the point, all I had was an inkling wandering restlessly in New York. From there to now—a team, a factory, the know-how, the connections, the working capital, a plan, a vision, and although grumpy an investor nonetheless!

About fifteen months, sixty-four meetings, fifteen cities, several train trips, countless phone calls, over 150 interviews, half a dozen few investor meetings were enough evidence that we didn't just *land* here.

Next was to receive my software crack team. Arunima's boys and girls were here. After some ice-breakers, and casual chats about the flight, the city, and their apartments, we were now ready to roll.

The boys, in their early twenties, looked observantly at the stuff on the walls. It was perhaps the first time in their careers that they were being issued laptops.

'Excellent sketch, Bharat,' Sindhu, one of our multi-disciplinary developers, another one of Govindan's protégé praised. Vinay eyebrowed unimpressed at this misappropriation of credit.

Jatin's team also arrived soon after. I opened the door and welcomed them inside. Soon we were fourteen people cramping up the living room, or should I say the first Base Camp of Bharat Kinetics.

'We are ready,' I walked up to Vinay and nudged him to commence the meeting.

'Cool,' he said and stood in front of the wall and began addressing everyone. I noticed that the glare from the tube light on the opposite wall was hugely distracting, and I made a mental note to call the electrician in the morning to have it moved around.

Vinay, however, continued, 'I can't believe this is actually happening. Around eight months ago, when Bharat and Aman came to see me in the hopes of reviving our unfinished college project, I played along to see how far we could get, but once we set out, it appeared as though the entire world was just waiting for us to begin.'

He continued for another five minutes or so, talking about why we were there, how we plan to progress, who all we have met, why this will take off, what's happening around the world, how rich everyone stands to become if they stayed the course, how proud they can be for architecting the world's best electric car hundred percent made in India, what it could mean for the country… and how it'd bind us all together. He also threw in an anecdote about three brick layers. The one where when asked what they are doing, each gives a different answer. While the first one says he is laying bricks to feed his family, the second says he is laying bricks to build walls. It is the third one who gives the fascinating answer that he is making the most beautiful monument on the planet.

He then posed the same question to everyone, what they thought they would be doing there?

'This is a start-up, and we are going to make an electric car,' Sindhu Singharyar said.

'Yeah, that's not entirely off the mark, Sindhu, thanks. Anyone else?' Vinay acknowledged.

'We will be making a fully made-in-India, super-fast electric car,' Sourabh Mahajan, another one of our programmers, pitched in.

'We are going to make India's best electric car,' Aditya Dixit from Jatin's team tried.

'Yes! Very close, Aditya! But it's going to be the *world's* best electric car,' Vinay remarked. Vinay then finally introduced himself and urged the others to do the same. 'I am a mechanical engineer by qualification, and I will strive to be a worthy colleague.'

Aman and I went next. I kept it brief and crisp, followed by Mr. Soni, Anurima, Aditya Dixit (from Mr. Soni's team), Sindhu(an electrical engineer who'd be helping Arunima with the operating system), Arun Kamath (from Arunima's development team), Rajat Chauhan (embedded system professional) and Ajay Bhindra (Jatin's floor supervisor).

We kept the rest of the evening light, just giving everyone a sense of what the next month was going to look like. Dinner was served, and there was going to be no booze as we had planned an early start the next day. One that would be hard to endure with a hangover, as we had asked the boys to show up at ten in the morning the next day. We could now see almost everyone yawning, and it was time to say goodnight.

It was Day 1 of the workshop. Aman, Vinay, Arunima, Sindhu, and I, along with Jatin and his trusted men Aditya and Ajay, showed up at 10:15 a.m. just in time. Our programmers, however, were running late. We waited for them for five more minutes before we finally began.

'So, let's start with understanding this car right here,' Vinay commenced the meeting. 'This car has about seventy-five parts, of which only fifteen are moving parts, compared to over 5000 in an internal combustion engine (ICE) that is used in a petrol or a diesel car,' Vinay continued explaining the make-up of the car while taking questions along the way.

His explanation came to a halt when the doorbell rang, and the boys finally arrived thirty-five minutes late. Despite such a heartfelt briefing the previous evening, we were obviously annoyed.

'Hi, sir, sorry we are late… we couldn't find an auto,' Arun sounded part apologetic and part nervous.

'That's fine. Now you need to make up for it. Do you want to know how?' Vinay replied in a rather casual and friendly tone.

The boys looked at each other uncomfortably, and Arun nodded.

'Okay, let's see. How about you make ten refreshing cups of tea for all of us?' Vinay proposed a rather simple atonement.

'Oh, but do you even know how to make tea?' I asked, and they both had a yes and no expression.

'No problem. Learn from YouTube. If you can help make a car, I am sure you can manage a few cups of tea,' Vinay said.

'Also, under this roof, "we don't know" won't be admissible. If you don't know, figure it out.'

The boys stood there looking unsure and slightly annoyed for being 'punished' like schoolboys, but with everyone staring at them, they reluctantly walked into the kitchen.

'Let me help you,' I joined them to help find the items they would need.

They indeed had no clue and had to resort to YouTube, and I stood by them to guide them if they were going horribly wrong. After all, I was going to be one of the consumers. The tea was ready, and I helped them serve it.

'Welcome to Bharat Kinetics!' Vinay said as he picked up his cup.

* * *

The day ended with Arun and Rajat making some thirty cups of tea by evening, and whether they understood EVs or not, they sure knew how to make a good cup of tea now.

The week progressed with sustained intensity. Our sketches were the basis for the design for Arunima, who began her 3D simulations with Arun, Rajat, and Sindhu. She looked sorted, and so did Jatin and his boys, who were giving her company and inputs to construct the simulation.

It was really Vinay and I who were left with no hands to help with making the battery. Plus, our involvement across all the work was becoming too much. We desperately needed a few assistants, a combination of lab assistants and trained electrical staff who could at least help with soldering, tooling, and assembling.

Next week was going to be spent at Jatin's workshop. The cashiers had been evicted to make space for Arun, Rajat, and Sindhu, and the front office was portioned off for Vinay, Aman, Arunima, and me. The visitor's lounge, too, had been partitioned for the team members who were yet to join.

Zila was going to be built like a super-secret undercover assignment. Jatin had made elaborate arrangements to conceal our operations from anyone visiting the workshop. And he didn't demand a penny for it.

'Bharat, hi,' Arunima walked up to me as I was chatting with Jatin and Vinay.

'Hey,' I replied with a smile.

'I know it would be expensive, but we will need a projector too. We can rent it. It will be cheaper that way,' she said.

'Sure, give me a couple of days. We will order,' I assured, without asking any questions. Vinay looked on, unconvinced at my lack of questioning.

'Great, thanks. I think we should install it in the apartment,' she suggested, and I nodded in agreement. In the process, she also passed a subtle message that she wouldn't want to operate from the workshop, rendering most of what Jatin had arranged for them almost pointless.

'That is fine, but we must work from both sites. Such a small setup shouldn't be departmentalized already,' Vinay intervened.

'No, I didn't mean that. It's just that it's more peaceful there. We can come here when the building process starts,' she clarified but seemed uncomfortable with Vinay's tone.

'That's fine, we can figure it out,' I added and diffused the whole thing. So much hinged on her being in a positive frame of mind.

'Thanks, Bharat,' she said and smiled, still not leaving the place.

I waited for a few moments, waiting for her to leave, but she stayed. I continued with my conversation with Jatin.

'Jatin ji, we need a place for battery manufacturing. I don't think we have factored that in.'

'Oh hell! But you didn't tell me,' he looked stumped.

'It just struck me. We need to figure something out.'

'We can use the terrace with asbestos sheets,' Arunima jumped in, eager to contribute. 'Asbestos is highly inflammable. We need to find a large basement somewhere,' Vinay replied, and I could tell some friction was brewing already. Both were trying to one-up on each other. It had to be conveyed to her that Vinay was the acting CEO, or it was best to let Vinay earn his stripes with the team himself.

'There are fire-resistant ones too,' she said and went on, 'I can find some useful links; we can get them here or from Jalandhar....'

'Arunima, the place will attract attention with that, plus you need permissions before erecting structures,' Jatin explained politely.

'Oh! Then?' she asked.

'That's what we are trying to figure out. I think it's a tall order. We will sort this out,' Vinay intervened and suggested she carry on with her work.

'Hmm... okay. Let me know if you need anything,' she added before reluctantly leaving for our home office with her little crack team.

'New challenges, young man,' Jatin Ji quipped at Vinay.

'Don't worry, sir, we will manage. Her ideas were bright, though. Can we not install asbestos structures?' He queried.

'No, no, no, let's look for a large basement with some kind of ventilation somewhere. We need to make a replica of what Animesh showed us at Varanasi. It needs to be as organized as his lab was, if not more,' I declared.

Three weeks went past, and I didn't see how I could leave for Dubai in another week. Not a single milestone had been achieved yet, and I had to recalibrate with Shantanu on when we could be back.

It was eleven in the morning, and everyone was back in the apartment working through simulations and operating system fundamentals. Once we wrote the principles, we had to send them to Govindan for his opinion. All departments were so intertwined, and I was already feeling burnt out. The new year was approaching. Some guys wanted to go home. How was this going to work out?

I desperately needed updates on where things were and decided to just walk into our makeshift development center set up in my room and ask.

'Hey!'

'Hi, Bharat,' they said and continued working. I didn't know how to react. I felt awkward, perhaps even unwelcome. Yes, in my own room! Nay in my own company! I was nervous about speaking to my own team. I had to figure something out. I couldn't just be ignored like some prying old man in the house. I wasn't even that old. If anything, I was younger than Arunima. Was that why she was acting tough?

I walked in firmly towards my suitcase and pretended to look for something in it, and thirty seconds in. It was more than clear no one was going to even look up from their screens. I walked right out to look for Vinay in our pocket-sized house.

'*Bhai*...' I said and took him out with me. We quietly descended the stairs and walked to the other side of the inner lane of the apartment complex. I leaned on the grey boundary wall of the park and lit up a cigarette, and so did he. I tried calming myself down. These were still early days, and I didn't want to transfer my anxiety to Vinay.

'Yaar, I need to set a date with Shantanu for my return to Dubai. I need to know how far we have come on simulations and the operating system,' I asked Vinay finally, feeling like an idiot.

'I know! She is hard to talk to, man! I have been asking for an update, and she doesn't even respond properly,' he vented. I felt better that I wasn't the only one feeling the heat.

'I know. I could feel the hostile energy. What the hell, man! Neither Arunima nor her guys are under control,' I lamented.

'Let's go together and demand an update,' Vinay proposed. I didn't think it was the best idea, but what choice did we have?

'Yeah, but no conflict. Don't poke the bear.' I cautioned.

'Don't worry. Let's do this. Someday we will need to... let it be today,' we punched our fists with determination.

'Hey guys... sit, sit, sit...' Vinay greeted as he walked into the room. Although no one had made any effort to stand in the first place. I just hoped things went smoothly.

'Can you bring up the design progress on the projector, please?' He demanded like a real boss.

Good job, Vinay, I said to myself.

'We are not ready, Vinay,' Arunima resisted.

'That's fine. This is no inspection, just taking stock. I have told you before that you can use my assistance. I train people on this,' he casually deflected her objections.

Although reluctantly, she connected her laptop to the projector, and after a bit of adjustment, we could see her screen clearly.

I was actually pleasantly surprised with the progress. It was all there already. Why was she holding it back, then? I didn't say much and let Vinay handle it.

'This seems to be in good shape. I didn't expect it to be a problem anyway, especially when you have the sketches already,' Vinay said. I was not sure how that landed with the team. If I was part of the team, I would have taken offense at Vinay giving all the credit to our sketches over their effort. *Wrong move, Vinay.* I thought to myself.

'We need to add a number of things. The angles, the pillar, etc., are still not accurate, plus this pirated software is not helping at all,' Arunima replied, sounding impatient.

'Sure, I understand, but this looks almost ready, so by when can we get a final look?' Vinay asked.

'Umm… give us two more days,' Arunima confirmed after being compelled to respond.

'Great! Good job, and thank you,' I said, and we walked out of our first formal review at Bharat Kinetics.

After this meeting, however, her team was in for a massive grind. No one left our apartment till four in the morning for the next two days back-to-back.

The next day Jatin Ji, Aman, and I visited some junk car dealers in Jalandhar. Jatin knew these guys well. The goal was to pick up a not-so-run-down car and some components like a transmission box, etc. We would use these to build an MVP, or a minimum viable product, and battery technology. Essentially converting a petrol/diesel/CNG car into an electric car running on a Zinc-air battery pack and see how far it goes.

Although most functional items were stripped out either by the seller or by the scrap dealer, if any were still left, the owners would spot them and sell them in the open market.

Finding working parts in the massive junkyard, though, meant screening hundreds of cars, which harded than finding a parking spot in Pitampura DDA colonies.

'Sir, this is getting too close. I need to leave before or by Christmas,' I confided to Jatin on our way back.

'I know! You must ask for more time, Bharat. Finalize the battery unit and hire at least a couple of assistants before you leave,' it sounded like Jatin was clearly not going to help solve this one for us.

'It will be hard, I will try, but I don't think Shantanu even has a choice,' Jatin was not impressed with my reply.

'You stay back. I will leave,' Aman offered, sensing Jatin's jitters. 'Best I leave per plan, get this whole thing sorted. I will handle Alan and everyone. You hire two or three people, finalize the unit and join me,' Aman proposed.

'See, that's it, problem solved,' Jatin remarked sounding animated and more importantly, relieved.

'Now leave Shantanu and Alan to me. I have your passport copies and will get your visa and everything,' Aman came to the rescue *again*!

Now it was time to tune in to Arunima's show.

# 15

# ZILA ON THE WALL

Arunima issued invites for eleven sharp. We moved the beds out of my room to create enough space for everyone to settle and get a good look at the projector.

Arunima and her team arrived thirty minutes earlier to set up the projector. She asked Arun to manage the laptop and projections while she and Sindhu were to take us through the semantics of the design. Soon, there were sixteen people in the room.

'Okay, good morning, everyone!' Arunima began with a confident and upbeat tone. It was hard to imagine it was coming from a girl who had barely slept through the week.

Everyone smiled while some reciprocated the greeting.

'Bharat and Vinay, you are not treating us enough. Look at the energies!' She commented at the lack of reciprocation.

'We are just scared of you, Arunima. Bharat, and I certainly are,' Vinay retorted rather childishly to puncture her comment.

And if that wasn't enough, some of the others joined him in the giggle. Aman and I looked at each other and then looked at Arunima, who, frankly, did well to sport a smile.

'No, I am not. The treat is on me, Arunima. You totally deserve it,' I spoke in her favor.

It was her show today. She had worked hard, and I absolutely had to make her feel important and a firm part of the inner circle.

For whatever my support was worth, I could sense from her expressions that she felt like she had scored a mini victory. 'Let's begin, please, Arunima,' I added.

'Sure, by all means,' she said and asked Arun to start the show on the big wall.

Arun brought up the first design, an SUV-like design with color options ranging from blue, silver, black, and white.

He explained the dimension in as much detail as he could. And was quite thorough with it.

The first design was of a compact SUV that will allow us to save on duties per Indian laws. It was 13.7 feet long, 6 feet wide, and 5.2 feet tall, along with other details like potential weight and aerodynamic coefficient, which essentially means how well a car will manage to ward off the driving drag. Formula 1 cars have some of the lowest coefficients.

'Let's move to the next one,' Vinay commanded, and I could tell that Arunima wasn't very impressed with this.

The next design was a full-scale SUV around 15 feet long, 6 feet wide, and 5 feet 5 inches tall with an 18-inch wheel diameter. Arun simulated color options, and everyone sat upright to take a look.

'I like this one; let's see a few more options before we decide on one,' Vinay commanded again.

'Actually, Vinay, we were only able to model two, given the time we had,' Arunima explained.

Vinay looked at me and thought for a moment. I knew he wanted to see some small car options too. I took over.

'Sure, never mind. I think we can go with a compact SUV design. Why don't we make some changes on the go till we find our Zila?' I looked around, and everyone seemed to think it was a great idea, so we began.

'Why don't we widen the lights a little?' one voice said.

'Nooo, not so much, yeah, slightly on the bottom right, widen it there,' suggested another one as Arun began to make changes.

'The doors need to have a slightly more smooth look. Right now, they look a little box-like.' I think it was Aman.

'The bonnet is facing down. Please lift it slightly,' said Aditya with no subtlety, almost like issuing an order. Arunima, to her credit, was dealing with this barrage of feedback quite patiently, in sharp contrast to the comment Vinay made earlier.

'The grill needs to have some marking of it being electric. Maybe design and depict some current flow?' I could no longer keep track of who was speaking.

'Yaar, you are not listening. The bonnet needs to be lifted, and the front grill needs to look like someone is smiling,' came another input.

'You mean "grinning"!' Arunima condescendingly corrected.

'See, in the interior, the cup holder is not deep enough,' comments just kept coming.

Someone had to put a stop to this soon.

'They are already 4.5 inches; how much deeper do you

need? Use smaller cups next time,' Arunima shut down the idea aggressively. I must say I smiled at her attitude

'Hi… the tail lamp… we can make it slightly sharper. It's just got a standard curve,' another one came. The excitement was understandable. How often do you get a chance to have your say in designing a real car? My idea of live edits had turned this whole thing into a commotion.

'Okay, everyone! Stop, please,' Arunima brought the house back in order.

'I have made some notes. Please give us a couple of hours. I will call you guys once we are ready.'

We agreed and allowed them to perfect the design, along with Jatin, for advice.

I waited in the living room and texted Aman and Vinay, who were on the balcony lighting up another cigarette.

Three hours in, Arunima came to tell us they were ready.

'So, before we show you to the car, let me explain how we have designed it,' Arunima recommenced.

My personal opinion of her design was that it needed a lot more work. It looked good, but it was nothing like the car I saw in my dreams. They had moved away from the sketches, and I was not okay with it. I worked for months perfecting our designs. Criticism coming from me publicly wouldn't have landed well. Hence, I stood back and listened to her open-mindedly.

Arunima continued, 'We have given the car a fluidic look. The head roof is placed at 5.2 feet, so not really a tall-boy model, but it has enough space even for someone 6 feet 2 inches tall. Beyond that, they will have a problem in any car.

The front grill has been lifted, and we have added a cute grin-like look and feel to it.

'The doors have been designed to look fluidic too, the seats have been made sharp, the boot has more depth, we have added metallic strips that resemble an electric current on both sides of the car, and it looks like a dream, especially in blue.

'Here is how it looks.'

Arunima unveiled the much-improved version. The front grill was indeed grinning on. The headlamps were designed like a waving flag, and there were subtle markings of + and – on the rear-view mirrors. The side strips were designed like AA batteries on both sides. Then they took us inside the car for a virtual tour. It could seat three at the back since there was no exhaust hump. The design was getting closer to the car Vinay and I had imagined.

It was clearly not enough time for the team, and I think getting there looked a little rough.

'Brilliant, I love this. This is amazing! I am so proud of all of you,' I announced. I wanted us to register a mental victory. For everyone had worked really hard for this till now and deserved to get appreciated.

'Gorgeous, this is just so gorgeous!' Vinay exclaimed, following my endorsement. *Idiot.*

Everyone was ecstatic, 'How can something that looks like this not succeed?' Jatin remarked, 'Boys, I am so glad to have known you!'

'Final? *Pakka?*' Arunima checked.

'Absolutely,' Vinay confirmed and hugged Arunima and then her team. I saw Sindhu walk away from Vinay towards me, dodging his excitement.

'*Woohoo*! Okay then! Thank you all. You were a great audience.' Arunima said and courtesied like a ballerina.

'You better get going if you don't want to drive in the dark,' Jatin Ji reminded, and I nodded and prepared to leave. My suitcase was already in the car, and it was time.

It was beginning to dawn on me that my corporate karma wasn't done yet, and regardless of how much I wanted to stay on, I had little choice but to take that plane. It was time to rescue hostage Aman.

# 16

# SAVING AGENT AMAN

The worst and the best thing about a high-pressure job like ours was that it lacked empathy. It didn't care for vulnerabilities, state of mind, health or family. If you are on the team, you better pull your weight. Nothing could remind you of this more than the rapidly burgeoning emails on your phone. From five unread emails the last I checked while leaving Delhi, it now stood at a towering 325.

'I am here,' I messaged Aman before mustering the courage to get back to my inbox.

Our days began at 7:45 a.m. sharp, yet, we would still not be the first ones in the office. Aman and I walked up all suited and booted. He brought up the presentation on the screen in a room with at least ten client representatives, all VPs and above. I began by introducing myself. I could tell something was wrong, and the mood was somber; no one welcomed me, no handshakes, none of the usual niceties of a first meeting.

'Gentlemen, we are worried if Bluewater INC knows what it's doing,' Mohammad bin Salim, I think that's what his name was, a peer of Alan, and a top shot at AL Grand spoke in a patronizing Arabic accent.

He continued to punch holes in everything Aman had to say.

I was just starting up, so I just stood there as a bystander sizing up the room for as long as I could. After an hour of hearing them out, I stood up to tell them that this was the best we could do and that if they held our invoice, we would have to pull back resources.

Alan was just waiting for one of us to hold our ground, so he could jump to our rescue. And he did so quite tactfully, offering to be the sane voice in the room, calming down emotions and speaking in our support. Stand up for yourselves, and before you know it, you will have allies to stand up for you.

He acknowledged the work we had put in and also point gaps in Al Grand teams, smartly emerging as the grown up in the room. He approved all pending payments and secured some commitments from us on how we plan to fix everything that was wrong.

'Good show, trust me, it only gets better from here, I have seen much worse,' Alan assured with a gentle pat on Aman's back as he left the conference room. We nodded acknowledging his support.

We placed our laptops on our desks to grab some coffee and some peace of mind, especially for Aman, who looked at least ten years older than he did while leaving Ludhiana, not that he had great odds, but at this rate his shot at love and family seemed really bleak.

'What the hell are you doing?' He asked me, getting agitated as I examined the grey of his hair.

'Nothing, just checking if you have begun balding too,' I sniggered, trying to cheer him up.

'So, ASK ME! I am most certainly balding and greying and perhaps dying. I might even want to get tested for diabetes and hypertension,' he exclaimed in frustration while I stood there and smirked.

'I am so glad you are here,' he said and hugged me.

'Things okay in Ludhiana?' He finally asked.

Let's party today,' I proposed.

'No, don't fall into that trap. We finish by 8 p.m., and then I need to prepare for the morning meeting,' he tried to reason with me.

'We are prepared. We are no Lord Shiva. We can't solve everything,' one of the many things I learned from Animesh.

'Guess you have a point. What the hell… bring the booze,' he announced.

Watching us both together, our teams started crowding us to begin narrating their horror stories. It was almost impossible to peacefully enjoy a cup of coffee and smoke. This grind continued till 8:30 p.m., when we finally packed up for the hotel. Alan saw us waiting for our taxi and quite graciously gave us a ride. He bucked us up and told us how well we were doing. Appreciating us, he also told us that we were running this project better than ninety percent of the projects he had seen in his life. This was certainly an endorsement of Aman's work ethic and competence. I had only just arrived. Alan was so awesome. Wish Shantanu could be a fraction like him.

I flicked open two beer pints as we sat on a sofa in my apartment. Everything was still like it was the last time. Pristine and exquisite.

'I will order. I can't cook today,' I announced, and he nodded, still engrossed in emails.

'It's your turn to get the next set of beers,' I said and settled on my couch, reaching for my laptop bag on the table. He was nodding to everything.

I opened the Bharat Kinetics mailbox, and Vinay sent the links to the four videos; we went through each one at a time.

### *Video 1*

'Hey, boys, what's up? Things are heating up here; we have begun work on the operating system. Govindan turned out to be true to his word and is now reviewing the design principles. You both must also look at this.' In a fifteen-minute-long video, he gave us a detailed tour of the design, the controls, the platform, the modules, and some timelines.

### *Video 2*

'I spoke to some young guys; at 15k a month, two of them work four days a week, Thursday to Sunday, on the battery. These are their profiles… I can at least get them to get to some groundwork. This one will take time, and I can't imagine doing it all by myself!'

The next few weeks remained almost exactly this way, keeping our heads over water at work, making sure Salim and his team were happy, and then tuning into Vinay's updates.

Weekends were spent on marathon phone calls with the team in Ludhiana.

The shuffle between both worlds couldn't be more contrasting: on the one hand, here in Dubai, we had millions in the budget, fancy apartments, and ultra-equipped offices, yet, all we could hear was commotion, stress, and politics, while back in Ludhiana, inside a loaned workshop, a basic apartment, Vinay was pulling off a unique invention with aplomb and passion.

Vinay was unstoppable, beating down our mailbox with his daily vlogs. It was hard to tell what he enjoyed more, the engineering or the videos.

### *Video 19*

'So, my *habibis*, behind me what you see—*Pandit ji,* side, please! Now look, those are the big clay supplies. So, as per our plan, we will now begin building the clay version of Zila. Jatin Ji suggested we add some plaster of paris to keep costs in check. Now, give me another moment. Let me show you more… okay? These are our ultra-advanced, state-of-the-art robotic clay milling arms,' he said and paused, like waiting for us to react, then continued, 'Okay! That was a joke! Maybe someday, one day, soon enough. For now, no money! No problem! We have used some makeshift drilling machines, changing their teeth and connecting them with a motor to control speed and precision. This should work…I hope it does.'

He went on a little longer. The clay building typically begins once the designs have been approved. Post this only, some minor changes can be introduced to the structure. Vinay couldn't wait for my approvals obviously so he perhaps went ahead and approved to keep going.

Life was now getting more on autopilot in Dubai; We even played weekend cricket matches with Al Grand employees… Our team members also found their feet, and things looked good for us at both Al Grand and Bluewater's.

With every passing day, my desperation to be with the team was only building up; getting my hands dirty, milling the clay, engineering the battery, being in the assembly line in a jumpsuit, fastening the nuts and the process, adding a bit of me into Zila. There was a feeling of envy. I smiled less on Vinay's vlogs and jokes these days. It wasn't even his fault! I should've been grateful to him. Maybe I missed being Mr. CEO, the leader.

God, when did I become so insecure? And it's Vinay, of all people! It should be a sin to envy of a genuinely fine human like him.

I confided in Aman, but he didn't take this too seriously and just remarked, 'Life is getting too easy for you, it seems. Let me add some more "stand-up" meetings' and laughed it off as a phase.

With less than a couple of weeks left before we finished our work in Dubai, Shantanu told us he would be there in a day or two. This would be when he introduced the new guy as our replacement and broke the story of us both carrying on with life. We were still tight-lipped, as passionate as ever, and neither Alan nor anyone else from the team had doubts about our plans.

'Where are you guys… come on? The team wants to talk to you,' Vinay messaged at around ten in the morning, at the peak of our meeting routine.

'Yaar! If I am calling so frantically, get out for a moment and return my call,' he sent another one after three missed calls.

'Boss, you are ruining all the fun. Please call ASAP,' he continued texting. While both of us wanted to eagerly get back to him, it was impossible. Aman and I did the bulk of the talking in these meetings. Finally, when we got free, we called him.

'What's the matter?' Aman and I called him from the only vacant room in the building.

'Dude, the team wanted to speak to the supreme leader. Now let it be,' he said in a dejected tone.

'I am sorry, buddy, but, you know, we are not on a picnic here,' Aman said.

Come on now, you are leaving in two weeks. Let it cool off now… anyway, it's all cool, and they are working through their daily tasks,' he concluded like he had given up expecting us to be available even in an emergency.

'That's fine. I will send you some videos. The guys really wanted to speak to you,' he repeated, not sure if he was emotional or just frustrated.

With another day behind us, we were now less than fifteen days away from throwing in the towel at Bluewaters. Shantanu was to arrive the day after.

'Vinay Aggarwal is sharing a file with you. Message from Team Zila.'

As the 600 MB video was downloading, I grabbed a few beers, changed into shorts, and settled into my lovely little couch, the one reason that could hold me back in this country.

'*Asalaam aleikum, bhai log,* whatsuppppp! We have the full team Zila here… everyone, say hi to Bharat and Aman Uncle,' Vinay began.

'Hiiiiii!' everyone exploded. Dark circles, and pale faces, but everyone seemed smitten by this guy's energy. Vinay had come into his own he had outdone himeself, a Vinay I hadn't known, maybe even he didn't.

He certainly had a presence.

'Alright, so we are here at Bharat Kinetics Global Development Center. Hold your breath and follow us to our little chamber of secrets!' He said using a misplaced analogy.

'What you see all around us are some of the most skilled craftsmen in the world. Leading them is this lady who is a full-time cursive writing enthusiast and a part-time software developer. That's Sindhu. Behind Arunima, our leading lady, are the *paanch paandavs,* who, after messing up their apartments, have now taken over mine: Arun, Rajat, Piyush, Ravi, and Tejas, our superstar coders! You guys better clean my house before leaving!'

So, who do we have next? Who do we have next? Oh yes, so from Paandavs to our Bhishma Pitamah, Jatin Soni ji, our guide, genius engineer, and scientist! Is there anything you can't do, Jatin ji?'

'This is group captain Jatin Soni reporting from the base. I am commanding my squadron of trainee pilots on a covert operation. Everyone here is out of control after not having slept for days together. Jai Hind to our able generals in Dubai!'

Even Jatin Ji wasn't immune from Vinay's charms. I could never imagine our Sheldon was now a Chandler.

'Alright, guys! So we are finally here. I am standing at the sacred Zila development zone or, as we like to call it, our little chamber of secrets! Don't mistake this for being a fifty-meter walk from the workshop gate. It may be a fifteen-minute drive from Ramesh Nagar to Bhagwan Nagar, but this journey has truly covered New York, New Delhi, Gurgaon, Patna, Chennai, Varanasi, and Bangalore… to settle all the way at Ludhiana, a place we now call home,' Vinay continued.

'Lack of sleep was still fine, but no booze? These boys even used this excuse for bathing only once a week! Our hands now permanently smell of clay and automotive paint, which is addictive! Bharat, man, what have you turned us into?

'So, after over 500 sketches, 1,000 hours of programming wizardry, countless handmade fonts, twelve to fifteen hours of daily workmanship, perfecting every curve, every line, my dear friends, take a good close look at the finest creation of our lives, a part of our soul, our darling… Zila!'

The eighteen-member crew together pulled off the veil.

AND THERE IT WAS!

Painted in silver, the first clay prototype of what was going to be amongst the world's best electric SUVs and certainly India's very best! It was breathtakingly beautiful.

The detailing was just otherworldly. Every angle, every curve, had meaning and utility. The very stance exuded such confidence, almost a personality, as if rubbing off of Vinay's. It was nothing like anything on our roads. It looked grand yet not intimidating. It felt welcoming and cozy, yet tough and reliable! I felt overwhelmed. Aman looked like he would break down any moment.

Vinay went on, 'And who better to take us through this gorgeous, stunning structure, than our resident wizard Arunima Banerjee!' Vinay said and handed his phone to Arunima.

'Okay, I can do this…' Arunima took a deep breath and smiled, 'Okay, so here we go! So, the front has these new-age grills in the shape of a heart-throbbing smile that took a while for everyone to form a consensus on. We decided to give it a lightning bolt or the charging-symbol design. A lightning-bolt smile for a lightning-fast car.'

I was now smiling and sighing in absolute admiration like a fan, but it was Aman who had his tears on edge, and they were to roll any moment. My impatience for the final design kept my tears at bay. I continued watching in rapt attention as Arunima kept the show going.

'But wait… what do I see behind this grill? Oh, right! Storage! Hundred liters of it! Enough to pack extra beers, ice buckets, and, who knows, perhaps an oversized teddy.

'You will never run out of space again!

'Now, from its smile to its eyes. These headlamps, my word! They've been modeled after the eyes of the cheetah and the wolves. These are outlined with dual-colored micro LED lamps, and when switched on, our Zila is a fierce beast on the prowl!

'To the feet… we gave it the exquisite fourteen-inch alloy wheels that come in the lightning-bolt theme; it's just so electric all the way!

'Shoulders and body are shaped like that of a swimmer, with one of the best air-drag scores. This will not drive but glide on the roads!

'A look below the shoulder, and voila! It has a door with curved window frames, not edges, but curves. And what's this? Oh… my… god! These seats are too wide and comfy!

'We also have such a cool-looking steering wheel with these fancy buttons to control volume, cruise, boot… even Iron Man will feel at home here!

'And to its left is her nerve center, a 14-inch touchscreen that controls everything from speed to music, navigation to air conditioning. I wish it could also boot out annoying co-passengers… but where will they go? Well… we can launch them into space…because… we have a sunroof! Yay!'

I couldn't believe my eyes! I had not experienced such unparalleled joy since my first ever 'foreign' trip to London.

Arunima continued, 'USB ports, AC vents, 5-inch cup holders, mobile slots, rear-seat vents, does it even fly?'

Every feature made our smiles grow wider and wider… the thought process, the presentation, the passion, the pride, and the love just radiated from every inch of Zila. I couldn't wait to be there to stand and stare at it for hours.

'They say behind every successful car there is a massive boot. What is it 450 liters? Are you kidding me? Who needs that kind of space? There is 550 liter of storage front and back, what are you going to pack, some noisy kids?' Arunima continued, 'And what does it say? ZILA, made in India, "The ZILA" with a flipped Z underlined by a wire design connecting it to the charging socket.'

They now moved the camera to the bonnet.

'So, who are the makers of this majestic piece of engineering?

They gently peeled off a silver sticker placed on the bonnet, one letter at a time, inscribed in the most beautiful cursive font possible, B H A R A T K I N E T I C S.

I had seen cars in India, and cars around the world, pretty, powerful, sporty, muscular, and with absolute regard to every engineer who had worked on each one of them. Zila was already looking like the princess in the pack.

My head and heart, I don't know which one, but something felt heavy, perhaps both. I wanted to let go of my tears, anything perhaps that could lighten the flurry of emotions inside me.

I looked at Aman. He had already teared up, his cheeks flushing red. We both sniggered in embarrassment, looking at each other. Bumping our fists proudly, we tuned right back in.

'Bharat and Aman, your two-man band is now an unbeatable clan of twenty most talented and perpetually sleep-deprived zombies. And this is for you both…'

*Zila, Dreamt and Designed by Indians.*

The video ended with the sound of the camera shutter and the picture of the entire crew around the life-size model of Zila.

Why the hell did the video end? We played it over and over, and the emotion was overwhelming. We were both overwhelmed, we laughed, chest-thumped, popped our beers open in the absence of champagne, hugged several times, and thanked our lord in our prayers.

'Zila… Made in India… Zila… freaking… Made in India!' We kept repeating it to ourselves. Almost an hour into this frenzy, we calmed ourselves down. It was not an idea in our head anymore or a graphic design. THIS WAS REAL! You could touch, feel, hug, and kiss it. Nothing was left to the imagination, and it was clear as day that Zila was going to be the most stunning electric car on the roads of India and around the world, one that anyone could drive and own with pride and love.

I knew at that moment that Zila will be the world's best Electric Car and go down as one of the most pathbreaking in the history of electric cars if not all cars ever made.

That was all the time we could be with Zila and after another phone call with Vinay, we had to re-focus on our next turbulent meeting rather than a summon. Alan was livid about learning our plans from Shantanu. He felt we had a greater bond than Aman and I anticipated.

He took us to a fine-dining Indian restaurant at Dubai Marina; the weather was rather pleasant, and we found ourselves a comfortable place in an open-air setting, facing the exquisite-looking creek. We could tell from his mannerisms he wasn't his normal self.

'So, guys, I thought we had a connection, and honestly, this news comes as a disappointment,' he sounded upset, and his British accent made it sound graver than it was.

'Sorry, what news?' Aman replied. We acted dumb, like we had no clue what he was talking about.

'Okay, don't tell me if you don't want to, but don't insult my intelligence.' His tone was reprimanding of Aman's attitude.

'Trust me, Alan, only we know how hard it was to resist discussing this with you,' I said.

'You should have; Well, I am all ears.' He prompted. He knew I was the loose cannon out of the two of us.

'I wish I could, Alan, but maybe another day,' I deflected his invitation as our first portions of grilled cottage cheese and grilled butter chicken arrived.

We waited for the person serving us to finish his thing before we could resume. I sipped from a pint of beer while Aman decided to stay sober for the evening. Alan simply enjoyed his wine.

'Food smells amazing,' I complimented the server just as he was about to leave. He thanked me and assured me he will pass this on to the chef, and left the place courteously.

'I assumed our connection transcended the boundaries of workplace,' he said. He clearly had walked in with an agenda. Were we really that brilliant that such accomplished men were falling over themselves to team up with us?

'One hundred percent, Alan. The fact that you have taken out time to meet us means a lot.'

I said.

'Oh, now come on! Spare me this rubbish!'

'I know, Alan, I hate to be so cryptic, you know, but just give us some time,' I rquested.

'Sure, I don't want to pressure you, but here is the thing, you know. You need the right promoters and the right support. I know you guys are going on your own. I didn't need Shantanu to cook up a silly story. I knew it the day I met both of you.'

'What did he tell you?' I asked instinctively.

'He told me you guys were taking a break. I should have told him to give *me* a break!' he said and cackled quite loudly at the cost of the comfort of the others around us. But, you know, he was white. He could do it. I could tell no one took offense; some even smiled along.

Mostly brown.

'What was he thinking? Two guys, best friends, want to take a break *together*? And I will buy it?' He continued.

'I knew it that day, Bharat. I could see in your eyes that you wouldn't do this for too long. Let me help you.'

'I will, Alan, I promise, just not now. I need to be clear about our plan and commitment. I promise I will come to you,' I reassured him.

'You promise?'

'Totally, the day our vision is crystalized in our own eyes, your phone will ring.'

'That is more than reasonable, Bharat. I am sure you are going to make it massively big. I am on your side,' whatever his motives were, his words were certainly encouraging, at the very least.

'Thanks, Alan, these words mean the world to me. Look out for our call, please.'

'Cheers to your new innings,' he said, and we raised and clinked our glasses.

With Zila turning out beautifully and support pouring from all sides, one would think we could breathe easy, but the devil was going to touch down tomorrow morning, and knowing him, I could expect any level of surprise.

# 17

# SMOKESCREEN

'Good to see you champions! How have you been?' He hugged us both tight. 'All good, boss. How about you?' Aman replied.

'All first-class,' Shantanu responded in his typical confident self.

'So where are we sitting down?' He continued and handed over a couple of bottles of single malts he had picked from the airport.

'My room should be good. It has a view of the Sheikh Zayed,' Aman offered.

'Okay, let's catch up in the evening. I need to meet both Alan and Salim and calm some nerves,' Shantanu explained, and we nodded.

'I also have a few meetings to finish. Maybe you both can start, and I will join you guys by about eight or so,' I suggested. Shantanu gave me a sheepish look like I was behaving pricey. How could I not abandon everything for the great man after all?

'Okay, big fellow, we will get started. I anyway enjoy Aman's company a lot more,' he quipped. 'Same here, boss!' I replied with wit as Aman nodded in disbelief.

It was about 8:15 p.m. as I walked towards the elevator through the long corridor. Members of the housekeeping staff wished me as they went by. One of them looked Malayali, and I immediately used my Indian connection and requested him to send a bucket of ice to our room 2201. He looked a little uncertain if this was the right process, and I tipped him so he doesn't signpost me to the phone in the room.

Shantanu changed plans and invited us to his room which was already open. I walked inside to release the door jammer so it could stay shut, it was clear they were in the conversation already, so I began arranging for glasses, water, and everything else we would need.

I couched as Aman continued to discuss our business. There was no mention of the project. It was purely Bharat Kinetics, Zila and I just tuned in intently.

The conversation soon went into overdrive, and Shantanu was now all over Aman. Around two hours and four drinks into the conversation, he got Aman to agree to an almost impossible precondition.

I still didn't say much. Anything I said at that moment would have created doubts about our progress and significantly undermined Aman. I just warmly embraced him and wished him good night.

This wasn't the same Aman who outsmarted Shantanu to invest. This was a more jaded, fatigued man counting down his days in Dubai. I shouldn't have left him alone with the wolf waiting to pounce and assume his alpha status in this partnership.

Well, we couldn't change what Aman was arm-twisted into, all I could do was to tell him that it was all okay and we will be fine. He remained stoic as we left for our rooms.

The only good thing about the evening was that the next day was Friday, and we didn't have to juggle our projects.

So the first thing we had to do was to bail out of the situation we found ourselves in, bail out as a team. It was time to get Vinay on the phone.

'Houston! We have a problem!' I began. 'Really?' Vinay sounded out of sorts.

'Dude, what's the matter?' I checked. I think I sounded a little riled up.

'This is complicated. I need you here, Bharat.' He sounded helpless.

'We have the electrolyte formula, plus Vinay's mind. What more do we need? I will be there before you know it. Final laps,' I assured him.

'Now come on! Is it Bharat Srinivasan I am talking to?' Vinay retorted, quite condescendingly.

I was caught slightly off-guard. This was like my blonde moment, 'So, then, what do you want?' I asked tentatively.

'I need someone to debate the composition with. I know I am almost there, but I can't do this without you,' he demanded and implored in the same breath.

'But you have Arunima and Jatin for now,' I suggested like he didn't know already.

'As in, you want me to make the same mistake Animesh made with us? Give them the keys to the kingdom? Everyone from the engineer to the programmer can now make a car. What they cannot build are a Zinc-air battery and high-tech power pack... What makes you think one of them won't walk up to the competition and trade this? After all, we took Animesh's formula, didn't we?'

'I told you I am losing touch being away from all the action,' I conceded, as I wasn't in the zone like he was.

'Now the problem is we will need some solid machinery. We can't do with this *jugaad anymore*. I cannot roll up 600 pieces all by myself with the help of some crude labor from Jatin's workshop. Plus, it's not even going to be industry-standard.'

'How much will it be? If we have to, then we have to,' Aman was out of it. He had no idea why we were even discussing this, given his conversation with Shantanu.

'Around ten lakh. I have spoken to suppliers. I can rent some of this, and the rest we can get second-hand. We need reliable machines for cutting, mixing, drying, and rolling.'

He went on, 'We also need to factor in for a generator, for power supply. The government will not provide the level of power that we will need to run our equipment, especially the oven that will operate close to 150 degrees Celsius.

'Okay, so let's do it then. You shouldn't have waited this long,' such things should be discussed well in advance.

'I know, I tried to avoid this cost...'

'Okay, so this will take at least three to six months, I presume?' I checked, prodding him to be real this time.

'Three months to a maximum of four months. I have already sounded off some suppliers. The lab staff can be trained ahead of time. You will also be here in a week,' he concluded.

'Let's take six months. Let's not underestimate the timeline,' I said. 'But the trouble is we need a running car in one week,' I said in my next breath, leaving him perplexed.

'Excuse me?' Vinay responded.

'Yeah, you heard me. Shantanu wants to see a running car before he takes the bet,' I explained.

'In a week? Buy more time. We will give him a real car,' Vinay urged.

'He is traveling with us to Ludhiana. This is no longer even a matter of debate,' I explained our predicament.

'And who made this commitment?' Vinay was now panicking slightly, and I couldn't help smiling at the absurdity of it all.

'That's not the point. We have a situation here,' I brought him back.

'It was me. I am sorry,' Aman spoke out.

'I suggest we come clean with him and buy more time,' Vinay advised.

'Really? And what do you think he is going to say, "No problem, boys, here is the money, let me know when you are ready with the car"?' I scoffed.

'Look, he is playing us, but we need to play along, alright?'

'Hmm…' Vinay responded while Aman nodded.

'He sees any signs of vulnerability, he will demand a bigger pound of flesh, and soon, we will be working for him again! I knew all along he wasn't happy with this ten percent arrangement. He will use this to bargain with us, but we can't budge an inch. So, we need to give him this.'

Vinay interrupted, 'We can go to others for investment. We have a solid prototype, team, production line, and design. He is not the only one you know.'

'You are right, but the one in hand, you know, is always better, and what's the guarantee that the new investors won't be such leeches too? At least he is a known devil…'

Give him what he wants. He wants to see 'A' running car, not 'The' running car. If you get my drift,' I checked with Vinay if he was ready for this game of smokescreens.

'You are such a cheeky genius. What the hell! Why didn't you say this straight away!' Vinay exclaimed, 'This is why I need you here. We will set the stage on fire!'

Aman didn't seem convinced.

'What if he finds out? It will be a disaster,' he said.

'We will see it then. He is free to walk away. Let's see if he can. This will be a last-ball finish, my boy. Now chill!' I tried calming his nerves.

'Now, act super confident when around him, okay? Also, just so you both know, we are not out of money. I have raised my loan against the property. Shantanu doesn't have the kind of leverage he thinks he does,' I informed.

'What the hell! Bharat! I told you not to! We must all pool in,' Aman argued,

'Yeah! Why not! Be my guest. Pay up now. All I am saying is we are not in a financial mess, and he must get this message loud and clear.'

'Sir, Vinay Aggarwal, are you ready?' I checked.

'Yes, Captain! Bring it on! *#lovelyludhiana*,' he replied. '*#Aaho*!' I added, as I forced Aman to fist pump.

* * *

Exactly eight days later, Aman, Shantanu, and I left the shores of Dubai.

Shantanu and Alan organized a grand farewell for us on the eve of our last working day. I don't think I was emotional. Nonetheless, I was grateful for the recognition.

Once we made our way out of the Ludhiana's arrivals terminal, we spotted Vinay, who was there to receive us. He was as good as a local now and could speak half-decent Punjabi, unlike Aman.

The plan was clear. Shantanu was going to be given a full tour of the workshop, and Vinay was going to lead the brigade. He had now entirely transformed the place. First steps inside our former humble little apartment, we could already see a top-notch mission command center.

Our easy charts were all gone, and the main wall was all repainted to resemble a racetrack. Each big milestone was denoted using a triangular golden flag—the Team, Design, Sample Models, Miniature Clay Prototype, Life-Size Clay Model, Battery-Pack, and so on, all the way up to the permits that needed to be obtained. First Zila on Indian roads, First Zila on international roads, 100,000th Zila on the road mouth watering milestones that could sway anyone. For a moment I did feel Vinay alone could be the CEO of this company.

Each milestone completed was stamped by a green dart, and by now, we had many green darts, including the completion of battery packs. Shantanu looked around curiously and asked some really basic questions, and Vinay hit all of them out of the park.

Shantanu was then escorted to one of the bedrooms, where the main wall had Zila animation video being played on the projector, with a hard-hitting commentary on performance, durability, battery life, cost per kilometer, and other stuff—enough to titillate a management consultant who had made an entire career out of fancy presentations and animation.

As per the plan, we kept him inside this mirage for as long as we could. Vinay ensured he drained him with as much detail as possible.

Some of it was irrelevant, some even made-up, just enough to overwhelm him, making him feel like he was now part of an EV renaissance. By now, Shantanu was itching to go to the garage. Jatin ji, however, sat him down for some tea and samosas.

The point of the whole thing was to hammer the power of our team deep inside his mind. While showing immense respect to him as our investor, we tried establishing that the scheme of things was much bigger than him.

He was smitten. And no matter how hard he tried, it was impossible for him to conceal how impressed he was with the whole process and our A-team, and he had barely seen anything yet.

Arunima was in next. She took him through her operating system demo and flowed—a demo he didn't ask for but was essential to further establish the depth of our technology, planning, and capabilities. Arunima was a natural, and once she was on, it was next to impossible to switch her off. We looked on with suppressed smiles as she tutored Shantanu on the essentials of the automotive operating system.

'Okay, Aru, I think we are good for now. There is a lot more we need to cover,' Vinay politely intervened. "Aru!" I thought and looked to Aman, who looked back at me with a blank expression.

Jatin Ji drove us all to our battery development center. Our lab assistants were given Zila lab coats, and we passed one to Shantanu as well as other accessories, like PPE kits, etc., one must wear while entering a high-end chemical lab.

Vinay began his tour and began explaining the concept, yet again, shamelessly drawing on Animesh's speech when he gave us a tour of his lab in Varanasi.

'You know, Shantanu, if science is the mind of God, then Maths is his language,' Vinay concluded. Aman shook his head at him, and I could barely control my giggles.

'I am sure… brilliant, you guys are up to something here. I am super-impressed, boys, proud of you all!' He was blown over to a point where I thought the visuals from this tour were going to dance in his dreams for many nights to follow.

'Thanks, boss. But you know what? What you have seen so far is all the work that goes behind the car. This is what makes Zila what it is. The process, the prep, the plan, the team!' Vinay continued with his hyperboles, and Shantanu stayed glued, making every effort to fit into the mix.

He might have thought he would walk in like a big auditor but was reduced to being a curious student.

Next was the big workshop tour. Soni Motors, in care of Jatin Soni.

Vinay knew the place like the back of his hand. He took him around the production line, the build process, the spray paint station, CAD developers, the tooling center, clay milling, and even the smelting and casting section that the team had created slightly away from the main workshop.

Shantanu was out of questions. He seemed to have been struck by an avalanche of information, knowledge, and craft. And we had still not shown him the big prize yet.

What also became evident was Vinay's passion. This man was living and breathing Zila. He knew every single tool that Jatin's engineers were using and randomly picked up a few of them and explained their usage. Shantanu gazed at Vinay, awe-struck.

It was time.

We arrived on the big stage. Vinay, Arunima, and others walked up and announced in a chorus, 'Presenting to you the world's best and fastest electric car. Made fully in India— The Zila Max.'

And there it was in the flesh! So stunning! Shining in silver. The video certainly didn't do justice to it. It was so finely detailed. I didn't let my mind wander too much, though. Arunima elbowed Vinay cutely in his abs and jumped in to take over the rest of the show taking Shantanu on the ride, literally and metaphorically.

She was another bundle of passion, knew every little curve and line on this car. There was nothing more to say or do. He wanted to see the car, and he'd seen one and much more.

Shantanu got his camera out to take a picture, and Arunima was quick to interrupt and politely requested him to put it away. He promptly complied.

Shantanu came up to me and complimented us on everything enthusiastically. He called his banker to ask him to release the funds that were on standby.

He had sniffed the early signs of success, 'Well done, everyone! This is phenomenal. I am super impressed! We are going to make history,' he exclaimed, and walked up to the stage again and just stared at the Zila from all angles. Arunima was quick to follow him and made sure he didn't click any pictures. But all he was doing was imagining where he was going to invest all the insane amount of money he was going to make from this.

For us, well, we had secured our first round of investment.

Shantanu couldn't stop looking at Zila. Aman, I, and Jatin ji looked at Shantanu's spellbound gaze while it seemed Vinay and Arunima couldn't stop their on and off sweet nothings standing on either side of Zila. There was such emotion here. Greed, ambition, pride, and, oh my god, now romance was also in the mix.

As for me, I was certainly relieved, but with this guy, I was always going to be wary. While our money was here, I knew it had come with a number of strings and riders attached, and I was bracing myself for the tricky times ahead.

But for now, it was time for the last leg of this tour, a road trip!

Jatin ji and Vinay had remodeled a Maruti Suzuki WagonR into an electric version using a conventional Lithium-ion battery pack, just in case Shantanu insisted on driving a prototype. We offered to take him around, but he declined. He had seen what he had to. Besides, how could Mr. Shantanu Vashishta be seen riding a WagonR!

Moments later, he offered to take the team out for dinner and drinks. I did not like his patriarchal tone as he spoke to the team directly. This was not Bluewaters, after all. I had to be on high alert.

'Boys, this is coming out really well. So it's going to be another six months, you think?'

Shantanu asked Vinay as we all settled in around a big table at a rooftop restaurant.

'Yeah, six to nine months should be realistic,' I replied out of turn.

'Cool, so you have your work cut out,' he continued, 'I am glad you kept in touch with your subject, Bharat.'

I smiled and nodded.

'Now, we need to keep the momentum going. Let's, please, set up a call once every week,' he went on.

Now, this wasn't going to happen. I was certain to keep him at arm's length.

'Boss, this stays here, whatever happens, whoever you meet—be it your driver or PM Modi, you will not give anything away,' I cautioned against any exuberance.

'Come on! Bharat, learn to trust,' he assured.

A few days went by, and Vinay quite reluctantly reminded me of the funds I had committed to him so he could procure the necessary equipment we needed to churn out industry-grade battery packs that could withstand some serious trauma, the kind we would inflict when we begin testing.

For some reason, something inside me was restraining me from using Shantanu's money immediately. Aman created a contract with the help of a lawyer-friend, and we emailed it to Shantanu. I also decided to request Shantanu for a more detailed chat about the money and his role before I even spent a rupee of it.

Shantanu joined us for a video call on a Sunday, fresh from a match of tennis, a new habit he had picked up in the last several months.

'How are you doing, my boys?' He began in an upbeat tone, 'Awesome, boss! What's up? You look fit as ever,' I replied, 'I am fighting fit!'

'Boss, so, first of all, a big thanks, we have received your investments! That's a big shot in the arm for us, but I wanted to discuss a few things with you before we even touch a rupee of it.'

'Sure, tell me.'

'Boss, so I want you to know—not that you don't already know—you have been well-informed all through, but still, however obvious it may sound… given that this is real money and your personal money, I wanted to state even the most obvious of things…'

'Bharat Srinivasan! Such courtesies don't suit your personality. Now, shoot!'

'Sure. You have seen our design labs, production units, car, battery labs, and the teams. What I need you to understand and appreciate is the battery tech is still in the labs,' I waited for his reaction.

'Go on,' he wanted to hear more clearly.

'Yes, sure. So, I don't want you to have an impression that everything is ready and we are ready to roll,' this time, I was direct.

'Of course! I understand.'

'And while we have everything in control, there is still a one percent chance that all of this may fold up. However heartbreaking it may sound, it's important that you don't think you have been deceived or feel that Bharat Kinetics lied to you.'

Now he was slightly shaken up, 'What do you mean?'

'I mean, life is uncertain, something could happen to Vinay or me, and we are the brains behind this right now, you know, so to that extent, I need you to be aware that there could be some unknown unknowns.'

'What's wrong with you? Is there something I need to know?' He sounded suspicious.

'No, right now we know the battery formula, we have the equipment, the team, and the real car is looking spectacular. I was just a little nervous with all this money, so I just wanted to talk it out with you, in all honesty.'

We spoke for another fifteen minutes and waited for him to confirm that he fully understood the setting, the situation, and the risks and formally authorized us to deploy capital using his money.

'Thanks, boss, all of this is your coaching. Just have one last request. I wanted to, you know, put pen to paper on everything we have discussed on this call and send it to you for confirmation.'

'By all means, Mr. CEO. It's your company, do as you please. I am just your mentor and coach, so you boys are able to overcome challenges above your weight…so, just out of curiosity, what technology are we going to use in the final car again?' Just when I thought I was through.

'Boss… It's called Zila.'

'Okay, very well, go build your Zila, my boy. I will see you soon.'

# 18

# THE ZILA POWER PACK

Armed with a fresh lease of oxygen and life, Jatin and his team took off. He hired a few more men on a contractual basis, expanded the garage a little more, and began the process of smelting and casting. Orders were getting delivered, and the shop floor was now brimming with action.

We could see the doors, the roofs, the wheels, the chassis, and the underbody being transported around. The plan was to build three units of the Zila Max, for which the engineers were now in overdrive. But what was going to be the point of all this if our battery pack and operating system weren't going to be ready in time?

Vinay, along with four other support team members, and I went about our business. We had known all along this was going to be tricky. Everything from charge, recharge, scale, safety, and tolerance to the material had to be right. Testing had to be intense, and quality had to be industry-grade.

It wasn't as though we weren't up to the challenge. Three months in, we had made significant progress, but each time it came from a round of recharge significantly weaker, barely lasting hundred full cycles before they went frail and eventually bust.

Meanwhile, Arunima also had her work cut out in building the software modules for Zila. The challenge was to build three and at least two separate operating systems; one for the core driving module, like drive control and regenerative braking and others, and a second one to control all the rest of the functions, like the infotainment system, navigation, air conditioning, etc.,

Now, these were in-vehicle modules. She also had to build a few out-vehicle modules, like a mobile application and control units. Finally, she had to encapsulate all of these modules in a cohesive structure that holds up when called upon to work together.

Arunima, unlike us, was a career software developer and a specialist in automotive software. Now, she also had a slightly bigger team than she did earlier. As a result, we were really able to push on with this.

Miraculously for us, Govindan arrived at his own expense to provide the final push and we knew the software module if no longer and in but only a when.

'Boss, I am telling you, you need to call Animesh,' Aman reminded me for at least the third time in three days.

'It's pointless. Which point do you not understand,' I curtly responded and got down to work.

'I called him, but he is not answering,' Vinay added, and that was it.

'Why?' I snapped and stood up aghast with Vinay

'What do you mean why?' He reacted like it was the most obvious thing to do.

'Really? We are here morning to night, and you didn't care to discuss it once with me? ' I was livid with them both for not trusting me with this decision.

'I just wanted to check if he answers. Don't make this a big deal,' he replied, dismissive of my anger and temper.

'Okay, whatever! That's it. We have done our bit; no more calls. Let's see if he gets back.'

'Let me try once. I had a better connection with him,' Aman offered his advice.

'No, no, no, that's it. We have done our thing. He only has himself to blame. Let's get on with it, PLEASE,' I almost commanded.

'Okay, if you two are confident, I will resist, but we need to make some breakthroughs soon. Otherwise, I will travel to Varanasi; the lives and careers of too many people are at stake now,' Aman announced as if he meant it.

We both partly nodded.

It wasn't like I wouldn't love for someone to come and build my battery, but Aman didn't get it. This was not going to be easy. We had seen Animesh's pack, and only Vinay and I understood the challenges in making it industry-grade. Even if Animesh was going to be here, I knew we wouldn't work as a team, so it was going to be pointless to pursue him anymore.

Aman left the place thinking it was my pride, while it was just logic. Everyone was getting slightly edgy about whether Vinay and I will be able to eventually pull this off. We had seen signs of success but several signs of breakdown. Jatin would routinely spend time checking on us. These were indeed nervous moments, I had gotten everyone on this bus with an assurance that battery was going to be a done deal when Vinay and I were on song, but no, it was more like a slog.

Sometimes even thoughts of shutting down the whole thing and cutting our losses began to surface in my mind, first in a hush-hush tone, which soon became shrill, to a point, I could no longer resist mooting it with Jatin, Vinay, and Aman.

There were multiple propositions we discussed. Why not sell our operating system as a stand-alone product? It was world-class, like a remote control for Zila. Fortunately, each time I mooted this theory, someone talked me out of it.

For all our faults, the one good quality we all had was listening to the elderly senior citizen in the camp, Jatin Soni walked in one day and told us to stop everything and take a break. We didn't see how that would but like we were listening and therefore we complied.

My despondency was going to be a recipe for disaster, especially for Jatin. This is not why he took a bet on rookies like us. He trusted us to go the full nine yards; maybe, Vinay and I were not the gifted engineers after all. Maybe smart guys, at best.

Shantanu wasn't making it easy too. Frantic calls for updates, sharply worded emails, and disturbing text messages kept coming from his end to get our reaction.

He wasn't going to make peace with my standard responses, so we invited him over to take a look at the real Zila, now made of metal, fiber, rubber, and plastic, a real car in every way, just without a motor and fuel cells. Arunima gave him impressive demos to keep him at bay.

But this time, he wanted more and sensed that something wasn't right, maybe from our body language or just his general sense of suspicion. He even sent random consultants from automotive backgrounds to help us with technical advice. The advice we didn't need.

I had to stand up and block any access to our apartment offices, workshop, or the battery unit. A move Shantanu implied as enemy action, and this is where our first real hostile standoff took root.

I had categorically asked, rather pleaded with him to keep this project discrete, and by sending some random consultants, he had dishonored a central condition of the partnership.

Vinay and I even suspected this to be some kind of a spy job. Aman might have been proud of the deal he had cemented, but Shantanu's second nature had come to the fore, and it wasn't helping anyone's cause, least of all his own.

We hadn't visited homes now for months. Our confidence levels were also dented every day we slept without a breakthrough. But, through all this, the best thing that happened to us was Shantanu's promotion to Bluewater's Global COO.

This meant that there were new pressure and restrictions on his time, shareholder meetings, more travels, press interviews, along with his running responsibilities. What a respite it was!

A residual part of our belief system was still alive, one that kept us going. Success was around the corner. A little more push and the bulb will light up somewhere.

After hours and nights of debate that took us back to our hostel dorm, our eyes finally fell on a treasure trove that lay right in front for so many months. We had dismissed such wealth of information as trash just because its author had abandoned it.

The break had worked like magic. Jatin knew more about fatigue than us, everyday people.

Several attempts followed with varying compositions, but with consistent principles, and after about another couple of months into this drill, some things did begin to work. Our battery was losing less power than earlier, and the dendrite formation was curtailed greatly.

All fingers were crossed as we began to put our invention through extreme torture. Another month in, and we had our first glimpse of the Zila Battery Pack, powered by Zinc-air technology Govindan and Jatin asked us to leave so they could test this objectively

1,200 cycles of charge! Yes, that's what our battery could endure enough to keep a vehicle running for 750,000 km before changing the battery pack. That's almost forever!

I was an inventor! We were inventors! We did it. Vinay and I did it! All of us, Bharat Kinetics and Team Zila did it!

This, this is what victory looks like, this is what success looks like, this is what a dream looks like. We yelled in excitement, cussed, fist-thumped, and, eventually, prayed and thanked the forces that were making it all happen.

There was something. I would be a fool to believe it was all just hard work, something divine. Someone's luck was working for everyone. I would like to believe it was mine. Who knows, after all?

Now, it was over to Arunima and Govindan to begin programming and configure the battery pack with her software to control power range and distribution, and while she perfected the whole package, we continued testing our

WagonR using the Zinc-air battery pack. The world's first Zinc-air EV was already on the road.

When Arunima and Govindan declared success, Zila Battery Pack was brought to the production line, and finally, it was time for the soul, body, and mind to come together and take its first breath of life.

The BIG day was here, it was going to be Zila's first day out!

Twenty-five of us now assembled around the production line waiting for Aditya and Jatin to confirm as they examined the Zila one final time.

As everyone waited impatiently in the hot sun, Aditya Dixit, our man, emerged from behind the boot, he winked, and thumbs upped with both hands, and THAT WAS IT!

Our moment in history had arrived. Zila Max was invented, and the world's best EV was ready.

Ready to roll, nothing virtual, not in clay, nothing left to the imagination. This was the real deal. We hugged, yelled, and kissed our baby 1000 times.

Finally, the coconut was smashed, and off we went for our first spin in the Zila Max. We drove for eight hours straight every single day for the next thirty days, clocking 5,000 km of testing.

Zila Max accelerated from 0 to 100 in seven seconds. Although we could increase it further, we held it back to suit our roads. It could charge from 0 to 98% in fifteen minutes with a range of 400 km on a full charge. What that meant for customers was that even a five-minute charge gave it a 130 km range. The battery pack Vinay and I built also guaranteed a life of fifteen years at least.

In the next fifteen days, we built four models of Zila Max against our earlier plan of three. One was to secure ARAI approvals and crash testing. The second was for internal testing, and the other two were for the All-Electric European Championship to be held in Munich in six months' time.

The rules of the championship were clear, and they had several categories, one for professional racing teams and another one for cars launched and selling, and the third was for 'Road Ready Pending Launch.'

The registration price was 100,000 euros which included one-way shipping of two units of the participating car model and return tickets for six members.

Every team was also provided a dedicated exhibition stall to showcase their models to both customers and investors.

As per their vetting and approval process, we had to reach twenty days in advance, and in case we failed their standards, we were given another week to re-appear. Those teams who failed both tests were going to be disqualified without a refund.

Now, this meant we needed a solid driver who could put Zila to some real test and demonstrate its full power and potential on the world stage.

And so began the hunt for the country's best car racer! Time for Zila to meet its match.

# 19

# THE DRIVER'S SEAT

From Greater Noida to Chennai, from Pune to Coimbatore, we were back in hippy mode.

We attended at least half a dozen races, during which we met and interviewed multiple drivers. Some refused to entertain us while others were beyond our budget till we finally landed in Coimbatore for a National Championship race.

In a country that's crazy about cricket, where even international sports like Football and Tennis are struggling, what are the odds for a domestic racing contest without any media superstars to have sell-out crowds? Close to zero.

This meant there were only a handful of people in attendance, and even then, most of them were either employees of the sponsors or friends and family of drivers. While this apathy is heart-breaking, it did give some of the best seats in the stands and allowed a vantage point of view of the contest.

Fortunately, though, the car makers didn't disappoint, and all the top auto companies in the country sent in their A teams and A Models to participate. And so, the stage was set. In total, sixteen teams will rough it up for ten laps on a 3.2 km long circuit to claim the title of the National Champion 2016 and prize money of five lakh for the driver and the crew.

Most of the audience were in their seats and glued in passionately, barring a few who were more engrossed in their phones. The committed ones were all charged and cheering for their favorite team, even sporting their merchandise. Some even had their caps and sunglasses to allow themselves an unglazing view of the action in the middle.

Car racing is an acquired taste, too was never a big fan of such events, and it was only now I realized how passionate one could get once this grows on you.

The teams took their positions and revved up their engines akin to conch cells making a battle cry.

The lights went off, and the drivers set off. Car 42, already in pole position, set the circuit ablaze, leaving heaps of dust behind as Cars 11 and Car 33 emerged through the dust storm, determined to stand up and be counted.

Behind the wheel on Car 42 was a thirty-six-year-old banker and a passionate racer Ravindra Kulkarni. Car 11 was controlled by a forty-year-old cement trader, and Car 33 was being steered by a BPO manager, also 30-something, while the three fought tooth and nail for the top spot. Car 61, driven by a twenty-year-old Neel KRT, started raging past accomplished drivers. Coming from behind, Car 61 shook the circuit as she started getting rude stares from the statesmen on the circuit.

He swiftly overtook 11 by the second corner in the fifth lap, squeezing past 77, 26, 33, and 84, and it was now it was a fight to finish as both looked to absolutely dominate the track for the remaining five laps, and the sound of their engines revving up along with all the other made for a mouth-watering contest.

Neel was now within millimeters of clinching the top spot, but Ravindra came across as a gritty customer who denied Neel even a whisker. Cars 11, 77, and 33 were now the only ones who could hope even of an outside chance for a podium position first two slots and were engaged in a tight battle for the title for their sponsors. Neel was testing out the banker to the limits with only one lap to go.

It was now only a war of nerves and temperament as both the machines had nothing more to give, who could keep up the case, who would handle the corners better, and who will be able to stake it all.

Neel was now tied and, in the next second, slightly ahead as both approached the most crucial corner of the race. It was the ultimate lap, and there was no coming back from here, no room to think. It's the moment when instincts take over. Both were now within meters of the corner and on the other side of the decisive turn, it was Neel who put everything on the line and emerged victorious by a margin of less than a second.

He was my guy! Had to be. The banker was good but there was something about this guy his sheer abandon and indifference to risk. My boy Neel.

Aman approached Neel's team manager, and we were able to secure some time with Neel KRT, and although he had finished as the champion, he wasn't going to be received by flashing cameras, and at the end of it all, he would have to look for an Uber or a kind friend to get home.

So, here we were at the coffee shop waiting for our star driver to arrive, and so he did, five-feet-ten or five-feet-eleven, lanky young lad, still in his racing attire with overgrown hair, brushing his shoulders covered by the cap. He was terribly tanned after braving the heat and dust of the track.

He walked towards us in a relaxed and wavy walk. It was hard to tell what he had in mind. He seemed like a regular next-door Gen Z kid.

'Hi. Aman,' Aman stood up and introduced himself with a firm handshake with Neel who still had his gloves on.

'Neel,' he said.

'Bharat.'

'Vinay.'

'Brilliant race buddy,' Aman began with a compliment.

'Yeah, thanks,' he said as he briefly lifted his cap and pulled his hair back, which exposed the tattoo of a spanner on his neck.

'We thought you were fabulous,' I added.

'Thanks, man! They must make better tracks,' he added.

'Coffee, Ice Tea? It's really hot in here today,' Aman continued.

'I will have a coke. Need some sugar high,' he said and chuckled slightly, still tired and disconnected.

'So, how long have you been racing?' Aman checked.

'Honestly, since I was sixteen, my parents used to hound me, so I could never do it regularly. It was only since the eighteenth birthday that I have been doing this full time,' we heard with patience as he continued.

'You know, in India, there are no college races, so you need to find these clubs which are really expensive, plus you have to fund your own car, modify it, you gotta be a driver, mechanic and most of all rich if you have to have any hopes of pursuing this,' Aman nodded and waited for his turn.

'Yeah, we know it's tough. So we are from Bharat Kinetics...' Aman started and did a good job of explaining Zila.

'So, electric, that sounds interesting,' Neel remarked.

We nodded, and he continued.

'So, sir, how can I help you?' He was still sounding tired.

'I think you can help yourself by getting rid of the heavy jacket you have on, and it's forty degrees,' Vinay added, both with ignorance of the subject and an element of heavy-handedness. Aman and I could sense that Neel wasn't particularly thrilled at this loose comment.

'Oh yeah, sure, there is a reason, but never mind, I will take it off.'

'Yeah, so we need you to join us as our driver and help test our car at extreme speeds and handling,' Aman continued.

'I would love to, but I only have experience in driving normal petrol and diesel cars,' Neel seemed to be honest kid

'Easy, that's fine; you will love the experience of 0 to 100 in five seconds. You will get it up at speed 200 even faster, and it will give you a greater high than this coke,' Aman continued like a denigrating big brother, 'You study? I mean, are you in some college or course?'

'Yeah, I am preparing to become a chartered accountant. I am trying,' Neel replied.

'That's great, so can you spare the next six months for this assignment?' Aman asked directly. 'Depends. What is the compensation and everything,' he continued engaging, in a wavy, convent-like accent, like English, was his first language.

'There is no compensation. We will pay for travel and the stay wherever we practice,' Aman added.

'No way! I am really sorry, I have much better offers than this.' For the first time during our conversation, Neel replied with conviction.

'How many of them are sending you to Munich to participate in a global championship?'

This dialogue was superbly crafted by Aman, and Neel was stunned.

'You want to continue discussing?' Aman looked him in the eye with a poker face. Neel's body language suggested he couldn't leave the table.

'Sir, now I have my expenses too. I can't do without money,' he tried explaining.

'List them down!' Aman ordered. He was back! And now, killing it with the young boy.

'I can't tell you all of them. I mean, come on!' He tried to protect his private space, but Aman wasn't letting go.

'Do you smoke?' Aman went on.

'I mean, sometimes, but how is that important?' He asked almost helplessly. The carrot of driving in Munich forced him to play along.

'Okay, let's assume 2,000 on smokes, another 2000 on booze. Don't worry, when with us, we will buy for you,' Aman had taken charge, and I couldn't hold back a gentle smile at this deal-making skills.

'I have to buy clothes, perfume, books, my phone bill, internet, and there is so much more.'

Neel was now desperately making a case to be paid for his time.

'Why clothes? We will give you Zila jersey,' Aman was totally unmoved.

'So, you mean I will always wear Zila jersey? And how about lowers?' I couldn't believe Aman had Neel justifying his expenses.

'Denim, which you already have. It's only a matter of six months. Cooperate, buddy. We are a start-up.' I had to now intervene before the hapless boy walked out on us.

'Okay, 2,500 for clothes, get a haircut, you will save on shampoo and grooming products,' I added.

'What the hell? Why should I cut my hair?' he protested, and I almost laughed at his face.

He, too, was being an idiot by indulging us and not being direct.

'You will look much more handsome. Tell me another top racer who has such long hair,' Vinay, too, joined in.

'This doesn't make any sense, but just so you know, there are many, actually, in NASCAR,' I couldn't believe he legitimized Vinay's question.

'Okay, now relax. 15,000 as a monthly stipend, ok?' Aman offered and confirmed. 'Can I think about it? If you don't mind,' he tentatively checked.

'10,000,' Vinay baited.

'Sir, come on! Don't do it this way. It's not fair,' he protested.

'Come on now! It's just a matter of 6 months. Experience Munich, make us all proud, and then see where luck takes you,' Aman said and continued.

'I will add to your offer some free CA coaching. I am one myself, 2006 Batch,' Aman sealed the offer, with his arms around Neel's shoulder, like a true elder brother.

'Okay, but I need to inform my parents.' Man! This boy looked really gullible. I couldn't imagine what he would do if he was put in front of someone like Shantanu.

At the end of the negotiation, Aman gave him his offer. We had made him so nervous that he was thinking of skipping reading the clauses in case it offended us. So he just gave it a cursory read and signed on.

'Okay, welcome onboard,' Aman congratulated him.

'Is there a clause for a haircut?' Vinay picked on him again.

'What's wrong, sir? That's not fair,' an unsuspecting Neel protested again.

'Nothing wrong, just kidding, my boy,' Neel shrugged his shoulders. Clearly, he didn't see the humor in our dad jokes. We had all aged before time.

The road ahead was now more than crystal clear. Race! Race and race till we land in Munich.

* * *

We landed back in Ludhiana with Neel and introduced him to the team as our chief racer for the tournament. While everyone greeted him courteously, they couldn't help but think about what this school kid was doing in the mix.

'Hey, what happened there?' Jatin ji asked Neel, pointing toward his neck.

'Nothing, it's just a tattoo.' The GenZ was given a hard time first by a millennial and now by a boomer.

'Oh, looked like some fungal infection. Never seen a design like that,' Jatin quipped, and after many, many months, we heard his unabated fit of laughter. Neel should have known what he had signed up for.

'Not funny, uncle,' he replied, clearly not impressed.

'Hey! Why are you getting angry at me? Your artist didn't do a good enough job. It looks like some serpent,' Jatin ji continued.

'I like it, uncle! Plus, it's on my body,' he shrugged his shoulders and kept walking.

'Oh, come on, everyone, watch him on the tracks, and he will show you what he is made of,' Vinay jumped to his rescue.

'So, what if he has a silly tattoo that didn't go right,' he added, stretching the joke.

'Now, chill, Neel. You are going to be working with us for six months at least, maybe even longer. This is harmless fun,' Vinay held his arms around his shoulder and took him to where Zila was parked.

'Yeah, I can work with that,' Neel remarked after taking a hard close look at the Zila from all angles.

'License,' Vinay asked and chuckled. Still poking fun at Neel.

'Seriously?' Neel replied, which gave me the sense, he was beginning to open up.

'It's automatic,' Vinay explained with pride.

'Wow! Good for you? You made this?' he checked, adjusting his seat and the rearview.

'Yeah, how is it?' Vinay asked with a sense of pride, almost suggesting how lucky Neel was to be behind its wheel.

'We will find out!' He said and gently pressed the start button.

'What? No engine sounds. No vibration! Is this a real car or a Golf Cart?' he exclaimed with contempt.

'Keep up with the times, young boy,' Vinay defended, and the banter continued.

'Do you wear seatbelts in this, or is this so modern that they strap up on their own,' Neel continued.

'Buckle up and be gentle on the accelerator. I want you to drive me, not take off with me,'

Vinay ordered like a senior.

'You should have thought that before taking the co-driver seat,' Neel replied with mischief and took Zila carefully out of the workshop, just as Vinay had ordered.

Or, so he thought.

He flew. Speeding past the Audis and Non-Audis, lined up on either side of the narrow bi-lanes of the city, missing them all by a whisker. He was breaking and turning on sharp corners, and I was certain to kill him if my beloved Zila sustained even the slightest scratch.

'Neeeeeeel, you moron!' yelled Vinay.

'Relax, big brother. We are just warming up. Let's see how good your invention is,' he remarked and slowed down just briefly before hitting the highway.

100, 105, 120, 140, 165, 180, and almost a cardiac arrest, when he applied breaks and spun Zila on its radius, leaving behind a big tire imprint. The sounds of tires screeching alerted every single vehicle and the pedestrian around.

'Stop right now!' Vinay ordered.

'This is no bloody joke. We didn't invite you here to get us all arrested,' he scolded.

'Don't worry. I was just testing. It will be smooth from here, I promise. Plus, you can pay off the cops from the money you have saved on recruiting me,' he added, now totally carefree.

He started going a little easy till his instincts took over as we clocked 110 again and slowed down again. Zila had its match and we were back at Soni Motors, alive!

Neel was a pro. We had our driver! Our champion racer!

'You have built a bloody monster. Don't release it like this on our road. This must be kept on the leash,' he remarked, his hand around Vinay's shoulder as everyone in the workshop looked on.

With Neel now warmed up to the team, it was nothing but aggressive testing and practice all around the country but mostly in Noida.

When all of this was taking shape, the Devil woke up again.

# 20

# THE DEVIL DRIVES A ROVER

To be honest, I never wanted to block him, and had he not behaved like a prick when the entire team was slogging twenty-hour days, I would have even invited him to inaugurate Zila, but given his attitude, everyone on the team now terribly despised him.

We knew none of this was healthy. He was, after all, our biggest and the only investor, so at Aman's behest, we agreed to draw a truce and invited him to take a look and drive in the all-new Zila Max, which now stood there in all its might and grace.

He drove to Ludhiana in his Range Rover Evoque. As we saw him approach the Soni Motor's gate, Aman and Jatin ji walked up to receive him. He warmly embraced both and entered the workshop as I stood out of their way.

Although he had his shades on, I am sure he was trying hard to spot me in the mix. The CEO not being present to receive the company's biggest investor was certainly not healthy.

Jatin ji gave me a stern stare, implying I must join them in this dog and pony show for Shantanu. He walked towards the stunning creation, which had now run over 15,000 km. It was still in great shape, given twenty people were attending to it day and night.

Jatin ji courteously held the door for him as he got inside to get his first real experience of the Zila.

There was no doubt. He was blown away at the first look itself. High-quality leather upholstery, the all-powerful steering, the touch screen, the rear space, headroom, legroom, the rear boot, plus the front boot, which he paid attention to only this time around.

Aman and Jatin took him around in the camouflaged version of the car and allowed him to drive, for the most part. I didn't check to hear tales of his fascination. I couldn't begin to imagine how he must have felt driving the real version when even the clay model was enough to blow him away to the point he released the money in an instant.

Aman sent me a text and asked me to come over to the apartment along with everyone else.

Arunima, Vinay, and I reached to try another round of truce talks with him as Aman and Jatin pampered him with some tea and samosas.

'So, as you would expect, Shantanu too now has a taste of Zila, and we don't need to tell you how impressed he has been,' Aman tried breaking the ice.

'I hope you were just as thrilled as us, boss,' I joined in, signaling my willingness to play ball.

'Superb, work of god! I swear. But I expected to see this on the 1st km, not the 15,000th,' he complimented and complained in a single breath.

'Boss, I know. We just wanted to test enough before showing it to you. Let bygones be bygones; everyone was under extreme pressure,' I persisted.

'The same attitude, even on your projects, you never gave me updates till I called, and even here,' he said and nodded in disapproval.

'See, we haven't changed, your very own protégés!' I responded playfully, trying to diffuse the stress.

Despite this, there was some uneasy silence in the room.

'I don't know what you think of it, but I have been giving active thought to a few ideas on how we must take this company forward,' Shantanu said and made his move.

He continued, 'In my view, you guys have done a fantastic job in getting the company to this point, but now we must get a professional management team to take this to the next level,' his remarks had dropped a bombshell.

I stood up gently and casually and walked around the living space, fiddling with darts placed on the Zila road map. This allowed me to keep calm and also think of a polite way of addressing this patronizing proposal.

'Boss, this is a professional management team,' I replied politely.

'No, sure! I don't mean we fire the team here. But let someone who has experience of running an auto company come in and take it from here,' he continued, and I didn't want the guys to hear this.

'You know, distribution, marketing, pricing, there is so much you have no experience of,' he spoke like he owned the company. I looked around for cues, but everyone was blank.

'Shantanu, we had no experience of building a car either, let alone an electric version with a battery technology that has no precedent,' I began defending with courtesy and patience.

'I am not opposed to getting top talent, and we will hire as we progress. The roadmap is right here for everyone to see,' I argued politely.

'Okay, now hear me patiently and with an open mind Bharat,' Shantanu began, suggesting I stand down and let him have his way.

'I have a few contacts who can run a study and recommend the right structure for us going forward,' he commented.

'They can also bring in several million dollars for this one-in-a-generation product,' he added.

'Boss, all thoughts are welcome. Let us, please, decide. You have made your points. We will think it over and see when we need to make these big changes,' I replied, assuring him I would look into it.

'I think it's necessary now, and I am nervous about my investments,' he argued.

'We have rejected this proposal, and boss, I don't know what you are trying to do, but whatever your agenda is, it sounds toxic, and we won't let it ruin everything we have built,' I, too, confronted more directly. Maybe I shouldn't have.

'Shantanu Boss, don't wreck this dream I plead of you. I don't want confrontation, especially when things are running so well,' Aman now stepped in, but Shantanu totally ignored him and addressed me.

'Bharat, you follow my advice and guidance, and we can all be happy. You act funny. You know me all too well,' this time he was threatening.

'Boss, don't chop the branch all of us have perched on. Let's avoid a new circus, please,' I responded with greater assertion.

'Don't test me, Bharat! You are still going to walk away with hundreds of millions. Just let the big boys take this from here,' he warned.

'Come on now. The big boys are in charge. You follow my advice for once, and you will walk away with hundreds of millions without doing a thing,' I almost yelled, and there was stun silence.

'Mr… Vashishta, Bharat, come on now! We have a world-class car, and we are going to be on the world map in three months. Let's only prepare for Munich,' Jatin ji announced, besieging peace.

'What, Munich?' He exclaimed.

'Munich All-Electric Global Championship and Zila is participating in three months,' I explained.

'And when were you going to tell me this,' he asked.

'You stop being a spy agency, and all the information will automatically come to you. Why can't you just sit back and enjoy your returns,' I said and sighed.

'I cannot approve of this madness,' he contested and stood up from his chair.

'You can email your dissent note, and we will archive it for records,' I responded.

'You are going to get more than just emails. This is my money you are playing with,' he tried to reprimand.

'Boss… with due respect, if there is anyone who is playing with his own money and everyone's time, it's you. Please stop!' Aman sounded tired yet assertive.

'I can't be talking to you. If this thing fails, you will hear from my lawyers,' he warned again.

'I really need to go now. You have already created a lot of stress in the team, but don't worry, like always, Aman and I will pick up the pieces, and you will get your returns,' I said and walked away, taking Aman and Vinay with my arms around their shoulders.

I felt like I was trembling like I was going to get some sort of a stroke. Not sure if it was Shantanu or just the fatigue from the lack of sleep, unending stress, and this little showdown that had perhaps aggravated my blood pressure or heart rate. Something wasn't right. I had to sit, and I sat on the sidewalk.

We were on the doorstep of experiencing life-changing success, and any spanner in the works by this man could prove to be absolutely devastating.

'Easy! Bharat! Don't worry. I have handled many such jokers in my life,' Jatin reassured me,with his hand on my head

I had always been bad at emoting freely. I wanted to, but all I could focus on was getting my breath in control and feeling a more familiar heart rate. Thankfully, Jatin comforting me seemed to have done a world of good.

I confided in Jatin and told him that I was feeling scared that this man could go to any extent, and I was now tiring out.

'I told you, don't worry. He is not a patch on the likes I have dealt with. We will be fine. Just focus,' Jatin reassured.

It was amongst the toughest days I can imagine, even tougher than perhaps Neel blowing it up on the circuit. I didn't dare to touch coffee or cigarette for the rest of the day. I didn't know what it could do to me. That's how susceptible

I felt from within. Fortunately, I survived to continue the battles to follow.

Jatin was confident of Zila getting the necessary road approvals, and our patent application was also on track to be registered in the name of us three. All we had to do was steer clear of troubled waters till we returned from Munich. And keep Zila a secret.

Fortunately for us, investigative journalism has been long dead in this country, and till you have a strong PR team or an established footprint, it's foolish to expect the media to uncover you, even if you are running the world's most revolutionary company in broad daylight.

With less than thirty days to go, the organizers wanted us to share the names of the team members traveling. Vinay called a meeting and announced that the team that would be on the plane to Munich.

'Okay, so here is the team that will be on the plane to Munich,' he began as we took our places in the cramped living room. Some sat on the floor; some stood. Aman grabbed a chair, and so did Jatin ji.

'Honestly, if it was left to us, all of us could go, but only six are included in the package. Still, we will travel as a gang of nine,' Vinay announced. By now, it was clear who these nine would be.

'So, Neel will be our chief racer, and Aditya will travel as a backup racer,' he continued, 'Arunima and Sindhu will support software updates and developments. Jatin ji, along with Ajay, for maintenance and keeping Zila in good health, Aman will manage investors and customers, and Bharat and I will be the stepneys, so everything from making coffee, fixing tires, writing code, or interacting with the media, will all be managed by us,' Vinay continued.

'Sindhu is going to manage the coordination with the organizers.

'Let's do this!' He announced, and everyone joined him in chorus. We had done an incredible job of turning around the mood in the room after the Shantanu episode.

Vinay, Jatin, Neel, Aditya and I spent our time training in Noida. While Aman was with the rest here in Ludhiana, keeping in touch with us.

We would return every week to spend time as a group and also take stock of everything else.

'Okay, Sindhu, do you have the passports and the documents?' Vinay checked, as the team was busy chit-chatting in one of our bedrooms over a movie on our rented projector.

'Yeah, but I can't recognize one of them. It reads Neelkantha Rao Thambe…' Even before Sindhu could finish, Neel stood up in protest.

'This is just so ridiculous and lame!' He lamented and sent everyone in splits.

'Really! Is that you? Oh my god, I can't believe this,' Arunima said, still laughing uncontrollably, falling and leaning over Vinay.

'The world calls me Neel!' He said and pointed to his tattoo with a sense of swag. None of it helped, and the two girls continued to giggle away at him.

'What? Are you like fifteen?' He was aghast, commanding them to shut up, but the more he reacted, the more everyone cracked up. Well, this joke wasn't going to finish here, nor was this budding romance.

But now it was time to strap up your seat belts and breathe in a bit of Europe!

* * *

We landed in Munich at six in the morning local time. From the time we exited the airport, it was like an 'Aman Show' at the stall and a 'Neel Show' on the tracks.

Aman had prepared for this opportunity silently yet meticulously with Arunima and her team.

Our stall had a massive banner that read 'Zila Max by Bharat Kinetics' embossed in Sindhu's cursive handwriting. The lightning bolt symbol was nothing more than par for the course at an Electric Car event.

Aman had pre-empted this in time, so he, Arunima, Sindhu, and her team built a high CG Zila video game.

Vinay, Aman, me, and Jatin dressed up in our best Italian cut suits while Arunima stood at the stall in a saree, taking visitors through the technology and operating system and also doubling up as the player two for gaming enthusiasts.

The game had multiple themes, like Racetracks from India to Monaco and Australia to Bahrain. We had a city mode, desert mode, and even a village mode, where Zila competed against models of the same specs using some pseudo names. Obviously, it was programmed to win, but that was not the whole part.

At the end of each race, the participant was told why Zila was winning. From Air Drag scores to Torque, it was the most experiential way to help investors and enthusiasts realize the power and value of owning a Zila Max.

This meant Zila became, if not the hot favorite, but certainly a darling for the visitor. Its underdog positioning, the giant killer video game outcomes, got us a number of meetings.

The requests were more than we could manage, but once inside the board room or a coffee shop, Aman and I ruled the roost.

His presentations and storytelling ability were never in doubt, I had seen it all the time, but here, he appeared to be on steroids. While we were sweating it out on the track with Neel, Aman was methodical, arranging every little piece of the puzzle, from marketing to stats, the game, or the experience.

The graphics, the numbers, the technology, and most importantly, the team composition, which comprised of a CA, two geeky engineers, one ex-Air Force pilot, two genius programmers, and a twenty-year-old maverick race car driver.

We positioned it as the greatest team ever assembled since the Yankees in 1927.

To add greater depth, we included pictures of our apartment, our development centers, design studio plus, battery labs, and photos of our early days.

While Aman was killing it in the board rooms, on the track, Neel was creating more than a buzz, and these twenty days leading up to the race were nothing short of a fairy tale. Those were the best days of my life!

Only if the race had turned out differently…

# 21

# THE WEDNESDAY MORNING

## *NIVEDITA*

Bharat smirked with pain as he spoke. I could tell he had not reconciled with the outcome yet. Even though he appeared to be collected and upbeat on the surface, he was hurting from within.

He gave everything he had and more to this; three years of prime youth, family, marriage, career, and even his house, but at the end of it all, he had a failed bid on a race track and a daunting legal battle.

'Any questions?' Bharat smirked as he asked.

'Are you hiring in your legal team?' I smiled back.

'Oh aren't you hired already! But looks like I may have to update my CV,' he remarked with dry smile

'You guys will have an army of lawyers one day, just don't lose this bond. You three are as rare as they come,' he nodded with a smile at my comment and looked up, thanking the almighty.

We needed to prevent Shantanu from going to court, which could only happen if he was convinced that we were desperate to drag him to court. This was a double-edged strategy, one all of us agreed to sign up for.

'So, it's all or nothing?' I checked.

'Not much choice. Go for broke. Won't blame you for the outcome, I promise,' he assured.

After some more prep work, we secured a meeting with Justice Bansal and Satish a week later.

It was a Wednesday morning, and we made our way to the Safdarjung Enclave. All of us drove in the Zila with Vinay behind the wheel.

'Winters in Delhi are so amazing! Why don't we have a beach here,' he said, cranking down the volume of a radio jockey, trying to preach using a rundown joke.

'Enjoy while it lasts. That idiot is going to turn up the heat inside,' Aman remarked, trying to keep everyone focused.

'Leave him with me. I will have him for breakfast, lunch, and dinner. You take it easy!'

Bharat remarked dismissively.

'Spare one course for me,' Vinay added.

'No way, he is all mine,' Bharat remarked, trying to appear battle ready. I am sure he knew he was in the heavy-weight ring.

'Whose Merc is that? Bloody… he had a Rover already. Now he has Merc, too,' Vinay exclaimed as we noticed a Rover and a Merc parked outside.

'Rover 6955, that's Shantanu's, the Merc, I think, is Satish's,' Aman tried clarifying.

'Oh, so intimidation tactics… are they going to be dressed in Tuxedos now?' Bharat scorned.

'We will find out. Now just relax and leave it to me,' I assured.

'You are telling us? Or yourself?' Vinay asked sarcastically.

'All of us, especially you. Behave like the inventor of the world's best car,' I replied in a stern tone, disciplining him.

'Oh! Oh! Co-Inventor, I worked as hard,' Bharat corrected.

'You can call yourself an Assistant Inventor or, say, intern on the Zila project,' Vinay mocked.

If you both don't focus, we will walk out signing a document that calls Shantanu the inventor,' Aman chided the two.

The four of us walked in, Aman and me, with civility while Bharat had his arms around Vinay's shoulder as they both entered after us.

'Good morning!' Bharat greeted both, and we all proceeded to take our chairs.

'Great car, the red Merc, looks stunning!' Bharat complemented, and Satish smiled with pride and acknowledgment.

'Special edition?' Bharat continued.

'No, the regular one. I have another limited edition, Aston Martin. This one is from a showroom in Connaught Place,' Satish surprisingly played along.

'Brilliant! You must take better care of it, sir. The dent near the fuel tank looks really bad,' Bharat commented.

'What the hell!' Satish stood up in anger.

'That wasn't his car! It was a different one, just some early-morning humor, Mr. Ranjan, easy!' Vinay clarified, and two high-clapped again.

'Really? You need to work on your humor, too. At least my

car isn't some stupid electric car, running on Zinc,' he chided aggressively.

'Stupid Zinc car! Oh…My…God! So, what do you call a person investing five crores in such a car?' Bharat continued.

'An idiot?' Vinay joined in.

'Vinay! Mind your tone. He is called Shantanu. Sorry boss,' Bharat took one more shot.

'Enjoy these silly chats, boys. That's all you are good for,' Shantanu came back well.

Just as Bharat moved to get back, Justice Bansal walked in, wearing a tan blazer, quite an age-appropriate, unlike Shantanu, who was in a red Superdry sweatshirt.

Everyone else also wore blazers. Bharat was in a blue blazer with silver elbow patches, teamed with a white round-neck t-shirt. Vinay was in a regular grey coat with black and some other shades and a round-neck t-shirt.

I was more conventional in all-black attire. Aman was carrying a blue blazer placed neatly on his chair and sat there in a black checked shirt, sleeves rolled all the way down and buttoned up.

We took turns shaking hands and greeting Justice Bansal before taking our positions.

'Alright, good to see all of you return. Looks like there is still some interest in a resolution,' Justice Bansal retorted in a satirical vein.

Satish smiled in acknowledgment. We all nodded and acknowledged him.

Both sides switched on their recorders, and the medication commenced.

'Ms. Das, if you don't mind, can I go first?' Satish sought permission, and I didn't resist. He stood up, and after Bharat's antics in the morning, Satish was going to come really hard at him.

'So, Mr. Srinivasan, in the last meeting, it was agreed that you ignored my client and your only investor's advice and participated in a race that turned out to be a disaster,' Bharat smiled like he was in disbelief at the inanity of the comment.

'Okay, is that it?' He checked.

'I have no time for mind games here,' Satish warned.

'Me neither, so, in the last meeting, we also concluded that your client is a predatory person, ignorant about the industry, and had throughout been trying to destabilize Bharat Kinetics,' he said and flicked his eyebrows.

'Mr. Srinivasan, please don't go the same road again! Everyone will end up in court,' Justice Bansal advised Bharat.

'Sure, sir, but all of this is being recorded, so we need to make sure the record is fact-based,' Bharat explained politely.

'So, let me put some facts here,' Bharat continued.

'Zila was the darling of the crowds. Even members of other teams were cheering for us. We led in forty-five laps out of fifty and returned with the award of top speed and handling. The Championship webpage lists us as the top five EVs to watch globally,' Bharat replied emphatically. He wasn't done yet and continued.

'No other car in this country has received such acclaim on debut. No doubt, even we were heartbroken for not being able to finish, but despite that, Zila had a glorious, glorious debut.'

Justice Bansal kept nodding while Shantanu sat nonchalantly, and Vinay thumped the table. Although not gentle enough for Satish, who gave him spine chilling stare.

'One can also call this beginner's luck,' Satish commented in an attempt to neutralize Bharat's self-praise.

'That's not bad! So, you concede, it wasn't a disaster, and your new hypothesis is that it was indeed glorious, but we were lucky,' Bharat interrupted before Satish could say anything else.

'It could have been much worse, my boy! That was your luck, now please, have the patience to listen carefully,' Satish curtly interjected.

'Let me ask you this. Did you have any racing experience?' He continued.

'We didn't have experience of building a car either…' Bharat replied promptly.

'Yeah, that's all the more reason you should have stayed away from venturing into starting a racing team,' Satish rudely advised and kept going.

'You had no experience in making a car, raising funds, or running a company, and while you were still learning the three most critical aspects, you added another one to your plate. This is a recipe for disaster,' he concluded, implicating Bharat for his misjudgment.

'Mr. Ranjan, you must understand that the teams we were competing with were also on debut, so it wasn't like we were going up against a Ferrari,' Bharat defended, staying close to logic, his all-weather ally.

'Except, all the others had a minimum of three million of funding, and this is from the championship page,' Satish now turned the same rule book back at Bharat.

Bharat nodded with another condescending smirk.

'Wow! That's some insight! But if you see, it's actually a compliment that we managed to not just build a world-class car for less than a million dollars but also compete and make an impression on the world stage. It just speaks volumes of how amazing we are as a team,' Bharat concluded.

'No, it doesn't, because you were short of money, and you hired a twenty-year-old, not a seasoned racer! Which made all the difference at the end,' Satish inferred, concluding his theory.

'You can apply the same logic to the entire team. But look, they have the greatest car in the world. Parked right outside this bungalow,' I came to help Bharat's defense, though he didn't seem to need it.

'My five-year-old niece also calls her toy car the greatest in the world, so let's please not get carried away,' Satish replied, fracturing my assertion.

'Hope you don't discourage her the same way,' Bharat commented.

'Watch it! Mr. Srinivasan!' Satish warned, red in the face as he had been since morning. The boys had managed to rile him up.

But he continued.

'Since you are such an expert, what's your analysis on what led to their Zila losing after being in second position for 25 laps and in third position for 15 laps,' Satish commented and briefly paused.

'Want this to be on record, Mr Srinvisan keeps saying, Zila was in the lead when it wasn't. It was in the second position, so please don't mislead,' he concluded.

'Your analysis is no different from an average cricket fan commenting on Virat Kohli's batting,' I replied, dismissing Satish's misplaced hyperboles.

'Very well, which is why I am seeking a qualified explanation from the man in charge,' Satish replied, asking me to let Bharat respond.

Bharat took a moment before responding, 'I have already provided my analysis. Neel drove Zila at 210 KMH for over three minutes. No car in the world designed for public use can handle that kind of stress, and because Zila kept delivering more power, Neel kept asking. It was a moment of indecision, and as a result, the security protocols embedded at the time of design were automatically invoked, causing forced deceleration, which Neel didn't anticipate,' Bharat explained.

'So, it was either an ignorant driver or the engineering team which didn't brief him well enough of the embedded safety protocols,' Satish interrupted and went to conclude Bharat's analysis.

'When people are working for fifteen hours a day, such lapses are bound to happen. The reason why they work fifteen hours is that the company can't afford it otherwise. And why can't they afford it? Because they won't even ask for VC funding. So how will this work then?'

'Anything else? No, keep going. Looks like you know more than I do,' Bharat remarked.

Satish was too hard-skinned to be sidetracked he continued his targeted attacks on Bharat. It's a strategy, break the strongest general, and the fort will eventually crumble.

'Mr. Ranjan, none of what you are alleging is coherent, just some random theories. You should have prepared better. Anyway, since you brought it up, let me give you some facts on racers,' I intervened after having heard enough.

I sipped a glass of water and continued, 'If you pick up the record books, drivers below twenty-four have won the maximum titles, which only supports the choice made by Bharat Kinetics.

And if Formula 1 drivers can debut at the age of eighteen or nineteen and even seventeen, there is no reason to suggest that Neel, who is beyond one of the fastest in the country, can't drive at twenty in an All-Electric Championship,' I continued. 'Now, if your bogus fables have been fully debunked, let me ask Mr. Vashishta a few questions that will allow me to understand his reservations better,' I looked at Justice Bansal for permission, and he gently nodded to confirm.

Shantanu moved uncomfortably in his seat and prepared for questioning.

'Mr. Vashishta, how many races have you attended personally?' I began.

'What's the point here?' He countered as he moved forward aggressively in his chair. Like he was suddenly woken up from a state of inertia.

'Can you name ten Formula 1 or any global drivers in any event for that matter?' I stuck to my line of questioning.

'This is all so pointless. Please can you move to the more substantive argument,' Satish interfered in Shantanu's defense.

'Easy, Mr. Ranjan. I am sure a top global business leader can manage his own defense.'

I brushed his points aside and continued, 'Yes, Mr. Vashishta,' I insisted, digging my heels in.

'I am not answering a patronizing question like that,' he resisted.

'Very well then, so I am concluding you are not even an enthusiast, let alone an expert,' I observed, smiling scornfully as I continued. 'So, on what ground are you objecting to Zila participating in a global event like this?' I asked, hoping he would react to this at least.

'My lawyer has already explained. They were biting more than they could chew, and I had to advise against this misadventure,' Shantanu spoke out confidently to Justice Bansal.

'How is taking a world-class Indian car to a world event a misadventure? This only reveals the promoter's vision of their company and confidence in their product,' I argued. 'Sure! By all means… But not in India first?' He protested.

'Then why did you travel to Munich?' I continued.

'Oh, let me guess! You were the seed investor, and you wanted to provide them with the guidance they didn't ask for,' I knew Satish would come to Shantanu's defense, and he did. 'Ms. Das, either ask the question or answer it,' Satish intervened.

'Since your client is being reticent, I am helping him find his voice,' I clarified and continued, 'Mr. Vashishta, why did you travel to Munich?'

'I wanted to be there for them if they needed anything,' he was now taking refuge in the victim's corner.

'So, Mr. Vashishta, sorry about that. Why did you go to Munich when it was such a bad idea?' I tried to bring back the conversation.

Just when this was getting intense on Shantanu, to my utter horror, I saw Vinay yawn. Bharat elbowed him, so he knew I had seen him. Vinay's thumbs upped, sat upright, and smiled conciliatorily. Aman nodded in disbelief, and Justice Bansal smiled along.

Shantanu waited for this little drama to finish. Maybe he had seen enough of this before, I judged, looking at his reaction.

'I told you, I cared for them. These are young boys. I knew they would need me,' he stuck to his logic.

'Stop it, boss! I feel like tearing up at your magnanimity,' Bharat remarked in a satirical vein. 'Bharat, shut up, please,' I ordered and continued.

'Sorry about that, Mr. Vashishta. So did you provide them with any guidance?'

Shantanu began, 'I tried. I set up several meetings, but Bharat Srinivasan systematically blocked me out of any team meetings. I was told I could only call him and no one else.' Shantanu spoke, and Bharat looked on with mischievous eyes.

'What kind of meetings did you need the team for?' I persisted.

'I had some investor friends, and I wanted to set up meetings,' he replied, suggesting he had holy intentions and nothing else. For once, even I felt maybe these two must have riled him up to this point.

I stuck to my earlier convictions and decided to explore this premise a little more.

'Then Bharat was more than sufficient for your meetings. You didn't need the team. Is there something you are not telling us?' I followed up.

'I wanted to organize a leadership session with a potential investor that would help the team learn and put up their best foot on the race day while opening up investment sources which the company needed so desperately,' Shantanu made his argument.

'Mr. Srinivasan is that true that you blocked a harmless meeting that would have only helped you and your team on the race day and perhaps helped with some easy investments, too,' I looked towards Bharat for him to be on record.

'Ma'am, he is bluffing. He pulled some random, white vlogger, posing as an investor, who was going to cover Shantanu as some wealthy chairman and the man behind Zila,' Bharat continued,

'And honestly, had he not lied to us, I would have arranged for a full interview with the team. He could have told us. He wanted a video for bragging rights in his circle and family. I have got so many for Vinay. Aman even has a few on his matrimony profile,' he said, ridiculing Shantanu's argument of setting up serious investor meetings.

'That's called PR! Obviously, you won't get it. Plus, what is wrong with me being clicked with the team and the car I funded?' Shantanu protested.

'Nothing at all, but for that, you first need to get the team behind you, which is going to be hard. If you hold their CEO by the collar in full public view…' This was the first time I hurled a direct acquisition that was actually damning.

'Let me handle that, Mr. Vashishta,' Satish took charge.

'Ms. Nivedita Das, I don't know about you, but if my life's savings were to blow away like this, on a grand racing circuit by a group of amateurs, ill-prepared so-called professionals, I would have gone beyond just holding this man by his collar,'

'You both make a great team,' Vinay added fuel with sarcasm.

'You will find out by the end of this,' Satish warned, and gloves were off straight away.

The day progressed without much break, though. We continued the meeting every day to get to a point when one side decided to either concede or walk away in the direction of a courtroom.

This daybreak was also the time to prep the three for the sessions that followed. If there was one thing Bharat and Vinay could learn from Shantanu, it was to listen to their lawyer and hold back.

The arguments continued. Shantanu progressed with puncturing my charge of physical assault.

'So, after blowing up investor money, my money, my lifetime savings, I see the guys making merry at a pub in a top hotel. I am obviously going to be furious; who won't? You tell me, Justice Bansal, what will you do?' Satish used this argument to neutralize one of our strongest arguments.

Though Justice Bansal didn't react, if these were to be heard in court, some of it might resonate with the presiding judge. Plus, the constant, callous comments by Bharat and Vinay could prove quite expensive.

So far, though, everything was hanging in the balance. I proceeded with examining Shantanu.

'Mr. Vashishta, is it true that Aman and Bharat were the best team members you had?'

'That's a pompous question, one I don't wish to answer,' Shantanu was extremely well tutored by Satish.

'It may be pompous, but certainly not untrue, given you promoted them six times in eight years,' I used his silence as implied agreement.

'They did well on the projects I assigned them but always under close supervision. The only time I missed, I had to pay with my life's savings,' he retorted.

'Given you supervised them so well, I am sure you must have demanded a business plan before investing?' I continued with my cross-examination.

'Yes, of course,' he replied, quite subdued compared to previous meetings.

'For everyone's benefit, here is a copy of the plan, a full account of the vision, the market, growth, risks, and areas of spending. The promoters have also clearly stated that no investor will be provided with access to company technology under the trade secret protection provision,' I called out.

'I am hoping you will get to your moot point soon, Ms. Das,' Justice Bansal chided me, and I was very unimpressed.

'Sure sir! So Mr. Vashishta, besides the plan, were you not provided with a full tour of the production line and design labs?'

'Yes, and I was also shown a prototype, following which they took me on a ride that hasn't ended since then. I was also made to believe that this was a test car running on their technology which will be much improved in the final version,' he narrated the journey.

'What was your reaction?' I probed.

'In case you haven't noticed, no matter how much your needle, I am not going to sing praises of your clients and their car. The fact I invested should be enough of an endorsement,' he replied with a straight and determined face.

'For the record, you said I am proud of you. This is brilliant, Work of God' I added. 'Ms. Nivedita, please get to the point,' Satish tried to rush me through, but I was consciously playing on their patience.

'The fact is, you were so impressed that you made the transfer even before the contract before someone else did,' I commented.

'An act of magnanimity is being reduced to sound like a desperate move. This is very disappointing,' Satish added in Shantanu's defense.

'It was not just an act of desperation but an act of greed,' I said and continued, 'Let me try. Desperate, errant, indecisive, or, let's say, insecure?'

'Ms. Das, badgering won't hold up in court,' Justice Bansal blocked my train of argument yet again.

'Mr. Vashishta, did Bharat not give you full disclosure of the progress before even a penny of your investment had been put to use with an option to withdraw, no questions asked?' I returned to a more regular line of questioning.

'Yes, but under a veiled threat that they will move to another investor if I find it risky.'

'Then why didn't you withdraw? Let me guess! Even the thought of withdrawing would have meant your several billion-dollar slipping away,' I continued my onslaught, pinning Shantanu down from his moral high ground.

'Let me handle that. Mr. Vashishta, you take it easy,' Satish intervened, and I knew he would.

'Ms. Das, come on now! What's this, greed and everything? Were your boys and their teams building some charitable hospital for the underprivileged? Please keep these value judgments out.'

After some more heated wiles on both sides, Satish began to question Bharat again.

'Is it true that you concealed that your technology was not ready at the time of your pitch?' Bharat looked up at Shantanu and spoke, 'You just walked in?'

'Excuse me?' An irate Satish checked back.

'Then what sir? Nivedita ma'am, has been telling you a detailed plan, and risks were stated up front and confirmed many times over. Still, you keep asking. Please be attentive. We all have better things to do,' Bharat replied with total contempt.

'Mr. Srinivasan, don't invite more trouble. You already have said enough,' It was now a common place for both Shantanu and Satish to threaten Bharat with consequences.

'You are on record, Mr. Ranjan. Please stop intimidating me!' Bharat replied unfazed.

It seemed like Satish got the message, which reflected in his line of questioning.

'Okay, very well, if you seem to think so, let me ask you another straight question. Hope you will give me a straight answer,' he replied and continued.

'Is it not true that all you had was a theory, a makeshift workshop, and a model that was made of clay at the time of seeking money from my client and your ex-boss?'

'Hmm… short answer, it's not true. Long answer…' Bharat moved to explain, but Satish interrupted again, 'How is it not true that you didn't have the battery technology and there was no car?'

'Yeah, my long answer would have helped clarify, but you didn't let me complete,' Bharat replied politely, still quite nervous.

'But you didn't have a working battery at the time?' Satish asked again, trying to pin him down.

'Mr. Ranjan, badgering will not hold up in court, see, you are not being attentive,' Bharat remarked and continued.

'My ex-boss and your current client were provided a full account of what exists and what's in the works before even a penny of his money was touched,' Bharat concluded, and even Satish gently smiled at his resolve and tenacity.

'Why not at the time of the tour? Why didn't you tell him then?' Satish wasn't going to let go.

'He didn't give us the opportunity. He called his bank even before he stepped down from the stage where the Zila Max model was showcased to him,' Bharat defended.

'Why not later in the evening?' He was now getting stuck into Bharat.

'Like always, he had called the entire team without checking with us. Had it just been us, we could have had a more freewheeling conversation about the ins and outs,' Bharat explained.

'Okay, let's step back. Why didn't you tell him this in Dubai or on the flight back?' Satish was playing hardball, and I had to step in.

'Your client wanted to see the car, and my clients quite transparently told him what he would get to see was a pilot model and nothing more. However, since he insisted, he was given a full tour,' I knew the argument wasn't going to be coherent for a lawyer of Shantanu's pedigree.

'A pilot car that works on Lithium-ion, when the final version is going to be Zinc-air based. Doesn't add up, Ms. Das. Anyway, let's examine this,' he said and looked at Bharat.

'Mr. Srinivasan, you had three opportunities, in Dubai, on your flight from Dubai and then on the eve of the meeting, but you chose to wait for the money to be transferred. You manipulated my client and deliberately allowed him to get neck-deep in his commitment to the point he couldn't go back anymore, only when you were 100% percent sure. When everything was done, you cleverly camouflaged the reality of your battery pack, which was nothing more than a concept,' Satish asserted, implicating the boys in fraud.

I stepped in to keep Bharat from getting into trouble. I knew though he was acting all cool and collected, he was now nearing his thresholds.

'Now come on! Mr. Ranjan here is a fifty-year-old man serving as a COO of a global consulting firm. Is he so gullible that he fell for an amateur con job?

'He had a full week to withdraw. The truth is that he knew how capable Aman and Bharat were,' I continued, 'He had already benefitted a great deal from both of them, had no doubts. If it wasn't him, they would have found someone else without much trouble, and he couldn't let go of such a mouth-watering proposition,' I argued.

Satish was obviously not going to surrender, 'I am hoping that you are not suggesting that this should be the template for start-ups to secure funding when dealing with unsuspecting angel investors. To tell them some part of the truth, take them through a window dressed office and fancy technology and after getting to the point of no retreat, give them the remaining twenty percent with a take it or leave it proposal,' he continued.

'It's like showing your best side to a girl when dating her and telling her just on the eve of the wedding that you are a cocaine addict and she can leave if she so desires. What your clients have committed is downright fraud.'

'Keep concocting analogies, but you and I both know there is no evidence to even suggest a spec of fraud or dirt on the part of my clients.'

Another grueling session came to a close soon after when Justice Bansal declared a thirty-minute recess.

Aman was highly impressed and couldn't stop complimenting my arguments, while Vinay and Bharat nodded in agreement. Although the mediation still hung in the balance, the four of us walked into the arbitration room with confidence, placed our recorders back on the table, and took our positions.

This time, it was Satish's turn to go first, and Bharat nodded his head as he braced himself for more vicious blows.

'The next charge by the complainant is that of financial mismanagement and lack of transparency in business and financial operations,' Justice Bansal read it out and handed the floor to Satish.

'Mr. Srinivasan, hope you are feeling fresh and rejuvenated after the break,' Satish began

'I was, in fact, missing you,' Bharat replied with wit, and everyone, including Shantanu, couldn't help but smile.

'Well, thanks, Mr… Srinivasan. I must admit I missed you as well.'

'So, Mr. Srinivasan, why have you not raised Series A funding for over a year of your car being ready?'

'We have been a bootstrapped company from the beginning, with a single seed investor. We had enough cash on books to start production on a limited scale,' I was relieved that Bharat was sticking to his entrepreneurial strengths and not doubling up as a lawyer.

'And what has been your source of income, given you have not sold a single car yet?'

'We have raised working capital debt, received three awards, plus a grant amounting to 35,000 Euros,' Shantanu nodded with a smirk as he read through the financial statements we had furnished for the meeting.

'And how long do you think before you hit your vision of 1,000 crores in revenue with forty percent margin per car? That isn't happening with this three crore fund infusion by way of debt,' Satish was now going to thread bear into the financial statement.

'That's an internal matter of strategy, one I can't disclose. But I know you will continue to persist, so let me give you an outline. We are going to start releasing in select markets. We have been given lucrative lending options by banks and even by the government. Once we hit the 1000 cars mark, we will go in for an IPO,' Bharat was economical with details but provided a broad wireframe at least.

'And is this what you promised Mr. Vashishta at the time of seeking money?' he brought it back to the second charge. He wasn't going to give up.

'This is one of the best outcomes for any investor. The company goes public, and their investment multiplies while Zila becomes a hot-selling product. This is a script every investor dreams of,' Bharat explained with ultimate resolve.

'Please answer the question. Was that the plan you promised to Mr. Vashishta?' Satish tried needling Bharat to evoke a reaction.

'It's in the business plan,' Bharat exclaimed like there was nothing to hide.

'Okay, we will come back to finances. How long was it before you invited Mr. Vashishta to see the final version of Zila Max?' Satish switched topics, and it was clear that Bharat knew his business better than anyone.

'The next day,' Bharat responded with complete clarity.

'This is such a lie. I was shown Zila after every man and his dog in that little shed of theirs had driven it. It was already the talk of the town in Ludhiana. They had appointed a racer and a coach for their racing team and even applied for government clearance before I was invited for a test drive,' Shantanu exploded.

'Mr. Ranjan! Looks like your own client is not paying attention to your question,' I intervened.

'Ms. Das, stop playing these mind games. All of us heard my lawyers' question and your client's lies,' Shantanu was now roughed up fully, and the boys were smiling, adding insult to his wounded ego.

Satish signaled to Shantanu with his right hand to stay calm and speak only when asked.

'Mr. Srinivasan, is it true that you had started driving cross country with Zila Max months before my client got his first preview?' Satish continued.

'That's what I tried explaining, but your client, like always, took off the racing process. The cross-country trip and the application for road safety licenses are all part of the testing process before the final version can be released, and once we were certain that our product worked, we immediately invited him for a demo and a test drive,' Bharat remained at his composed best, and now Satish was out of ideas.

'You don't believe your top investor has the right to be part of the production process. Your car was being tested, it was beginning to even make news, but Mr. Vashishta, who provided you with the vital line of oxygen, was denied all access,' Satish continued.

Justice Bansal intervened, 'Mr. Ranjan, What are you trying to prove? Please move to your next point. Nothing is coming out of it. The boys told the investors when they thought the product was ready. There is nothing here; please move forward.'

'Sure, Sir.'

'Ms. Das?' Justice Bansal handed the floor to me.

'Mr. Vashishta, why did you send consultants to Bharat Kinetics premises?'

'The boys had no experience of making a car. I was nervous and only sent help at my own cost,' he explained rather politely this time.

'Did you bother to check the affiliations and profiles of the consultants?'

'Yes, they were highly qualified automotive engineers who had served around the world in top auto companies, not like some rookies riding high on a fluke,' Bharat and Vinay smirked mischievously at Shantanu's response.

'Since you have admitted that you had researched their profiles, you can longer be excused for ignorance. So this was a deliberate attempt to embed foreign moles inside the shop floor,' I waited for him to defend himself.

'My research didn't reveal their affiliations with competition, and none of them was in any active engagement at the time,' only Shantanu, instead of defending, ended up confessing.

'Mr. Vashishta, why did you file this notice? Do you realize the mess you've got yourself into? Following this meeting, I will recommend my clients press charges against you now. You have assaulted the CEO in public view, constantly disrupted operations, and, worst of all, attempted to plan 3 moles, who are today contracted with German and Chinese companies trying to build the exact same technologies. This amounts to corporate espionage. In fact, national espionage,' I could tell he was now totally breaking down. His dreams of a penthouse in Westminster, an early retirement, and a business icon headline were all coming down crashing, and he could blame no one but himself.

'You cannot intimidate my client, Ms. Das. This behavior is deplorable. Justice Bansal, I expect you not to permit this,' Satish stood up in protest.

'Let's call time on our meeting today. Let's get together again in a couple of days. Mr. Ranjan, you better have something more solid; you are clearly going down,' Justice Bansal concluded as we packed up.

# 22

# THE FINAL LAP

The week was now up, and we all assembled at Justice Bansal's place, which was undergoing some kind of renovation. We couldn't blame him. He had planned for this to be well over by now.

I led the boys into the meeting room. I wished Justice Bansal, but I couldn't help but notice a new member on their side. Seated next to Shantanu, this was downright cheeky, and had this been a court of law, I would have objected and bought more time to examine the new witness.

I looked at Bharat, Vinay, and Aman, and it was clear that it was some old association. Vinay went to wish the man who was dressed up in a brown checker shirt.

'*Namaskar Gurudev*, so good to see you,' Vinay spoke, almost elated at his sight, while Bharat and Aman were not at all amused.

The Gurudev though, didn't bother to respond and looked at Shantanu like he was his master.

We occupied our positions, and Justice Bansal began, 'It was brought to my cognizance by Mr. Ranjan that they have clinching evidence of plagiarism against the promoter of Bharat Kinetics and would like to invite the victim of this sinister and downright criminal act Mr. Animesh Tripathi, who is an accomplished scientist and an honest professor in Varanasi.'

'Ms. Das, hope you are okay to continue with the meeting in light of this new development,' I could have stopped, but Bharat nodded like he wanted to be done with this.

'Justice Bansal, honestly, I would not want to, and best handle this in court, but given everyone has made time, I will just uphold my regard for you and agree to continue with the proceedings.'

'Mr. Vashishta, why don't you begin and give us some background.'

'Justice Bansal, it is clear. These boys are conniving fraudsters who have manipulated me all along. Their confidence to continue with their unethical ways has been further bolstered now that they are armed with a strong lawyer, but what is more painful is that it's not just me they have frauded. They didn't even spare an honest gullible scientist in the holy city of Varanasi.

'They tracked him on YouTube and met him in the guise of being young, spirited entrepreneurs, won over his confidence, exactly as they did to me, and duped him into showing them his humble little lab. Slowly trapped him into showing his life's most cherished creation, a Zinc-air battery formula. The boys being engineers, carefully made notes, and eventually, when the man asked for his fair share, they robbed him of everything he had and left him in the cold.

'And when the news of their Zila Max flying on the international scene was making ripples all over, the poor man couldn't have felt more cheated, and my fight now is not just to expose these scheming little pricks but also to fight for the rights of every such scientist in the country who is being bullied by such impersonating thugs.'

We thought he was through, but he continued, 'And the worst part is that they made me part of this epic scam which, when exposed, will not just send these three to jail but massively dent the nation's reputation now that they have taken this to the world stage,' he concluded and took us all by shock with this closing act.

'Now, Ms. Das, with your permission, I would like to ask a few questions to Mr. Srinivasan,' Satish was obviously not going to let this go, and his desperation to pin down Bharat was more than visible by the twinkle in his eyes.

'Mr. Srinivasan, did you meet with Mr. Mishra in Varanasi under the pretext of building an electric car?'

'That is correct, but not under the pretext. We have indeed built the world's greatest electric car,' Bharat turned to me after his response, and I signaled he was doing okay with a gentle blink of an eye.

'Did he take you to his laboratory?' Satish remained focused.

'That's right.'

'What did you learn in his lab?' Satish's line of questioning and his tone sounded like he had nabbed a criminal in the act.

'We were given a tour of the battery manufacturing process, most of which we knew already. Mr. Mishra then helped us get hands-on practice in building a rechargeable Zinc-air battery,' Bharat tried not to be bothered by Satish's prowling posture and kept his response fact-based.

'So, how did the experiments go?'

'Fabulous, we had no doubts that Mishra was a hidden gem and this country is full of enormously talented individuals like him,' Bharat spoke with poise.

'Mr. Srinivasan, if this generous praise is a tactic to lure Mr. Mishra out of this case, then you are making a grave mistake,' Satish warned.

'I am just stating how I felt while I was there. Even after leaving Varanasi, I continued to respect Mishra Ji, and I maintain that even today. He is one of the brightest scientific minds I have ever met.'

'Wow! You are an amazing man, Mr. Srinivasan. You respect Mr. Vashishta for his support, yet you want him out, then you generously express your regard for Mr... Mishra and yet rob him of his life's creation. I get a sense that you are quite a twisted person,' Bharat nodded and smiled at Satish.

'I will not respond to your observations of my character. Let me just address the specific point on stealing Mr. Mishra's life's work, and the answer to that is that we haven't stolen anything from him. He is free to use his chemistry even today,' this response stunned everyone.

'Mr. Srinivasan, thank your stars you are not in court, else you could be held for perjury,' Satish warned.

Bharat looked at me for a cue before answering, and I blinked my eyes, granting permission.

'Mr. Ranjan, if there is anyone here who should thank his stars for not being in court, it's your client, and if you are through, can you please hand it over to Ms. Das?' Animesh looked like a wreck and was clearly overwhelmed, while Satish and Shantanu drew a blank face.

'Mr. Ranjan, if you have no further questions, can I have the floor, please?' Their scripts had been overturned by the honest and unambiguous response.

'No, I am not done yet. Please, if I may finish?' I nodded and granted Satish more time.

'Mr. Srinivasan, your car runs on a Zinc-air battery formula which was first shown to you by my client, and although you might have used a slight variant of his model, it still qualifies as plagiarism, make no mistake,' Satish almost threatened Bharat to confess.

Bharat now looked to me for help, and I gladly jumped into his defense.

'Mr. Ranjan, without passing judgment on your understanding of electrochemistry or even basic science, but just so you know, even as we speak, there are scientists in Israel, Taiwan, and China – working on the same formula. In fact, why even go outside the country; there are several scientists working on a Zinc-air combination right here. Despite Mr. Mishra's devotion and talent, he doesn't hold proprietary over this technology. If anything, he could claim IP on his model and nothing more.' As true as it may ring, I knew Satish was too dogged a lawyer to be silenced by this defense.

'Ms. Das, these arguments are all too convenient just because you have switched the combination slightly. It doesn't get your clients off the hook. I am still open to an out-of-court resolution if your clients are willing to confess to their crimes,' his empty threats were going to have no impact, and I had seen enough of it.

'Mr. Ranjan, don't worry. If anything, I am all too eager to take Mr. Shantanu to court and watch him get convicted and humiliated for his evil intentions of destroying a dream as sacred as science. But before that, let me, please pose a few basic questions to Mr. Mishra,' I looked at Justice Bansal to mediate so I could do my job.

'Mr. Ranjan, you may please hold on to your thoughts. Ms. Das has been really patient,' Satish reluctantly retreated. I waited for him to settle before I began.

'Mr. Mishra, I have heard a lot of praise about your scientific abilities from my clients, and I am so glad to be able to meet you finally,' I was hoping for him to at least smile back, but he stayed straight-faced and committeed to the script, he was asked to rehearse.

'No problem, so if you don't mind, could you tell us after your fall out with my clients at Varanasi, did they ever try to contact you?' He looked to his masters, and they granted him permission to answer.

'Yes,' he replied tentatively.

'Great, how many times,' I furthered my point.

'I can't remember, but a few times,' he responded as everyone seemed totally glued in.

'Quite a few times, in fact, a total of twenty-seven times spread over three months, starting with calls and the messages both from Vinay and Aman,' I continued, without seeking validation from him. 'So, why didn't you reply even once?'

'I did reply and told them that my demands will not change,' he replied with a sense of pride and authority.

'Don't you think that was unreasonable?' I asked in an effort to unfurl the full story.

'I don't think so. Without my battery, there was going to be no car, and I had very reasonable demands,' he had still not let go of his pride, and this was another proof to me that Bharat is an honest man.

'So, a 15% stake, setting up a production line in Varanasi without consulting anyone in the team, along with complete autonomy for you to build the battery, were reasonable demands?' Even at the risk of repeating myself, I tried confirming.

'Absolutely, it's one of the biggest inventions of this generation,' Satish chimed in support.

'Oh, I see. Then why is it that Mr. Animesh hasn't been able to find another taker for it? Well over a year since he met Bharat Kinetics?' I looked at Animesh and flicked my eyebrows to elicit a response.

But it was Satish who came to his defense again.

'Mr. Mishra is simple and not industrious like your clients. You must show empathy for people from small-town Ms. Das.'

'I come from Dhanbad, Mr. Ranjan. I will still wait to see if Mr. Mishra ever spoke to another company to present his creation of the century?' There was still no response from Animesh.

'Let me guess, I am sure he did, but he was informed that his battery, although brilliant, will burn out in three months, correct me if I am wrong, Mr. Mishra,' I waited again.

'No, that is not correct. It's only the combination I showed Bharat Kinetics guys that could last for three months. Since then, it has greatly improved,' Satish knew this was curtains, and it was evident in the way he shut his notepad and clicked his pen.

'Need I say more, but still in the interest of concluding, Mr. Animesh Mishra, who is, without doubt, a gifted scientist, found my client to be some amateur boys he could shortchange, and he wasn't wrong. After being rejected by everyone they met across the country, they immediately fell for this. But you know, Kashi Viswanath's blessing is not yours alone, Mr. Mishra. They, too, had a divine light guiding them, which saved them from the monumental disaster as you decided to call it off. When they simulated your learnings, they realized that they had been gamed by this unassuming, gullible, small-town scientist, but fortunately, even as humble as they looked, both Bharat and Vinay were the top scholars in class, and they were able to invent what was, in reality, the invention of our generation.'

'And Mr. Mishra, just so that you are able to sleep in peace, the boys didn't just meet you. They met some other PhDs as well. Some didn't value their own thesis, but thankfully it fell into the right hands. So your trickery, treasure trove of literature, and their own engineering genius are what ultimately led to this magical invention.'

I looked at Animesh for defense, but there was none coming. Shantanu and Satish were livid as this scientist had gamed them too, and now there was nothing left to say except prepare for the wrath that was going to follow.

So, I continued, 'Justice Bansal, all of us have witnessed how a vicious case was concocted against three honest, competent, and committed men trying to make a mark for themselves and their country. Nothing stopped them from sourcing cheap material from China or Taiwan, but they stuck to making it right here. Two years of no salary, no sleep, and no revenues, the company you call a science project meant both Aman and Bharat had their savings and their homes mortgaged to keep the company going as your client kept serving one blow after another. Vinay gets paid only every alternate month, all of this while making sure not one member of the team goes unpaid on payday.

'While going through all this, the only goal that kept them going was to build a world-class electric car that anyone could own. They dared to dream and dared to fight everything out too.

'Now, please make note, especially you, Mr. Vashishta, since your lawyer will still be counted as one of the country's top lawyers, and it's you who are going to face charges of Espionage, Anti Company Activities, Malicious Charges, Destabilizing Management, and Physical Assault that could have resulted in the closure of what will be India's 1st pure-play electric car company which holds the potential to be bigger than Tesla or any other company in the world.

'We are filing a lawsuit demanding damages of hundred crores plus a legal fee to compensate for the mental, financial, and reputational damage brought upon my promoters along with a prison term of at least one year for Mr. Shantanu Vashishta.'

There was stun silence in the room. Even Bharat, Aman, and Vinay maintained a straight face, but Shantanu was turning pale, and so was Animesh, who wanted to somehow wriggle out of the mess he had brought upon himself. Satish gently batted his eyelid in appreciation of my pursuit, one only I could see.

'Okay, why don't you all hug and kiss each other? I will wait,' Satish stood up, almost unfazed.

'Now, if you are through, I want to bring this argument to a close,' Satish said, and Justice Bansal nodded.

'First of all, I don't understand this whole twenty hours a day, hard work argument. You want to start a company, and you bloody work hard for it. What's new in all this? I have worked just as hard as a lawyer, Ms. Das, and you have, so had Justice Bansal. This is just an emotional argument that amounts to nothing,' he continued, and I wasn't surprised. Satish doesn't leave a case without a chunky pound of flesh.

'And this whole thing about making India proud, it was my client's money that allowed this kind of self-indulgence that these bunch of boys make. They are not doing a favor to the country, and even if they are, by chance, since the car has indeed turned out well, it was their own lookout. The people didn't petition them to make an electric car when we have so many other problems to solve.

'That aside, the core of the issue is that they have mistreated their first and only investor, who took this bet on them, without which there wouldn't be a car. There wouldn't be any national pride. There would be no reason for the team to feel proud of their efforts.

'And even for a moment, we believe there was no plagiarism, and it was indeed their own the invention, it doesn't absolve them of misuse of funds and investor harassment.

'You tell me, Justice Bansal, are you willing to risk your savings? Are you willing to be kept in the dark by the boys you mentored at some stage? My client offered professional help, and personal advice, all of which were rejected,' he paused and sipped some water after turning the matter on its head, leaving us all deep in the woods.

'Still, we have one final offer for the promoters. If they want to part as friends and not drag this to the courtroom,' he paused again to check for permission to table his offer.

'Final offer, valid for the next hour and no more. The company has cash on its books. We need the entire sum of three crores to be returned immediately, plus a sum of another five crores to be paid through a payment plan over the next twenty months. In exchange, my client will surrender his shareholding after this. They can make India proud, Pakistan proud, Asia, and the entire world proud. We don't care, but it can't be at the cost of Mr... Vashishta when he is not even going to be respected in the very company he helped create.

'Ms. Das, you are a smart lawyer take this deal and my client will withdraw all his claims on the company and surrender his shareholding, you know this legal battle will destroy whatever is left of this experiment,' Satish called everyone's bluff and made his fine move on the board.

We broke out into a different room so I could understand what the boys had to say.

'This isn't a win, is it, Ms. Das?' Vinay sounded like I had failed them.

'You are stupid! This is a massive win,' Aman and Bharat fist-bumped.

'I am going to now sue you both. What is cooking here?' Vinay hated when Bharat and Aman didn't bring him in on matters of money.

'Easy, nothing's cooking. We can pay him off and get him off our back. Five crores is our final offer, ma'am,' Aman announced.

'Six! He won't agree less than that. Plus, it's fair to give him his money back,' I challenged with a counter.

'Whatever you feel is right, ma'am,' Bharat stepped in with implicit trust.

A win or a loss was now a matter of perception. I think both sides left licking their wounds. Shantanu was off their backs but this battle brought the company to its knees along with more debt. Everything was now mortgaged.

# 23

# DOLPHINS MEET THE SHARK

Given the blows Bharat Kinetics had taken through the mediation process, Shantanu had created enough compulsions for the boys to go back to him for reconciliation, and six months since we closed the mediation settlement, Bharat, Aman and Vinay came home for a little reunion.

'Congratulations, boys! Proud of you,' I said and embraced all three of them.

'Heard you have also made peace with Shantanu?' I asked Bharat. 'He called, or you did?' I asked him directly as Aman and Vinay moved in their seats uncomfortably like they had something to hide.

'I did, had little choice,' Bharat broke the silence.

'Well, okay, I am listening,' I suggested that he goes on.

'Honestly, I did not expect that he would call us for dinner. We arrived at his penthouse's newly renovated terrace garden, overlooking the spectacular Gurgaon skyline,' Bharat continued narrating as we all sipped our coffee.

*'This one is a special single malt. Only a hundred of these exist. I had been saving this for when we become a billion-dollar company,' Shantanu bragged and kept it aside.*

*'But given your situation, I think even a Black Label is a luxury do,' he chuckled with contempt.*

*I responded with an understated smile, perhaps suggesting I wasn't impressed at all.*

*'Bharat, I need to give you a hug. I am sorry about Munich,' he continued.*

*'That's fine, boss. What will you apologize for? Let's not go there,' I remarked, and it was enough to spur him on.*

*'You still think I need to apologize?'*

*'All you had to do was step aside after making a good car and let the big boys take over. You would have walked away with millions. But here we are now!' he lectured with authority.*

*I moved to respond, but he blocked me and continued, 'You know, this is the problem. You have always done well when I have been the mentor figure. Just that you suddenly took yourselves too seriously, anyway.'*

*'I heard no work is happening at your Soni Motor plant; that's what you call it, don't you?'*

*'Yeah, we chose the wrong investor, paying the price,' Vinay remarked quite seriously for a change.*

*'Okay, I am sorry if you felt bad. I am actually here to help you both. See, end of the day, I have always deeply cared for both of you since the time you joined my team,' he began again, and we nodded.*

*'If you are okay with it, I am okay to forget the whole thing and revive Bharat Kinetics. You truly have a good product. Don't let it go to waste for want of money,' he continued, and we kept tuning in.*

*'Such a shame. Come on. You can keep drinking. That's fine,' he commanded. We nodded, without sipping, just suggesting he goes on.*

*'I think we can save this sinking ship, take back your six crores, and forget everything that happened. No need to return any of the money to me. Life goes on as if nothing happened. You know how to make products, brilliant products. I know you both, and even you, Vinay, but making a company is different.*

*How many were we when Bluewater's started here? Sixteen! And how many are we today? 1600! Why do you think I am the COO globally and CEO of India? I know how to build a company.'*

*'Are you with me?' He checked again, and we nodded as if we meant it.*

*'Great! So here is my offer. Consider it practically, especially you, Bharat, lose the emotion.'*

*I looked at him and let my eyes talk, signaling he continued without advice.*

*'Six crores goes back to you all, plus a 3 % stake; 1% to each one of you without the dilution of ESOPs that you have issued to your team members. I will retain all your staff members and give them the same respect, better salaries, and a real career. Sell the 70% remainder stake to me and just sit back and watch your company grow. Your 3% will be worth millions in less than a couple of years. Exit then. Travel the world, buy your farmhouses, penthouses, yachts, whatever,' he took a sip and waited for a reaction.*

*'I will even pay a handsome retainership amount to the three of you till we make an exit,' he added to sweeten the offer.*

*'Why didn't you make the offer earlier? We could have avoided this legal circus,' Vinay asked.*

*'Honestly, I never expected you guys to get this far, I knew I could exit even if you deliver 50% of your business plan, but you went all the way and beyond,' he continued, 'And that gave you the false sense of self-worth. You were not open to negotiating*

*then. I tried making this offer, remember? In your run-down little apartment in Ludhiana,' we listened to him as Aman lit up a cigarette.*

*'And this was always the plan, wasn't it? Throw us to the wolves and then emerge as a messiah with a gun to our head. I underestimated you. I thought this was just an ego trip,' Aman looked into Shantanu's eyes and spoke every word with utter contempt.*

*Shantanu didn't have the patience to explain or atone for anything.*

*'You have time till tomorrow. Call me if you want to keep the company. Sorry, I didn't plan for dinner,' he hoped we would leave after this epic dressing down*

*'Night's still young, boss. We can talk,' Aman said rather calmly.*

*'Well, so you indeed need my money and support. Now, lose the ego and take this offer. You can be angel investors yourselves after this,' he was back on the table.*

*'Who ran the numbers for you? If I may ask?' Aman was now talking.*

*'We can rework the stakes if that's your issue,' he had once again fallen to Aman's deal-making skills.*

*'We will come to that, Shantanu. I am thinking, what would have been the value of your 10% if we were a billion dollar valuation today?' Aman didn't let him reply and continued, 'Looks like your guys didn't run any research on Bharat Kinetics.*

*'What were you thinking, Shantanu? You thought we would be so silly to take you on without another investment and order book.' Shantanu was red in the face now.*

*'What do you think I was doing with my Italian suits in Munich? Who do you think went with Alan for dinner a night*

*before you arrived,' Aman said and paused so Shantanu could take another sip of whiskey.*

*'Why don't you google Bharat Kinetics?' Aman didn't let him say anything and flashed his phone, which read, 'Indian Electric Car Maker Bharat Kinetic receives pre-orders of 5,000 units and funding round of $200 MN ...'*

*'Get out of my house, you son of a b...'*

*I splashed my whiskey on his face. 'Now we are even, just why I came to see you.'*

*'YOU BETTER LAWYER UP, BIG MAN. WE ARE COMING BACK FOR YOU,' I announced, and we left the place, leaving him with his rare single malt.*

'Woohoo, so now am I hired, Mr. CEO,' I joked.

'Ma'am, you are the best! See you at Munich 2018, and this time we are in it to win it,' Aman said and handed me the keys to a special edition Zila Max. Made in India.

The Shark is the fiercest predator in the ocean until it meets a bunch of spirited Dolphins.

# ACKNOWLEDGEMENT

Writing a book is lonely but getting it out to the world is impossible without the universe working for you.

Well, my universe starts with my wife Pallavi, my best friend, critic, coach, and almost a co-writer, but for her, I would have been done at chapter 2.

Varun Chopra, Founder Foster Reads, the younger brother I never had.

Harshil Shah, for calling upon his wealth of experience in managing one of India's most respected bookstore chains.

The vibrant team at Hub Hawks and Nu Voice for platforming my work and helping me navigate the tricky terrain of publishing, marketing, and distribution.

My friends, colleagues, and family who doubled up as early-stage reviewers, Amit Tiwari, Rajeev Sharma, Yamini Murthy, and Nisha Gandhi

Giridhar (Mr. Barrel) Soundararajan – Founder and Managing Director Barrel Motors for reviewing the story as a reader, entrepreneur, and technical expert from the automotive space.

Finally, Mr. Nitin Gadkari, Minister of Road Transport & Highways, Government of India, for taking out time from his super tight schedule to review my work and provide his priceless feedback. As a champion of electric vehicle adoption in the country his endorsement comes as a massive dose of encouragement.

And above all the blessings of my Guru and guiding light Sai Baba